Justice Secured

RANDY RAWLS

Rawls, Randy
Justice Secured / Mystery-Thriller / Randy Rawls

Amazon Author Page:

www.amazon.com/author/randyrawls

Website:

www.RandyRawls.com

Cover art and design by Victoria Landis

Copyright 2017 by Randy Rawls

ISBN-13: 978-0989990431 (Randy Rawls)
ISBN-10: 0989990435

PREVIOUS TITLES

Tom Jeffries Series:
Thorns on Roses
The Runaway

Beth Bowman Series:
Hot Rocks
Best Defense
Dating Death

Historical:
Down by the River

Ace Edwards Series:
Jake's Burn
Joseph's Kidnapping
Jade's Photos
Jingle's Christmas
Jasmin's Fate
Jeb's Deception

DEDICATION

Especially for Tracy and David, my children, with my love.
And for Ronnie, always My Honey.
For those who tolerate me and critiqued this writing:
Ann, Gregg, Richard, Stephanie, and Vicki.
For Joanne at *Murder on the Beach Mystery Bookstore*,
a friend to every author.
AND, **especially,** for readers everywhere.

ONE

Josh Hawkins drove north on US 441, heading for his fiancée's house in Delray Beach. Rush hour was on the wane, but traffic remained heavy enough to stack up at traffic lights, which were frequent. That set up a scenario reminding Josh of a NASCAR restart, many of the cars jockeying for position and attempting to get ahead of their *competition*. Josh stayed in the center lane as the circus swirled around him. His mind wandered.

The image of Jaden, his fiancée, appeared, bringing a warm feeling. How fortunate he was to have found her. It seemed a dream to him. How could an old Special Forces operator like him have gotten so lucky? Not only was she intelligent, beautiful, and talented, she was sharp enough to have landed a position as an Assistant State Attorney in Broward County. However, he'd learned not to question luck. If it was good, relax and enjoy. If it was bad, he'd work his way through it. He frowned. Her mood had been down for the past few evenings because of the case she was prosecuting.

Josh's phone rang, returning the smile to his face. Jaden.

"Hey, Sunshine. What's up?"

"After the day I've had, up is not the right word. I'm too much of a lady to say what comes to mind. However, life goes on and tomorrow is another day. Ooh, did I mix clichés?

Anyway, you get my intent, I hope. And part of that life is dinner, and I'm hungry. How about swinging past Publix and picking up a few things?"

"What do we need?"

"A couple of rib eyes—make mine a big one—and baking potatoes. Check the asparagus. If it's fresh, grab a bundle. We have some Texas Toast in the freezer."

"Got it. Anything else?"

"Yes, salad makings and a nice bottle of wine, maybe a Cabernet Sauvignon. And if you want something to drink, get that, too."

Josh chuckled. "Is this one of those nights I've read about when I'll have to pour you into bed?"

"Could be, my love. Could be. Now, quit jabbering and get your butt home. I miss you."

"Miss you, too," Josh said as the phone went dead.

Since he was on Route 441, he had no problem finding a Publix Supermarket—one every block or so, or no less than every major intersection. There were other markets—a limited few—but Josh preferred Publix—in spite of the fact it would be mobbed with folks grabbing dinner. He frowned, picturing the jostling for position that would take place. The aisles of a supermarket were almost as dangerous as a South Florida parking lot.

He grinned, thinking of Jaden's order. Usually, she ate like the proverbial bird, picking over a salad or going lo-cal. But when she was upset, look out fridge. She must have picked up a dessert on the way home since she didn't remind him to get anything sweet.

Josh pulled into a shopping center that housed a Publix and other smaller stores. It was L-shaped with parking in the open area. As he drove toward the base of the L, he saw a disturbance along the sidewalk—four people hassling one another.

Slowing, Josh studied the situation, wondering what was happening. Mouths appeared to be working, and there were a couple of shoves. Then one man punched another, knocking him into the driving lane in front of Josh. The other two laughed and patted the attacker on the shoulder, showing Josh who allied with whom.

The scene didn't fit Josh's theory of fairness—three against one—especially when Josh saw that the victim appeared older. He swerved to the right, toward the three men, and blew the horn. That got their attention, and they stepped back as he nosed up to them, placing his car between them and their patsy.

He got out of his car and walked to the old man. "What's going on here? Are you okay?"

From his prone position, he looked at Josh, fear in his eyes.

Josh reached to assist him up, noticing that his features appeared Asian.

"Hey, asshole. You stay out of this. It's a private party." The words came from behind Josh where the three attackers stood. Laughter followed.

In a slow, deliberate manner, Josh helped the old man to his feet, then turned to the threesome. "Was someone speaking to me?"

"Who else could it be? You're the only asshole I see."

Josh looked at the Asian, who teetered, but appeared to be gaining strength. "Will you be all right while I take care of some business?"

The look hadn't changed, but his eyes seemed to be clearing.

Josh walked around the front of his car, studying the situation. They appeared to be in their early to mid-twenties, and each had a shaved head and a muscular chest. The muscles looked like they came from a gym rather than hard work. They wore shorts that dangled to mid-calf and T-shirts. Flip-flops or sandals and numerous tattoos completed their attire.

"Would one of you call 9-1-1, please?" Josh said. "He

might need medical attention. Also, tell them by the time they get here, there could be other customers."

"Huh . . . Do what? Are you nuts? Yeah, he's gonna need a doctor—and you too, if you don't get the hell back in your car and move on."

"Watch your language, please. This is a public place, not your bathroom. There are women and children who can hear you."

"What kind of fool are you?" The speaker stood about five-eleven and puffed himself up to look tough. "Get out of our way. We got business to finish. These damn slopes got to learn how things are done in our country." He glanced at his friends. "He either pays, or he gets hurt. We done been patient with him."

The other two laughed and did high fives like his comments were hilarious.

Josh studied the one who'd taken charge. He spoke accented English, and his features were Latino. His referring to the old man as a *slope* piqued Josh's curiosity. Was his target Vietnamese? During Josh's days in the military, he'd heard Vietnam vets refer to them as *slopes*. He glanced at him. Could be. It was obvious the three thugs had a grievance against him. Josh wondered what he'd blundered into.

"Look," Josh said. "I'm sure he's willing to forget what happened if you boys want to go on your way and promise not to return."

"Boys?" The leader snickered. "You must come from some *ba-ad* country, maybe someplace in Asia like this *slope*. There ain't no *boys* here—unless you count yourself."

"Cute. My opinion hasn't changed, though. Leaving now would be the smart thing to do."

The leader slapped one of his friends on the shoulder. "Smart? Are you smart? This man, no make that this *dead-man-talking*, says leaving would be the *smart* thing to do. Stand by while I 'splain to him he needs to get his ass in his car and move on." He wheeled back to Josh. "We got work to do, and you're in the way. Mr. Trung don't understand American ennerprise. Hell, he don't even talk American. It's our job to help him with both."

A woman ran out of the storefront behind the threesome, sputtering in a language Josh didn't understand as she passed them. She hugged the victim who tottered in the roadway, his hand holding his jaw. Her words continued to pour forth, but in a softer tone. He responded in kind and pointed toward Josh.

She kissed him on the cheek and looked at Josh. "My husband say you save him. I be forever thankful," she said as she helped support him.

"Yes, ma'am," Josh said, eyeing the three attackers. "If you'll just stand by, I have some unfinished business here. It'll only take a moment, then we can take care of your husband."

He gave full attention to the three. "Since you're being stubborn, and I don't have time to play your game, let's move this along. I'm sure I'll be talking to the police, and they'll want to know what happened here. It would be nice to have names to give them. You, boss man. What's yours?"

Again, the three laughed and did high-fives.

The spokesman said, "You may call me *Mister* Alvarez. That's all you need to know because you won't be here long enough to remember any more. Now, move it, or I'm gonna smear you all over this sidewalk."

Josh could see he wasn't going to talk his way out of the confrontation, and it didn't appear coincidence would produce the police in time. He turned to Mr. Trung and his wife. "Please, sit in my car while I reason with these youngsters. I don't want you hurt by a flying body. And, soon they will be scattered in different directions—face down."

As they followed Josh's suggestion, Alvarez said, "Hold it right there, Trungs."

The woman opened the door of Josh's convertible and helped her husband in before walking around the car and opening the driver's side.

Alvarez watched, then turned to Josh. "You sonafabitch. I've had enough of you. You done stuck your nose in too far." He jerked a switchblade from his pocket, flipped it open, and twirled it. "This is for you, funny man."

Josh studied the knife, then the thug. Both appeared capable of doing bodily harm. Alvarez held the weapon low, near his waist, flipping it from hand to hand, as if he were ambidextrous. Less chance of having it swatted away if the adversary didn't know from which side the attack would come. His eyes were cold, squeezed into a slight squint of concentration. Josh guessed he'd drawn the blade before— and walked away successful. His confidence was obvious.

Josh's best bet was to force him to move, to commit in haste. Maybe he could goad him into action. "Okay, bright boy, you've got control. A smart drill instructor I knew said don't draw a weapon unless you plan to use it. And, if you plan to use it, don't dither. It's a sign of weakness. Sounds like you think you can talk me to death. Why don't you quit waving that pigsticker around and show me how well you use it? So far, your moves are weak, signs of a rookie. Look, even your buddies see it."

Alvarez glanced at his friends who watched with big eyes.

Three steps. That's what Josh figured separated them, two at the least. Alvarez would cover the space before he extended his arm. He'd want the extension to drive the knife home in Josh's midsection with his final lunge. He didn't appear to be a finesse fighter. He'd go for the biggest target.

From experience, Josh knew knife fighting was an inexact science, sometimes driven as much by luck as skill. Many a survivor was not the best trained. An opponent misjudged and dodged in the wrong direction. *Voila.* Fight over. Josh didn't intend for that to happen.

No matter how he rationalized it, facing a switchblade was a dangerous contest that Alvarez could win. The good part was that, once committed, Alvarez could not change his mind, could not alter his thrust, whereas Josh had several options. Time to get game-on.

Josh made a show of looking at his watch. "Are you going to play with that thing all evening? I have better things to do than admire your lack of finesse. Maybe you need a shot and a beer to find your courage."

"You bastard." Snarling, Alvarez sprang toward Josh, knife low in his right hand and close to the body as expected. Good attack discipline. Josh lifted onto the balls of his feet.

TWO

Three short steps, more like mini-bounds. That's what Alvarez took. Josh set himself and pivoted sideways at the last instant. He guessed right. The knife missed by less than inch as Alvarez reached for Josh's middle, the biggest part of his target. Although Alvarez had himself under control, as any good fighter would, his momentum carried him a half step too far.

As the arm straightened, Josh clamped it to his right side, grabbed the shoulder with his left hand, and brought his knee up hard against the elbow. There was a crack, a scream, and the sound of steel on pavement. Josh pushed the punk away where he landed on the concrete several feet away from both Josh and the knife. Josh whirled toward the others.

They were relaxed, grins on their faces, not expecting their friend to fail. Their eyes followed Alvarez to the pavement, then they wasted more time by looking back to Josh. Each appeared to realize his predicament and moved.

Number two went for his rear pocket as Josh stepped forward and smashed the base of his palm into the thug's nose. Blood sprayed as the bone crumpled. Down for the count.

Number three's hand was coming away from his back holding a revolver in his fist. Josh was two steps away. He had to hope the punk was a rookie, or the night might not

8

end well.

A purse slammed into the thug's face, knocking him backward as it appeared to blind and distract him. He staggered, his free hand rubbing at his eyes. Josh jumped and grabbed the pistol, cupping the cylinder so it couldn't move, and twisted everything upward. The trigger finger snapped and the gun came free in Josh's hand. In the same moment, Josh kneed him in the groin and backhanded him across the cheek. The punk settled to the pavement, one hand supporting what all men hold dear, no thoughts of fighting in his mind.

Josh threw the pistol under his car, out of reach of the three. He kicked the knives after the revolver.

"I told him not mess with my husband," Ms. Trung said, grinning, her purse in her hand. "I told him I get him."

"Thank you, ma'am," Josh said. "You saved my life, but you could have been injured. I asked you to stay in the car."

"Young man, I fighting all my life. I don't stop because bad people want my money."

Josh smiled and reached out a hand. "I'm Josh Hawkins. It's a pleasure to meet you. Now I have some shopping to do. I'm sure you can take it from here. I don't think they'll give you any more trouble."

A patrol car with siren whooping turned into the shopping center, freezing everyone in place.

"I call them from inside store," Ms. Trung said. "But we don't need them. You already fix things."

Two police officers got out of the cruiser, their hands hovering over their side arms. "What's the problem here? Who hit 9-1-1?" the driver said.

Ms. Trung stepped forward. "I did. These three attack my husband because he would not pay. They say we need pay, or our store might burn."

The officer looked at the three, who were in various sprawled positions on the pavement, then spoke to his partner. "Call for EMTs, an ambulance, and backup. Could be a busy scene."

To Ms. Trung, he said, "Your husband did this? Is this him?" He nodded toward Josh.

"No." Ms. Trung giggled. "He too young. This Mr. Hawkins. He rescue my husband. They beat him. My husband in car."

The policeman studied Josh a moment, his hand never leaving his service weapon holster. "May I see some ID, please?"

Josh said, "Of course. Stay away from your gun while I reach into my back pocket, though. I promise not to get fancy."

"Do it."

Josh removed his driver's license and PI license and gave them to the officer.

"Stay right there." The driver gave the cards to his partner. "Run these."

He turned back to Josh. "What's your version of what happened here? Did you take out all three?"

"As Ms. Trung said, they were pounding on her husband. He looked like he needed help, so I evened the odds. I recommend you put cuffs on them. Their injuries aren't serious, not near as serious as the hurt to their pride. As soon as they get their heads back, they won't be happy."

"He broke my arm."

"He broke my finger."

The third thug sat, holding a handkerchief over his nose.

The officer looked at the three. "Good point, Mr. Hawkins, although I wouldn't quite describe them as unharmed." He nodded to his partner who had come up to him. "Anything?"

"He checks out. Both licenses are current. No outstandings. EMTs are on the way. Want me to take care of those three?"

"Yeah. Put the ties on them, then see if you can get IDs. If Mr. Hawkins and the lady are right, they need an escort to the hospital. In spite of what Mr. Hawkins says, they don't look so good. I'm no doctor, but that looks like a broken arm."

Two more patrol cars entered the parking area, followed by an EMT wagon. Everyone bailed out and went to work.

Josh said, "If you're through with me, I need to hit Publix, then head for home. My fiancée is waiting for dinner."

"Not yet. In fact, I need you to come to the station for a statement." He looked at the Trungs, who were now side-by-side, holding hands. "The two of you, also."

Josh nodded. "I bet you aren't married, are you?"

"No, but it wouldn't matter. I have three injured people she says attacked her husband, and I have the knight on the white horse who rode to their defense. That's three statements that have to be taken. Then, unless I miss my guess, someone will have to sit at the hospital waiting to interview the three alleged bad guys. Dinner? I figure I'll be lucky to find time for breakfast, much less dinner. So, Mr. Hawkins, I suggest you call your fiancée and tell her you'll be very late tonight."

Josh looked at the EMTs working on the three he'd put down. "Okay, but don't believe a word they say. If you don't mind, I'd like a bit of privacy when I make my call. I hate to get yelled at in public." He shrugged.

The officer smiled. "Sit in your car. Just don't try to drive away."

Josh started toward his convertible, then stopped and turned back. "Before I get too close to my car, you might want to check underneath. You'll find a pistol and a couple of knives I took away from those wannabe bad guys."

The officer got a quizzical look, but walked over and knelt. Using his nightstick, he swept the weapons out and stared at them. "You say these belonged to the injured men?"

"Yes. I disarmed them and kicked the weapons under the car."

The policeman stared at Josh as if doubting his words. "What are you? Some kind of superman? No, forget that. I'll bag the gun and the knife and have them checked for prints. Make your call."

Josh crawled into his convertible, took out his cell phone, and punched in Jaden's number.

She answered with, "What's taking so long? I'm starving."

"Sorry, Sunshine, but I'm afraid you'll have to open a can of soup. I seem to have gotten myself in a situation here."

"Situation? Oh, Josh, what is it this time?"

"Three punks beating on an old man. You wouldn't want me to pass that by, would you? Well I didn't, and now the police want me to go downtown and make a statement. Since the Trungs will be with me—"

"Trungs? Who are they? Is that singular or plural. How many are there?"

Josh chuckled. "The old man is Mr. Trung. I don't think he speaks much English. His wife is Ms. Trung, and she's a real pistol. In fact, she might have saved my life."

"Oh, yeah. That clears things up. Should I meet you at the station—or call an attorney for you?"

"Not necessary. This is pretty cut and dried. As soon as I give them a report of what happened, I'll be on my way. Should only take an hour or so. Save me some cold cuts."

"Wait. You said three punks. Did you take on all three?"

"Yeah. No problem. They flunked mugger 101."

"Are you hurt? How bad are they hurt? Are you sure you don't need a lawyer? I don't want to end up prosecuting you in court."

"Can't happen. It's out of your jurisdiction. Sorry, the officer is giving me the eye. I need to hang up and get ready to talk into a recorder. I love you."

"I love you, too, you big lug. Although you manage to get yourself into some of the damnedest situations. Come home when you can."

The line went dead, and Josh hit the off button, frowning. A steak sure would have tasted good. He was hungry. Maybe he could get a hotdog on the way to police headquarters.

THREE

Once at the police station, Josh asked his escorting officer, "Do you mind if I contact the Coral Lakes department? There are a couple of detectives there who know me pretty good. I think they might answer some of your questions."

The officer hesitated. "Okay, give it a try. Anything that shortens the paperwork."

Josh scrolled through his phone and found Detective Phil Summers' number. Phil was the junior partner of Lieutenant Jim Richards. While Richards seemed to have a perpetual suspicion of Josh and all PIs, Summers was friendlier and defended Josh to Richards.

Josh called the private line and got an answering machine. At the tone, he said, "Phil, Josh Hawkins here. Call me, please. I need a character reference—yeah, that's what I said—character reference. The Boca Raton police would love for you to tell them what a sterling person I am. Anytime in the next thirty seconds will be good." He chuckled, hoping Phil would know he was joking about the time element. "Thanks. I'll owe you one."

He shrugged, then told the officer, "I'm sure he'll get back to me as soon as he gets the message. We've worked together before."

"Okay. In the meantime, have a seat with the Trungs. This place is like a Jewish deli before the holidays. Someone will take your statements as soon as possible."

Two hours passed with the three of them sitting on hard plastic chairs and waiting for the police to find time for them. However, it gave Josh an opportunity to learn about the Trungs. Ms. Trung told him their history as she eyed the comings and goings of the police, suspicion and fear in her eyes.

They were born in Chu Lai, a small village in Quang Ngai Province, South Vietnam and spent their early years ducking the Vietcong. Their parents collaborated with the Americans during the Vietnam conflict, putting themselves on the VC kill list. When the U.S. withdrew, the two men had no choice but to take their families into hiding. For the next six months, they moved from friend to friend, hole to hole, often using the tunnels the VC had dug for ambushes and to cache weapons and ammunition. Above ground, there was a frenzy of murders as the Communists extracted their brand of justice on anyone they suspected had worked with their enemy. Quick *trials* were held in the village square, and the verdict was always the same. The punishment followed in the same square, witnessed by the population of the village. The message was clear. Disagreement would not be tolerated.

When it became obvious there would be no pardons, the parents plotted to escape. They lived close to the coast, so the two families moved to the water's edge and hid in an abandoned American bunker, hoping fate would show them a way to freedom.

By day ten, after dodging patrols that came to the beach to swim and bathe, they were giving up hope and looking to return inland. Then at twilight, a leaky round boat with one broken oar floated in on the tide. The men grabbed it and half-dragged, half-carried it to the bunker. For three days, they worked on repairs to make it seaworthy, weaving palm fronds into the existing wicker. There was nothing they could do for the oar except eliminate the jagged edges of the shattered end.

On the fourth day, they secreted themselves in the jungle, praying the soldiers would not return. While they sweated from tension and the sweltering heat, the sun drifted across the sky. They ate as much as they could, stuffing themselves, knowing space on the boat was limited. Whatever supplies they could load would have to last until they were rescued—or captured—or died at sea. After what seemed like several days, the sun sank behind them. As soon as dark descended and before the moon rose, they filled the little boat with fresh water carriers, their food, a few of their possessions, and cast off into the South China Sea. They took the partial oar, but could do little with it because of their overloaded condition. Any movement threatened to sink them. Again, their prayers were answered as the sea remained calm. A rainsquall would have been too much for their survival, given the perilous condition of their craft and the burden it supported.

For fourteen days, they floated without direction or compass, knowing little except they were drifting farther from land. The palm trees morphed into a green blur on the horizon, more indistinct each day. Then their eyes saw only water. The coast was out of sight. They watched in consternation as their fresh water and food supplies dwindled, despite the rationing they imposed. Their skin reddened and threatened to blister. Although they were outdoor people, they were not prepared for the unrelenting sun beating down on the South China Sea. Without telling the children or the women, the two men estimated they had enough for three more days. After that, they'd have to depend on catching fish for food and drinking the fluids in their bodies.

They awoke on the eighteenth morning and immediately forgot their sunburns, dehydration, and their gnawing hunger. A glorious surprise awaited them. An American warship steamed a few hundred yards away. They almost sank the round boat in their excitement as they waved items of clothing and screamed themselves hoarse.

Sailors on watch for escapees saw them and alerted the bridge. Once taken aboard, they were on their way to the United States, a dream held by millions of Vietnamese—a dream not realized by many.

After processing, they were relocated to a small town in Minnesota, along with several other Vietnamese families. Mr. and Ms. Trung grew up as playmates and best friends in neighboring apartments. While her family took to the American way, learned English, and insisted it be spoken in the home, Mr. Trung's parents, as well as many of the other émigrés, stayed loyal to the old ways, conversing in Vietnamese among themselves and with friends. Consequently, Ms. Trung spoke good English while Mr. Trung's was limited.

It was inevitable they would marry, and they did when he was eighteen and she, seventeen. It was also inevitable they would move to a warmer clime as soon as they could. The weather was a major topic of conversation whenever families gathered. The adults yearned for the heat and humidity of the homeland and passed that desire to their children.

Within a span of two years, all four parents died, and the Trungs made plans to leave Minnesota. With many tears of farewell, they made their move, relocating to Boca Raton where they'd lived for the last five years. To support themselves, they opened a small Vietnamese grocery store. It was in front of that business that Josh met them.

The three hoodlums were not strangers to them. They had visited before, demanding protection money. The Trungs refused to pay. On those occasions, the three threatened and punctuated the threats with a few slaps and groceries thrown around. Today, they came with a different attitude, and as soon as the Trungs said no, began to punch Mr. Trung. One of them slugged Ms. Trung, knocking her behind the counter, leaving her woozy. When her head cleared, she saw what was happening outside, called 911, and rushed to help.

Josh knew the rest of the story.

Ms. Trung asked, "Mr. Hawkins. Maybe you tell me how this happen in Florida? It never happen in Minnesota. We live there many years and everyone was friendly. Florida is paradise. Florida is everything beautiful. But it has people like those three. It seem impossible."

"I agree," Josh said. "Unfortunately, human nature is what it is, and there are rotten people everywhere. What we must do is put them in jail. That's what it will take to make our streets safe."

Ms. Trung nodded. "How we help?"

"Fight back. Call the police. Press charges. Testify in court. Tell other storeowners to do the same. There is strength in numbers. Punks are cowards. If you stand up to them, they will crumble." He felt like a hypocrite. He didn't trust the justice system, but he couldn't tell the Trungs that. No, he'd keep his true feelings to himself. What he said to them was the right thing to say.

His cell phone rang—not his distinctive *Jaden* ring, but his everybody else ring. The window read *Phil Summers*.

"Phil, how are you?"

"Laughing my ass off. That's how I am."

"What's so funny? Let me in on the joke."

"You. You're hilarious. A character reference? That's what it sounded like your message said. Do you have any idea how many pounds Richards will take off my butt if I give you a sterling character reference?"

Josh chuckled. "Yeah, I guess it does seem a bit funny, but here's the deal. I broke up a three-on-one where the one was an older man and the three were young punks. The police seem to think I used more force than necessary. I need someone to let them know I'm just a big teddy bear."

"This is too good to pass up. Put someone on the phone." Phil's voice gave him away. He was relishing the moment.

"I'll have to call you back. We've been decorating some

hard plastic chairs for the last couple of hours. I don't know what's happening in the back rooms here. I'll ask around for someone who'll listen to you."

"You're on. I'll stand by. Ring when you find the right person." Phil hung up. The last thing coming through the phone was his laughter.

Josh rose and approached the officer tasked to keep an eye on them. He was engrossed in a crossword puzzle.

"Excuse me," Josh said. "Could you ask whoever is in charge tonight to come in? I have a detective from Coral Lakes who needs to speak with him."

"Sure," the officer said. "He's pretty busy, though. Might be awhile."

"Give it the best you've got."

As Josh returned to his chair, the policeman picked up his phone and punched in a number. Looking at Josh, he spoke into the mouthpiece. He hung up and said, "He'll be out as soon as he can break away."

Josh sat, looked at the Trungs, and shrugged.

Thirty minutes later, the inner door opened, and a man in civilian clothing came out. His basic blue suit showed the wear and tear of a long day. His white shirt had lost every sign of freshness. His eyes were red-rimmed with bags under them. He walked to Josh and the Trungs.

Josh stood to greet him. The Trungs rose beside him and bowed their heads.

"I'm Detective Kelly. Mr. and Ms. Trung, Mr. Hawkins." He nodded toward the couple. "I'm sorry to have kept you sitting here so long. We had several things to work out in the back. For your info, the three men you put in the hospital are doing fine. They'll be healthy enough to hear the charges against them tomorrow, even the one with the busted elbow. We found witnesses at the scene who support your story. Everyone says the young men were the aggressors. Someone from the State Attorney's office will be in touch with you. Please cooperate with them. You're free to go."

He shook hands with the Trungs. "We appreciate your cooperation. It's good citizens like you who help us do our job. For the next couple of weeks, you'll see more patrol cars passing your store. We hope this was an isolated incident, but we'll stay in touch in any case. If you need us, call. I promise we'll respond."

He stepped away from them and concentrated on Josh. "Mr. Hawkins, your situation is a bit different. I received a special request that you return in the morning. Would nine o'clock be convenient?"

"Why?" Josh asked. "I'd rather get things wrapped up tonight. Hopefully, I'll have a life to live tomorrow."

"Sorry. The word comes from outside the department, from a much higher level. I have no control over it—except to pass it to you. Oh, the word is it's a request, not an order. You have every right to say no. There will be no ramifications. Will you be here?"

Josh puzzled a moment. "Should I bring a lawyer?"

"Your choice. I've told you all I know. I need to pass the word back up the line."

Josh tugged at his ear lobe. "You present an intriguing situation. A special invite? Yeah, tell'm I'll probably be here—but not to hold things up if I don't show."

Kelly took a deep breath as if relieved he'd delivered his message and had a response. "Good. I'll relay it as you said it. Now, I'll get an officer to drive the three of you to the shopping center. Enjoy what's left of your evening."

FOUR

Josh walked with the Trungs to the police cruiser, wondering what he'd missed. Why would he be *invited* to the police station in the morning? That made no sense—none whatsoever. Someone was spinning a narrative that Josh was not familiar with. Who? Why? Yeah, he'd be there in the morning. If, for no other reason, his curiosity demanded it.

He took out his phone and called Phil Summers. "The police changed their minds and turned me loose for the night. I'm keeping your number though. They want to meet with me in the morning."

"Good," Summers said. "That'll give me more time to figure out how to whitewash all I know about you. Never fear, though, I have a fertile imagination. They'll never get the truth out of me." His laughter ended the conversation.

Josh stared at his phone, a smile on his face, and mumbled, "Sometimes you never know when you're making a special friend."

He and Summers had bonded during a previous case. While Josh tracked the criminal, Summers tracked him—following orders from his superior, Lt. Richards. When things came to a head, Summers was close enough to see that everything Josh did was legal and his hunches were correct. During the subsequent inquiry, it became clear that Josh's approach had shortened the investigation and Richards' plan

21

would not have worked. The embarrassment had further damaged the relationship between Richards and Josh. Richards did not appreciate being shown up. Summers remained objective in spite of his boss's antipathy.

Josh checked the time. Eleven. He hoped Jaden was in bed and asleep, but doubted it. She sounded too wired when they spoke earlier.

At the Trungs' grocery, he walked with them into the store where they closed things down for the evening, then he escorted them to their car. They had parked in a reserved space in the back alley. Each step of the way, Josh kept his eye out for trouble. It was possible some of the punks' friends might have stayed in the area, waiting for them. Fortunately, everything remained quiet.

At their car, Josh handed Ms. Trung his business card. "Here's how you can contact me—any time of the day or night. Do not hesitate to call. The people of Florida are not like those three, but we have our share of hoodlums. Be careful. If anyone bothers you, let me know, and I'll do whatever I can to help."

Ms. Trung bowed her head. "Thank you, Mr. Hawkins. You are good friend. My husband and I feel very humble."

After watching them drive away, he resumed his trip to Jaden's—no steaks, no potatoes, no asparagus, and no wine, but a good feeling he'd helped a couple who deserved it. He hoped it wasn't the first wave of tsunami that would see more *collectors* sent their way.

* * *

Driving toward Jaden's, Josh reflected on how he'd gotten to such a position in life after starting out in a small town in East Texas. He smiled, remembering what a poor scholar he'd been in school. Hunting, fishing, and days roaming the woods were much more important to him than nouns and verbs. Fortunately, he had a natural bent for mathematics, and it was math that pulled him through high school.

Following graduation, he was all set to pick up a nothing job and spend as much time as possible in the forest and along the lakes and rivers. However, his parents had a different idea. Mom wanted him to go to college, something she'd harped on throughout his high school years. His dad stayed neutral—somewhat—on that subject, but made it clear Josh was not going to lay around the house. He could select one of two choices. Go to college or get a real job and move out.

With those options facing him, Josh enrolled in college. It only took a short while for him to figure out he had little to no desire to be there. He was ill-prepared for the academics and surrounded by city-boys, most of them skating through life on their parents' money and reputations. The fraternity culture seemed to rule the campus, and Josh had little interest in it. He went home for the semester break, sporting a two point five average, and announced he would not return.

His mother was distraught and tried to get him to change his mind, but his father accepted his decision. Of course, he reminded Josh this meant he had to get a fulltime job and move out of the house. Josh agreed.

After six months and two different jobs, both menial, Josh heard an Army recruiter speak at a civic meeting. That did it. The next day, Josh drove into the county seat and enlisted. He departed for boot camp three weeks later, leaving his mother crying and his father smiling.

At first, like the other recruits, he found the ways of the Army strange. Spit and polish in the barracks, nitpicking inspections, cleaning weapons they never fired, everything built around *hurry up and wait*. They marched everywhere they went, whether it be a training site or the mess hall. Forced march, followed by standing in formation, sometimes at the position of attention, sometimes at parade rest. If someone was found inadequate, he ended up in the front leaning rest position. While it was no fun, Josh adapted and soon became a favorite of the drill instructors. Basic Combat Training fell behind him in a eight-week chunk, and he shipped out for Advanced Individual Training—Infantry in his case—where he excelled. The similarities to his upbringing—hunting and living off the land—made him an ace, finishing first in his class.

His top finish gave him the opportunity to volunteer for Army Airborne School where he won his *jump* wings. After serving eighteen months in the 82d Airborne Division at Fort Bragg, Ranger School beckoned, and he transferred to Fort Benning where he again finished number one in his class.

Eventually, he earned his way into Special Forces and never looked back.

* * *

He pulled into the driveway at Jaden's and grinned at the light shining through the windows. She had waited up for him. However, that meant she had questions. He'd get a thorough grilling before either of them slept.

He let himself in the house and called, "Hey, Sunshine, I'm ready to confess. Trot out your interrogatories."

Jaden walked into the living room, a stern look on her face. "Don't make it so easy. I need the practice in cross-examination." She smiled, walked to Josh, and kissed him. "There, that should soften you up for the interrogation phase of the evening."

They both laughed. Josh pulled her down onto the couch and returned her kiss with more passion. "If that's how you greet witnesses in court, you'll never lose a case."

She untangled herself and said, "I didn't get my steak, so you owe me a full explanation. Talk."

Josh spent the next half-hour giving her a detailed report on the evening.

When he finished, she said, "Interesting, although much of it sounds like one of your war stories. Why do they want

24

you downtown in the morning?"

"No idea. But, I need my rest, so I'm sweeping you off to the bedroom now."

* * *

The next morning a few minutes after nine, he walked into the police station and spoke to the officer on duty. "I'm Josh Hawkins. I'm supposed to meet someone here."

"Yes, Mr. Hawkins. I was told to expect you. Pass through the scanner, please, then follow me."

The officer led Josh through the maze of hallways and stopped in front of a door labeled *Conference Room.* "In here," he said. "Apparently, they started without you."

Josh opened the door and pushed into the room. Four pairs of eyes turned in his direction—three men and a woman. The closest was Detective Kelly, whom Josh had met the night before. He nodded at Josh. The others were strangers. Josh took a moment to examine the room. A scarred conference table with four chairs on each side and one at each end. Walls needing a fresh coat of paint. A dirty and worn rug on the floor. One picture hung on the wall—a cheap copy of a George Washington portrait. Josh was not surprised at the furnishings. Police departments seldom got money for creature comforts. They were too busy fighting for enough to pay their officers and keep vehicles on the road.

The man sitting at the end of the table glared at Josh, a look of scorn on his face. His clothing screamed bureaucrat—navy three-piece suit with a pale blue handkerchief sticking out of the breast pocket, starched white shirt with wide collar, and yellow power tie. He wore designer frame glasses with a pale blue tint. After a few heartbeats, he said, "I assume you're Hawkins. Is that correct?"

"Yes," Josh said, stepping forward with his hand out.

"You were told to be here at nine. It's after nine. I guess the Army didn't teach you promptness. Well, you're no

25

longer in the Army. This is a civilian forum. From now on, you'll get a quarter-hour cushion so maybe you can be around for the opening bell. Now, sit down so we can begin our discussions."

Josh lowered his hand and looked around the table. Kelly shrugged. The others kept their heads down.

Josh dropped into a chair at the table.

The man stared at Kelly, then opened a file. "Last night, you stuck your nose into an ongoing investigation and ruined months of work. If I had my way, you'd be cooling your heels in a jail cell and would stay there until I chose to have you released. Someone else made the decision to let you walk. The last thing we need is a nosy amateur messing in things he doesn't understand. From now on, you'll receive your orders from here and follow them to a T. I have no patience—"

"Excuse me," Josh said, standing and glaring at the man. "I must be in the wrong room. I can't be sure because no one told me the reason for the gathering. However, I'm pretty sure I would *not* have been invited to attend a session on how to act like a puffed-up jerk." He shoved his chair out of the way and started toward the entrance, his fists clenching and unclenching.

"Hawkins," he heard, but continued walking. He opened the door and almost bumped into a man reaching for the doorknob. He wore a well-tailored dark suit, white shirt, tie that matched, and carried a folder in his hand. He was shorter than Josh, balding, a paunch protruding through the lapels of his jacket. A pair of glasses perched on the end of his nose. He appeared surprised, but recovered quickly. His deportment said he was not accustomed to being startled.

Josh's instinct was to shove past him.

"Oops," the newcomer said. "I didn't realize anyone would be leaving so soon." He looked into Josh's face. "Oh, you're Josh Hawkins, aren't you? Sorry to be late, but I wanted to re-read your file. It's a real pleasure to meet you."

As he reached to shake Josh's hand, his expression

changed, and he stopped in mid-stride. "What's going on here? Why were you leaving?" Looking around Josh, he added, "I see ugly faces all around the room."

Josh looked at the man's hand, then into his face. What was going on? Who was the newcomer, and what part did he play in the group? Maybe it was time to relax and go with the flow.

Josh said, "My mistake. I barged in on an ongoing meeting. The subject was *How to act like an ass*." He nodded at the man at the head of the table. "I don't enjoy being the target of the hour, so I'm removing myself before I lose my temper and get into trouble by breaking someone's face."

The newcomer frowned, then stared at the man Josh indicated. "Agent Sutherland, I don't recall telling you to start without me. I don't recall telling you to chair the meeting. And I don't recall telling you to show your arrogance by insulting a person *I invited* to attend. So, I think it's safe to say you're out of line, way out of line, so far out of line I'm tempted to lock this door and let Mr. Hawkins have his way with you. This is not the first time, but it will be next-to-the-last. If it happens again, even the tiniest of indiscretions, you will be on a quick flight out of here."

Sutherland's mouth flopped open. "Sir, I only—"

"Shut your mouth before I change my mind and ship you off to Washington now. Don't open it again until I tell you to speak. And get the hell out of my chair."

Josh feared his mouth hung open in shock as the speaker moved to the head of the table. Sutherland grabbed his papers and scurried away in the opposite direction, taking a position on the side of the conference table beside the woman. She leaned away from him as he sat.

The newcomer put his papers on the table and took a moment to compose himself. After several deep breaths, punctuated by disgusted looks at Sutherland, he said, "Mr. Hawkins, I am Isaac Newsome. I apologize for the crassness of my subordinate. While I wasn't present to hear his words, based on experience, I can guess his attitude. Please have a seat and give me a moment to make a phone call. Once we put the call behind us, I'll brief you on why *I* invited you here. I want the whole group to hear the conversation so I'll put it on speaker."

As Newsome dialed his cell phone, Josh stared at the others. Kelly shrugged again. The woman smiled. Sutherland's veiled eyes reflected scorn and disrespect, while the other studied papers laying on the table in front of him. It seemed a strange group and Josh wasn't sure he wanted to be there. However, his curiosity won the day, and he took a seat at the table.

Newsome laid the phone down.

"Isaac? Twice in one morning. Must be a special day."

"I wish, Em. This call isn't as pleasant as the first."

"Oh?"

"I'm calling to let you know I'm close, very close, to sending Sutherland back to you. His childishness . . . no, his churlishness is getting to me. If I didn't have so much invested in this team, he'd be bouncing down the street today."

The phone was silent for a moment, then Em said, "I have total faith in your judgment. You know the reasons I selected him for your effort, but if he's being a deterrent, send him home. I ask one thing, though. If you fly him out of there, make sure he has a coach seat in the last row—one that does not recline—and send him by the longest route, maybe a quick stop in Greenland. That will give him an opportunity to get used to being uncomfortable before he gets to my office. When he arrives, I can promise him a temporary position as a seat warmer in the outer circle—far outer circle—while I manipulate the bureaucracy to have him fired. His time on the plane could best be used drafting his letter of resignation."

Isaac chuckled. "You're tougher than I am. One good fact to share with you, though."

"Fantastic. Tell me something positive."

"Josh Hawkins is here, and my first impression is he lives up to his billing. He was walking out on Sutherland when I arrived. I suspect he'd have preferred to teach him manners." He chuckled, while looking at Josh. "I believe he could have done it, too. But enough of that. My next chore is to undo the damage Sutherland did and convince Hawkins to work with us."

Em said, "Mr. Hawkins, welcome aboard. I hope you'll stay. Isaac says you're perfect for us, and Isaac is the best. Thank you for all you've done for our country." Her voice shifted. "Gotta run now. Lots of meetings to attend to plan future meetings." Her voice carried a smile as it faded away.

Isaac Newsome put his phone in his pocket. "Sutherland, that was not a joke. I was dead serious. Screw up again, and you're gone. Please tell the others who Em is."

Sutherland mumbled something incoherent.

"You don't have any problem being understood when you're playing *big wheel*. Try again."

"Emma Morgan, Director of the FBI."

Wow, Josh thought. This guy has a long reach.

"Right. Your boss." He glared at Sutherland a moment longer, then relaxed. "On to more pleasant things. Mr. Hawkins, I am glad you accepted my invitation to join us this morning. My lateness was because I was re-reading your file—fascinating, couldn't put it down. You have quite a background."

Josh squirmed in his chair. "I'm not sure what you mean, Mr. Newsome. I—"

"Please. No false modesty. After I heard about your little disruption—or more specifically, the effectiveness of your disruption—last night, I decided to find out more about you. I find three to one odds fascinating, especially when the one carries the day. In case no one has told you yet, we were watching that operation." He sighed. "Anyway, I had your files pulled and, lo and behold, I think I found my man." He looked at the folder. "Do you mind if I remind the group of a few things? They didn't have as long to study you as I did."

Josh said nothing, but his brain raced. *They were watching a shakedown of a Vietnamese grocery by three thugs. What have I walked into?*

"Sutherland, make sure you listen. In fact, I want you to serve as secretary for the meeting. Mr. Hawkins is an ex-Army Special Forces operative and an officer. He entered as a private and left as a captain. Received a direct commission supported by everyone in his chain of command. Unfortunately, a Reduction-in-Force came along, and the Army let him go—their loss. Reading between the lines, it looks like some petty bureaucrats held his lack of a college degree against him. Probably over-educated jerks like you, Sutherland."

FIVE

Newsome paused and turned his attention to Josh. "On behalf of our country, I apologize for the Army's stupidity in not recognizing the asset they had."

Josh nodded, wondering what was coming next.

Newsome switched back to the others. "While in uniform, Mr. Hawkins was involved in numerous operations, most of which remain classified at the highest level. Commendations for jobs well-done fill his file. If he tried to wear all the medals he's received in the open, it would weigh down his chest. I had his classified file pulled, but even that was heavily redacted. All I got were his list of awards and hints at what he did. The citations for several are buried deep in security. That probably worked against him during the RIF, too. Most likely, the board only had access to unclassified records.

"After leaving the Army, he joined the police force in Fort Worth. He began by walking a beat and ended as a detective. Several years later, he left them—again with commendations in his file—and became a private investigator. We are fortunate to have him here in South Florida. Those are the highlights. I suspect the details are worthy of several Hollywood blockbusters. What I'm trying to impress on you is Mr. Hawkins is a true American hero." He paused and looked at Josh. "Did I misstate anything?"

Josh felt himself blushing. "You left out the choir humming the *The Battle Hymn of the Republic* in the background. Other than that, you managed to overstate about everything."

"I don't think so. If you stay with us, you'll learn I'm not one to use hyperbole. It's a pleasure to welcome you to our little group. I hope you'll become a permanent part of it. However, before I say any more, I need to tell you that anything—and I do mean anything—you learn in this room must remain in this room. Are you willing to agree to that?"

Josh frowned as he looked around.

Stoic expressions met him at every position.

Rubbing his chin, he said, "Sure. If I didn't know it when I came in, I don't need to carry it out."

"Thank you," Sutherland said. "With that out of the way, let me introduce the others. First, our lady, Rosalyn Waters. Roz represents the DEA. Across from her is Lowell Randolph. He's from the Florida Department of Law Enforcement. That's Robert Kelly, whom you met last night. Robert is a member of the Palm Beach County Sheriff's Department. And Bradley Sutherland. Brad is our liaison with the FBI, at least for today. As I said earlier, I am Isaac Newsome. I represent the Attorney General's office. This is the nucleus, the planners, so to speak, of the task force. There are others scattered around that you might meet along the way."

Each of the members, other than Sutherland, acknowledged Josh with handshakes and a "nice to meet you." Josh returned in kind, wondering again why he was there.

Newsome looked around his small group. "Any other housekeeping I should get out of the way before we get down to business."

Josh smiled. "I have something, sir. So far, I have no clue why I'm here. Perhaps you can fill me in. And while you're doing it, I'd love to know what this task force is all about."

He closed Josh's file and picked up another. He opened it and studied the first page a moment, making Josh wonder if the whole truth would be told or some limited, sanitized version. After all, Newsome said he was from Washington, the home of obfuscation and non-speak.

Newsome appeared to gather his thoughts before speaking. "This task force was formed at the request of the Attorney General. Our sole reason for being is to take out by whatever means necessary one Henri Blanc. Blanc is a French-Canadian who began operating in the US about ten years ago."

Sutherland interrupted. "Sir, don't you think—"

"I don't recall giving you permission to speak," Newsome said with a slashing look. "Go back to taking notes. I want a detailed memorandum of the meeting when we finish. Don't leave anything out."

He returned to Josh and continued in a quieter voice. "Blanc maintains his Canadian citizenship and spends enough time in Canada to stay legal. They suspect, as do we, that he plays a key part in much of the crime that plagues South Florida. As far as we know, he stays legitimate while in the north. Have you heard of him?"

"No," Josh said. "Afraid not. What's he into?"

"Pick something, and chances are strong he makes money off it. Prostitution, drugs, car theft, money laundering, burglary, bank robbery, extortion. He collects a percentage of what you walked into yesterday—the old protection racket. It works as good today as a hundred years ago. If there is a crime in South Florida, the perpetrator either pays a percentage to Blanc or runs the risk of disappearing. He has a well-oiled operation with fingers in everyone's pockets."

"If you know so much about him, why haven't you pulled him in?" Josh asked.

"Don't we wish? First, Blanc has layers of insulation wrapped around him. Peeling those away is a legal nightmare and hasn't been accomplished yet. Second, he seldom stays in one spot for long. As far as we've determined, the only time he's not on the move is when he's in Canada. There, he settles down and relaxes. Kind of his vacation time, I suppose."

"So, why not ask the Canucks to bag him and extradite him?"

"For what? He doesn't break Canadian law, and we have never been able to make anything stick to him. Every time we've tried, his bevy of lawyers make him out to be holier than Mother Teresa. We get a black eye while his halo gets another coat of polish. He donates to charities, political parties, and to candidates across the board, both American and Canadian. That's why my boss decided to assemble the task force. Each of these people is an expert." He indicated those at the table. Our mission is to find a way to dismantle the Blanc empire."

"Even him?" Josh asked, nodding in Sutherland's direction.

"Excellent question," Newsome said. "In the government, we always have our chaff, those who must be given purpose because they're on the payroll. Agent Sutherland's expertise is computers. He has received months of specialized training. We brought him along to try and break into Blanc's networks, but that has been fruitless so far. All we've determined is he uses several layers of ever-changing encryption for everything. Sutherland has pulled a few things down that I sent off to NSA. They're working on it, but tell me not to bet my next born on the results."

Newsome paused, then said, "As good a time as any to introduce the others in depth. Roz knows every trick there is to slipping drugs into and around the country. She's found several shipments we believe function under the Blanc umbrella. However, she didn't pick them up until they were in country and ready for the street. We were only able to stop some of the distribution. Even if we had caught them early, there would have been no ties to Blanc. The importer would have taken the fall."

He indicated the man across the table from Roz. "Lowell is our Florida expert. If it happened in the last twenty years and affects Florida, he has the details. Thanks to him, we determined that Blanc gets a piece of almost every illegal dollar. We're not sure how the money flows, but we hope to get there. That's Lowell's primary job—sorting out the people chain while Sutherland attacks the electronic chain. The shakedown you stepped into last night is part of that. We're pretty certain Blanc would have gotten some percentage of the protection money had it been collected. What we don't know is how the money would have traveled from the punks on the street to Blanc."

Kelly was next. "Needless to say, Robert knows crime in South Florida. He is our *Mapquest*. If we learn of something going down or hear of something that went down, we turn to him. Thanks to his in-depth knowledge of the geography, we've thwarted several operations that would have placed cash in Blanc's vault." Newsome hesitated and smiled. "Again, the one you stopped last night is an example."

Newsome paused, appearing to think. "That's enough for now. As we work together, you'll fill in the details."

"And me," Josh said. "What am I?"

"I'll defer that answer for later. Let me continue about Blanc. As I'm sure you can guess, there are others interested in his empire. Other crime leaders have tried to take him down. Each has failed . . . and disappeared."

"Disappeared? How?"

Newsome smiled. "I'm sure you're aware you live in the perfect part of the country for disposing of bodies. To the west, we have the Everglades, filled with meat-eating predators. On the east, the Atlantic Ocean which seldom surrenders those wearing cement boots. Not to ignore the thousands of miles of canals which swallow cars and bodies without a burble. You ask how? I'll let you fill in the blanks."

"You haven't answered my question. Why me?"

Sutherland broke his silence. "Sir, I don't think he's the right man," he said, his voice surly.

Newsome gazed at him. "You're talking again. Since you are, you may give us your opinion. Why not?"

"His record shows he has no respect for authority, and he's uncontrollable. We have no way of knowing what he'll do, or how he'll do it. He could compromise the operation. Or worse, he could revert to some of his old Army tricks and embarrass the task force. I, for one, will not tolerate any illegalities, no matter how honorable he might think they are. Remember, the Army threw him out."

"Strange," Newsome said. "We read the same reports and came to different conclusions. Were you perhaps reading with an agenda?"

Sutherland puffed up. "I resent that, sir. I am a true professional. All my ratings have given me top numbers in professionalism."

"Uh-huh. We're not here to discuss your past ratings. You should spend your time worrying about your next one— the one I write. Now, don't you have some computer work to do? You stick with software. I'll make the personnel decisions." He closed his file folder. "Let's take a break. I have a bad taste in my mouth. Sutherland, you come with me." He rose and left the room with Sutherland following.

Randolph and Kelly stood. "Time for a pit stop," Kelly said.

"Yeah," Randolph said. "Never pass an opportunity. This meeting could last for hours."

They walked out, trailing Newsome and Sutherland.

Roz stood and moved to the table holding the coffee pot. "Can I get you anything, Mr. Hawkins?" She smiled, nodding toward the doorway. "You'll get used to that. When Isaac gets exasperated, he calls a break. I guess he doesn't want us to see him throwing things. Sutherland tends to get under his skin."

Josh looked at her. What was going on here? Being left with the lovely lady was simply too coincidental. Did Newsome think she could soften him up for whatever they had in mind? Strange, very strange. "I'll have a coffee," Josh said, rising. He followed her to the pot and accepted a cup. "Please don't call me Mister. I'm Josh, just plain Josh. From the little I've seen, Sutherland could irritate anyone. Glad he's not my problem. Do you know why I'm here?"

She hesitated. "Be patient. Isaac is slow and methodical, but he gets there—one of the finest men I've ever worked with. A major strength is he never shoots from the hip. When he thinks it's time, he'll tell you."

"Patience has never been my strong suit. The Army tried to drill it into me, but the lessons didn't always take."

She stared at him. "Yes, I can believe that. You remind me of a taut spring, ready to launch if a switch is flipped."

"Ouch. Maybe Sutherland's personality call was right."

Roz chuckled. "That would be a first." She returned to the table, picked up her papers and briefcase, and took a chair across from Sutherland's position. After sitting, she looked at Josh and smiled.

He raised a quizzical eyebrow, then returned to his seat and sat, sipping his coffee.

Newsome re-entered the room, followed by Sutherland, Randolph, and Kelly, and took his chair. "Okay, let's get back to it."

Josh said, "Anytime you're ready to fill me in, I'm ready to know."

"In a moment, I promise. I have a couple more things to tell you. As I said, Henri Blanc gets a payoff from most of the crimes committed in South Florida. We're not sure how he collects them, but know he does. This, of course, has him rolling in money. He lives an extravagant lifestyle, always on the move. And, as I said before, he donates to politicians across the board. But that only accounts for a small percentage of what he accumulates through his illicit activities. We can trace his legal donations, but what is untraceable and somewhat in the speculation stage is the money he gives *under the table*. Plus, we're reasonably certain he has funds in hidden accounts in other countries. In other words, Mr. Hawkins, we do not know the extent of his ill-gotten fortune." He glanced around the table, as if seeking approval.

Everyone except Sutherland wore a pleasant expression. Sutherland scowled.

Newsome took a deep breath. "We don't know how Blanc's operations function. For all we know, he could be supporting terrorist groups in the Middle East. It's simply not in our knowledge base. Whatever his actions, he must be stopped. And that, Mr. Hawkins, is why we invited you to join us."

Newsome went quiet and leaned back in his chair. No one said anything.

Josh shifted his gaze from person to person. Other than Sutherland and Roz, no one met his eyes. Sutherland stared, a sour expression on his face. Roz smiled and nodded. He realized he had a potential enemy in Sutherland, although he didn't know why. The other men seemed not to care one way or the other, and Roz . . . well, she could still be carrying out her assignment. In any case, he was tiring of Newsome's ducking.

Josh returned Sutherland's stare until Sutherland broke contact. He suddenly found something interesting in his notes.

"Mr. Newsome," Josh said, "I've never been patient at word games or at reading between the lines. Why don't you just lay it on the table? What do you expect from me, or for me to do?"

After a moment of silence, Newsome said, "Yes, I suppose it's time to state your mission."

SIX

Gazing at Newsome, Josh said, "What? Plain English, please. No more bureaucratic double-talk."

Newsome hesitated, staring at Josh's folder. "We want you to do what you did in the Army. Neutralize Henri Blanc."

The room was so quiet, Josh imagined he could hear a fly buzzing against the window. If anyone was breathing, it was in short, quiet breaths.

"Mr. Newsome," Josh said, leaning forward, "I don't claim to be a smart man. I don't have a stack of fancy degrees to tack onto my name. I don't work in Washington and have no desire to. I live in a simple, straightforward world. When I have something to say, I say it. I'd appreciate it if you would do the same. If your *neutralize Henri Blanc* means assassinate him, please say it that way."

Newsome flinched. He stared at Josh as if trying to see into his soul. "Yes. We want Blanc dead and out of sight and don't care how it happens. I believe you're the person who can do that. Is that simple enough?"

Josh pursed his lips. "Thank you for your directness." He looked at the people at the table. Still, no one met his eyes except Roz. Sutherland had his head down, writing on a legal pad. Roz nodded as if saying, *you're our man.*

"When last I wore a police uniform," Josh said, "there were laws against killing people, no matter who they are. I suspect that at least one of those laws protects Mr. Blanc. Am I wrong?"

"Mr. Randolph, would you take that one?" Newsome said.

"One of my jobs on the task force, representing FDLE," Lowell Randolph said, "is to insure we stay beneath the radar. Should Henri Blanc disappear, it will be assumed he returned to Canada."

Josh studied Randolph's face, looking for a clue. There was none. "And if the Canadians have no records on his re-entering the country?"

"Not our problem," Randolph said. "We will shrug and say he left South Florida, flying his private plane. There will be a flight plan supporting that. He could have crashed somewhere north of the border or, perhaps, deviated from his stated itinerary."

"Ms. Waters?" Newsome said.

Roz said, "DEA's position, if asked, will be that a source advised us Blanc would be making an inspection trip to Colombia. We have long suspected he has extensive holdings there on which he grows coca plants and converts them to cocaine. We believe he made that trip, but have no further knowledge."

"Mr. Kelly?"

"We'll follow FDLE's lead. As far as we know, he took off and hasn't been seen since. For sure, he did not crash in Florida."

"Sutherland?"

"The FBI will cooperate with the cover story."

"There," Newsome said. "That's how we'll play it—no local or national investigation of his disappearance."

Josh fingered his jaw. "That might work. However, aren't you concerned that if he disappears, someone else will step into the breach and business will go on as before?"

"Of course," Newsome said. "However, not the way you summarized it. We believe there will be a scramble for the" top, with several of his lieutenants and other gang leaders vying for number one. The war that follows will cripple illegal activities throughout Florida. At the same time, it will flush them into the open where the police can track them. Within six months of Blanc's disappearance, we think we will have broken the back of local crime. And," he paused for emphasis, "with internecine battles going on here, problems throughout the country will be lessened." He sipped his water. "However, it all starts with the disappearance of Henri Blanc. In other words, Mr. Hawkins, it all starts with you."

Josh rose, walked to the picture of George Washington, and nudged the bottom left corner. He stepped back and stared at it. "Much better." He faced the group. "Can't seem to get over my military training. Lines should be straight and squared."

He returned to his chair and looked at Newsome. "That's a lot to swallow at one meal. I'll need time to sort through the pros and cons of assisting you."

"If necessary. Although I'd like an answer sooner, rather than later."

"Understood. You will put everything in writing, won't you?"

Newsome chuckled. "How many times did you go on a military operation with written orders in your pocket?"

"So, I'm supposed to trust you—to believe you'll protect me if things go south?"

"Yes, that's it. Not unlike your past experience, is it? The government demanded deniability then. On behalf of that same government, I must have it now. If something goes wrong, you cannot be identified with the government. However, that's not as cold as it sounds. If Blanc grabs you, we'll do everything in our power to get you back. We, too, believe in *Leave no man behind*. The trade-off, of course, is that you do not reveal anything to Blanc that will hurt our future efforts. But, if you get picked up by the police, you'll be on your own. Deniability, remember?"

Josh looked around the table. "Even more reason for me to give it serious thought. When I wore the uniform, there was no one else to consider. If I disappeared, so be it. Now, I have a fiancée. I need to discuss it with her."

"I'm afraid that's not possible," Newsome said. "She's an assistant state attorney. Her advice has to be for you to turn me down. In her position, I'd do the same." He rubbed the back of his hand. "But I'm not in her position. I'm in mine. And I need you. I need your expertise."

Josh stood. "Okay. How do I get in touch once I decide?"

Newsome held out a business card. "Call me. That number is personal. There'll be no one except you and me. Before you leave, though, I have a secrecy oath I need you to sign. Similar to the ones you signed while in the military. No tricks, just an agreement to not reveal what we're doing. To reiterate, everything you heard today, including the existence of this task force, is Top Secret and must stay that way."

Josh nodded, knowing the purpose of nondisclosure agreements—protect the government. With that, each of the others, except Sutherland, held out a business card to Josh. Josh accepted them and stuck them in his hip pocket.

"Time to move on," Josh said. "Where do I sign?"

* * *

Josh drove away from the police station, his mind swirling. He had no reason to doubt Newsome's story. After all, he was in South Florida where the unusual was the routine. Henri Blanc could be everything Newsome said.

However, Josh's consternation came from the request made of him. Did he want to get involved in an assassination on his home turf? Operating in denied areas against enemies of the country was one thing, but this was different. If he had gotten caught before, it would have been a quick end. If he were caught on an operation such as this, it would be months of court followed by years in prison, struggling to stay alive amidst the dregs of society. Not a pretty thought.

Per Newsome's description, taking out someone of Blanc's stature could produce more heat that anyone could tolerate. Despite Newsome's assurances the task force would have cover stories ready to release, Josh didn't have a secure feeling. He expected those cover stories to be in place to protect the task force, not him. All it would take would be one curious bystander, and Josh would find himself hunted by the police. Not good.

His common sense told him to reject Newsome's request. Play it safe and continue to enjoy his newfound life with Jaden. Yet, his concept of justice said Blanc needed to fall, fall hard—if Newsome's description was correct. Newsome asked him not to discuss the situation with Jaden, but he couldn't do that. If he were getting involved with something that could destroy them, she had to at least know the outline.

He had nothing on his calendar for the rest of the day. Perhaps he could watch Jaden in action. Her appearance in court should be starting within the hour. Good idea, he thought. Maybe she'll find a way to put Rodriguez where he belongs.

Thinking of Rodriguez forced a groan from Josh. He was a lowlife the justice system *needed* to take off the streets. He had been in Jaden's crosshairs for the last year—a wife-abuser she prosecuted in court. He beat the charge by bringing in friends to testify that his wife, Sophia, was accident prone and tripped a lot. A *doctor* testified her bruises at the time of Rodriguez's arrest could have come from stumbling into things and falling. The jury bought the story, and Rodriguez walked free. Jaden's only option was to accept the verdict, believing he'd be back, and cringing at the thought of why.

And he was, on a charge of murder. A few weeks after his acquittal, he killed Sophia. This time, Jaden was confident she had him, but a smart defense attorney worked the loopholes in the law like an eighteen-wheeler plowing through a field of wheat.

Jaden's mood over the past several evenings had been down, touching Josh's heart. She trusted the justice system and immersed herself in her caseload, believing hard work would lead to the punishment of the guilty. She would not accept that there was a bias favoring the miscreants who committed crimes in the community. Josh vowed it would not save Rodriguez again, would not allow him to walk away from murder. If the court didn't make him pay, Josh would. His dilemma was that Jaden knew his opinion of the justice system and had asked for a promise he'd stay neutral this time. His reply was nothing to be proud of—weasel wording at its best.

He drove to the courthouse, found a space, and parked. After getting out, he raised his trunk lid to stow his weapons, then remembered he was unarmed because of the trip to the police station. He walked into the building and cleared the metal detector. The courtroom was on the eighth floor so he took the elevator up, then squeezed into the back of the room.

Jaden was approaching a man in the witness chair. "Mr. Camacho, thank you for returning this morning. I know you're taking time off from your job, so I'll keep this as short as possible."

Camacho shifted in his chair and stared at her.

Jaden flipped a page on her legal pad. "Yesterday, you told us that you saw Ms. Rodriguez fly into a rage on several occasions. Is that right?"

"Yes, ma'am."

"I'd like, and I think the jury would like, to know a bit more about those rages. When did it happen last?"

"I don't know. I don't keep a calendar on stuff like that."

"Good point," Jaden said, glancing at the jury. "Was it last month, two months ago, six months . . . I'm not looking for an exact date, just a time frame."

"Uh," Camacho said, looking at the defense table. "Maybe a month before she died."

"Fine. What were the circumstances?"

"I don't understand. We were just there, and she went off on us."

Jaden again glanced at the jury. "What were you doing? What was she doing? What was her husband doing? Did anyone say anything untoward to her?"

"Uh, what? I don't know what you're talkin' about."

"My mistake. I'm sorry. Did anyone say anything nasty to her, anything to insult her?"

"Naw. We was just watchin' the game, and she went crazy."

"Where were you, and where was Mr. Rodriguez?"

"Let me think a minute. I was settin' on the couch. Santiago was . . . I'm tryin' to remember. Yeah, he was comin' out of the kitchen with a coupla beers. She come out after him, screamin' she was gonna kill him. That's what it was. I remember now."

"So, Mr. Rodriguez was in the kitchen with her before she went *crazy.*" She made finger quotes in the air for the word crazy. "Did you hear them talking?"

"No, ma'am. I didn't hear nothin'."

"So, he could have said anything from 'I love you' to 'I'm going to beat you to death.' Is that right?"

"He didn't do that. That last, I mean." His voice rose, a bit of irritation showing through.

"How do you know? You said you couldn't hear them."

"I just know, that's all. Santiago never touched her."

Jaden looked toward the jury, saying, "How do you know that?"

"Objection, your honor," the defense attorney said. "She's badgering the witness. He answered the question."

"Not at all, your honor," Jaden said. "Since he's so sure of himself, I think it's important for us to know why."

"Overruled, but get on with it, Ms. Archer. I'd like to

finish this trial this year."

"Thank you, your honor." Jaden turned back to Camacho. "So, how do you know Santiago never touched her?"

Camacho squirmed, staring at the defense table. "Uh, he told me so."

"Who told you so?"

"Santiago. He said she just come after him. He didn't do nothin'."

"And you believe him?"

"Of course. He's my friend. He wouldn't lie to me."

"Isn't it convenient that Ms. Rodriguez isn't here to disagree?"

"Objection."

"I'm finished with this witness, your honor," Jaden said, walking away. "Thank you for your patience."

During Jaden's cross-examination, Josh watched the jury. They appeared to listen, some with passive expressions and others whose faces revealed their feelings. He hoped to see changes that showed they sided with Jaden, that they doubted the witness. However, except for one woman, there was little change. In her case, it appeared her irritation grew with each question Jaden asked—at the question, not the answer.

He sighed. Jaden had done a good job, but it was wasted if the jury didn't see though Rodriguez's buddy. That was the problem with the justice system. Too often it came down to the best actors, the best prepped, those whose friends were the most accomplished liars. Rodriguez killed his wife, but was blessed with the right kind of friends.

He slipped out the door, his plan for lunch with Jaden abandoned. If she ate at all, it would be with her notes in front of her, studying, looking for the chink in Rodriguez's defense, trying to find a way to get the truth to the jury. He shook his head, convinced once again the system slanted toward the guilty. The innocent were pawns to be sacrificed to make the game look official.

He'd heard enough. He figured he should get home first tonight with last night's dinner order in hand and have the charcoal hot and the wine chilled and poured when Jaden arrived. Perhaps, it would give her ego a boost. His meeting with Newsome and company popped into his mind. He needed to discuss it with Jaden. Then he remembered the secrecy oath he signed. He'd spent his life in loyalty to his government and couldn't change that now. He'd have to keep Jaden in the dark. Of course, with the way the trial was going, she'd be too busy to notice his preoccupation with something else. What he preferred to tell her was not to worry about Rodriguez. No matter what the judge and jury said, Rodriguez would receive his punishment.

SEVEN

Josh stopped for lunch and took a table in a rear corner of the restaurant. He needed to think and didn't want people disrupting him. If he decided to go after Blanc, there were major logistical problems to solve. If a task force of the US Government couldn't track him down, how could one man like Josh do it? He needed intelligence, he need logistics, he needed backup. Operating as a lone wolf was not his style.

Josh ordered a bacon cheeseburger, fries, and iced tea. Then he took out a small lined pad and began to doodle. Maybe something would flow through his fingertips that he didn't know he knew. His meal came, and he ate without tasting. Such was his concentration.

He tried to put himself into Blanc's head. If he were going to run an operation like his and demanded tight security, how would he do it? Josh wrote the first criteria.

1. Knowledge of Blanc and his whereabouts would be limited to one echelon below.

2. Each echelon would practice the same level of security.

Josh stopped and thought. That was pretty much it. If the knowledge of each level of the organization was limited to one layer below and one contact above, barriers to penetration were in place. To get to Blanc, an outsider, such as Josh, would have to break through at a base level and work himself upward without committing a fatal error. One slip and he'd disappear. Jaden would be a widow before she became a bride. And Josh had little doubt that Blanc and his people knew many ways to make a body invisible.

At which tier could Josh effect a penetration? Perhaps Newsome could introduce him in at a mid to high level, but Josh doubted it. His feeling was that Newsome was as much in the dark as Josh. Both had a mission with no idea how to accomplish it.

Josh doodled and thought. Thought and doodled.

"Refill, sir?" the waitress said, a sweating pitcher of iced tea in her hand.

"Oh, yes," Josh said, looking up and realizing he'd been so engrossed he hadn't seen her coming. Was that a clue to his decision? Was he already so lost in Blanc that a cute waitress with a plunging neckline could materialize beside him, and he not notice? He had to think yes. Before he committed, though, he needed more info. Maybe Detective Kelly would talk to him. Besides, Kelly was local. If Josh were swept up by the police, having an ally in Kelly might save him.

He took out the business cards of the task force, remembering the hostility Sutherland had projected, and found Kelly's. Before dialing, Josh considered Sutherland. How should he handle him? For reasons he didn't understand, Sutherland appeared to have taken a distinct disliking to him. He was a threat Josh would have to watch. He grinned. Of course, if Sutherland became too much of a pain in the ass, he might join Blanc on a long trip to nowhere. Josh wondered who would miss him. From what he'd seen, no one on the task force.

He punched in Kelly's number. When a voice answered, he said, "Detective Kelly, please."

"You got him."

"This is Josh Hawkins. I wonder if we could meet. I have a few questions you can answer, if you're so inclined."

There was silence on the line, then, "Things seem rather

clear to me. I don't know that I can add anything."

"I assure you that's not the case. Seems to me we're the locals in this deal. We must have something in common."

Again the silence. "Yeah, you have a point. I can break away for about an hour. Where are you?"

"How about the Coral Lakes library on University. We can either talk there or go somewhere else. Your choice."

"Fifteen minutes." The line went dead.

* * *

Josh walked in and looked around. A plaque by the door said the library had been open for five years. It was a two-story building tweaked to the needs of modern patrons. There were few reading niches. Where, in years past, comfortable chairs would have been, wooden rectangular tables filled the spaces. From previous visits, Josh knew students poured in after school and clustered, waiting to be picked up by parents. Some did homework, but for most, it was social-hour. Two uniformed guards walked the floor, attempting to keep the kids quiet.

There were also rows of computers, most of them in use. Josh frowned. Having grown up in a small town with a one-room library, he had a great deal of respect for the libraries he'd known in the past. However, he accepted they had evolved from places where normal conversation was *shushed* to an environment catering to youth and the electronic age. He couldn't imagine trying to sit and concentrate on a book. Too much noise, too many distractions.

In the middle of the lower level, there was one small area with three soft chairs around a circular coffee table. Josh sat and watched the front door, waiting for Kelly to come through.

As he looked at the computer activity and the few patrons examining the bookshelves, he realized this was not a good place to talk to Kelly—no expectation of privacy.

They'd have to shift to somewhere better suited to the conversation Josh hoped to have, perhaps to a nearby restaurant.

Kelly entered, stopped, and studied the room.

Josh rose, waved, and went to meet him. "I appreciate your coming," he said. "I realize now I didn't make a good selection. Guess I forgot how libraries have changed."

"Yeah, I wondered when you named this place. I haven't had lunch. How about a restaurant I know around the corner?"

"Works for me. I can always use another coffee."

* * *

Leaving their cars in the library parking lot, Josh and Kelly walked to the Irish Pub a block away. The pub prided itself on its selection of international beers, but also had a limited menu.

Once they had settled in a rear booth, the waitress came over. Kelly order a hamburger, fries, a Guinness, and a glass of water. Josh selected a Killian's, chili dog, and water.

When she finished writing and walked away, Kelly said, "Okay, how can I help you?"

"I'm concerned about how much support I'll get if I decide to take on the task Newsome offered."

"In what way?"

"C'mon, Kelly. Don't play cute. If something goes wrong, is my butt going to hang out for sacrifice? I'm not interested in being a public enemy. I've spent my life in service to my country. I'm not anxious to be remembered otherwise. Now that I think of it, I'm not interested in *being remembered* at all any time soon. I'm engaged and looking forward to a long life with the woman I love. You're been on the inside with this group for a while. Give me the straight skinny."

Kelly unrolled his napkin and put it in his lap. He played

with his silverware, positioning it, then repositioning it. When he spoke, it was in an almost whisper. "I don't know. I want to believe we'd go all out to save you, whether from Blanc's people or from the police. But I can't guarantee it. From what I've seen, Newsome is a straight shooter, but my gut says he won't let the government be embarrassed. So, if it comes down to your good health or admitting the US government is attempting to kill a private citizen, who happens to be a foreigner, I wouldn't rush to trade places with you. I suggest you build your own escape mechanism if you take on the mission."

Josh took a deep breath and let it out in a controlled flow. "Fair enough. I suppose it's the answer I expected. Now, another. What's with Sutherland? What's his problem with me? Can I expect a knife in the back from him?"

Kelly smiled as the waitress approached with their meals. After she settled the plates with the usual banter and left, he said, "That is much easier to answer. In a nutshell, Sutherland is an ass. He doesn't have anything against you. He's just a control freak and thinks he should be in charge. When I first met him, my impression was similar to what I take yours to be. So I did some discreet inquiries. It wasn't hard to find people who would talk. He's an interesting case—if you find such people interesting."

"What I find interesting is what you just said. Care to explain?"

Kelly took a bite of his burger, chewed, and swallowed. "He grew up with a silver spoon up his butt in DC. His father is a major league lobbyist with lots of money to spread around. That allowed him to move in the power circles. For reasons that defy logic, young Sutherland decided he wanted to be an FBI agent. Chances of his selection were slim, so his dad took care of it for him. He dropped the word in a few ears, and young Sutherland received a gold-plated invitation to join the FBI.

"That's when the real problems began. At the Academy,

he was argumentative and always knew more than the instructors—much like you saw yesterday. He even attempted to lead a mutiny against one particular exercise. That should have gotten him bounced without a goodbye party, and it was about to happen. However, Dad stepped in, swung his clout, and ensured he graduated on schedule—bottom of the class, but graduated.

"Once on the street, he continued his ways, arguing with those above him and, generally, being a pain in the ass to everyone. It got to the point no supervisor would take him. However, with his pop hovering in the wings, the big boys had to find a position for him. About that time, the FBI was expanding its cybercrime operations. Some brilliant bureaucrat recommended Sutherland for ADP training. Off to schools he went for a year, where neither his personality nor his father's influence changed. His grades allowed him to squeeze by, always last in his class with low evaluations. Following graduation, his cybercrime assignment came through, but his performance didn't improve. When this task force appeared, his supervisor found a perfect way to get rid of him—dump him on us. His computer skills are basic. Roz's are much better. If you need any in-depth research done, ask her."

Josh smiled. "You, indeed, have done your homework. Good report."

Kelly sipped his Guinness. "However," Kelly continued, "while I have no respect for Sutherland as an agent or as a human being, remember his political clout. You heard what Newsome told Emma Morgan. 'Next time,' he said. Can you guess why he didn't send him packing on the next plane *this time?*"

"Political clout," Josh said.

"Right," Kelly said. "Watch your back. But don't feel like the Lone Ranger. He'd knife any one of us to further his career. Backstabbing is his best tool to get ahead. He knows he'll never rise up the chain based on talent."

They quieted while the waitress topped up their water. When she moved away, Josh said, "What about Lowell Randolph? Does he have an axe to grind?"

Kelly sipped his water. "He's one of us and is as fed up with Florida's reputation as I am. And, like me, he knows that rep is well earned. If Blanc disappears and the gangs start killing one another off, Lowell will smile and be ready to arrest the survivors."

"What about Blanc? What's his security set up, and how can I get to him?"

"Sorry, can't help you. The guy's a spook, almost invisible. We assume he's protected, but don't know for sure. Get to him? That's the ingredient Newsome hopes you bring to the team. We've had little to no luck. Heck, we're even unsuccessful in pinpointing his goings and comings to Florida. Most often, we hear a rumor he's in the area. It's news to us."

Josh sipped his beer, then said, "Okay, one more, then I'll let you finish eating. Who else is involved with the task force? There has to be more than the five of you."

"If I knew, I wouldn't tell you. Yes, there are others. They're out there circulating in dangerous territory. The less anyone knows about them the better. Newsome keeps that information on close-hold."

Josh thought about what he'd heard. Other than loyalty to his country, there wasn't much to recommend the job. But crime within the borders on the scale Newsome described was a threat as real as many of the missions he undertook while in uniform. Blanc had to be stopped and stopped in such a way a message was sent to those wanting to emulate him.

"Okay, I lied," Josh said. "Another question. Would you take on the tasking?"

Kelly ducked his head, then stared at Josh. "No way. Of course, I don't have the training you've had." He reflected a moment. "I hope you will, though. We need you." He shoved the last of his sandwich into his mouth and looked at his watch. Using full-mouth talk, he said, "Gotta run. I have a meeting to attend. Lunch is on you."

Josh watched as Kelly left the restaurant. He had much to think about and a tough decision to make.

However before he made that decision or spoke to Newsome again, he needed to do his spadework to see if the task appeared doable. The only sure entry he knew was through the Trungs. He'd stop by to see them, to make sure they were okay. Plus, there was a Publix in the same shopping center. He still owed Jaden a steak off the grill.

EIGHT

Josh parked between the Trungs' Vietnamese grocery store and Publix and walked toward the Trungs'. He was glad that all was quiet along the sidewalk, just the usual number of pedestrians. He flinched, picturing Mr. Trung being thrown around by the young punks. Then, he pictured them lying on the pavement, all the fight gone out of them. That produced a grin.

When he walked in, Ms. Trung looked up and gave him a huge smile of recognition. "Mr. Hawkins. Don't tell me you eat Vietnamese food."

Josh chuckled. "No, I'm afraid not. I just want to make sure you and your husband are all right."

"Yes, we are fine. Dai is sore, but, thanks to you, not bad hurt."

"And, of course," Josh said, "I had to stop by and thank you for saving me. If you hadn't been so fast with your purse across his face, that punk could have gotten the drop on me."

Ms. Trung blushed and hung her head. "He make me mad. I act without thinking. Not very ladylike. I glad I did. I don't understand young people like him. What could his parents have taught him? Do you think they know?"

"My guess is they do now. I suspect the police were in contact with them today."

"I feel sorry for them. Such shame to bring to their

house. How can we pay you for saving us? We don't have much, but I can fix you a wonderful meal or give you the ingredients and recipes."

"Not necessary. There is one thing you can do for me, though. I need to make contact with the people who tried to steal your money. Did anyone give you a phone number or an address?"

"You want to meet with them?" Her eyes were large with questions.

"I think it's a good idea. Perhaps I can reason with them and convince them they shouldn't be bothering the merchants around here."

"That would be nice." Then Ms. Trung laughed and shook her finger. "Mr. Hawkins, you are wonderful man, and I thank you for saving my husband, but you are terrible liar." She held up her hands, palms out. "Don't worry. I don't need to know why. I sorry. I do not know how to contact them. However, if they come back, I will call you right away, and will ask for phone number."

Josh smiled. "That will work. Call me anytime, day or night. Do you still have my card?"

* * *

After leaving Ms. Trung, Josh went into Publix and shopped per the instructions Jaden gave him the previous night. Two rib eye steaks, each an inch and a half thick, two large baking potatoes, a bundle of asparagus, salad makings, and a bottle of wine. Checking his watch, he saw that if he moved fast, he could get home and have the charcoal stacked before Jaden arrived. That would allow him to kiss her and hand her a chilled scotch and water when she entered the house. While she changed out of her work clothes, he would get the potatoes into the oven and prepare the steaks for grilling. As she sipped her drink, prepped the asparagus, and mixed the salad, he'd have a beer and light the charcoal. His goal was to allow Jaden an opportunity to unwind after her day in court. She deserved it.

He loaded the bags into his car and pulled onto Route 441. He hummed as he allowed traffic to sweep him north, a smile playing around his lips, an evening with Jaden uppermost in his mind.

His phone rang. The caller ID showed a number he didn't recognize. "Hello."

"Mr. Hawkins, this is Hoa Trung. You said I should call if men come back. They are here, two of them."

"What are they doing?"

"Demand money. They want one thousand dollars tonight. I told them I need call my banker."

"Good thinking. I'll be there in twenty minutes. Tell them I'm bringing the money. If they try to leave, ask for a name and someplace I can get in touch with them to deliver the cash."

"Yes sir, I do that."

Josh heard a clunk, then in a fainter voice, "My banker be here soon. He bring the money." Smart woman, he thought. She put the phone down and left the line open.

At the next intersection, Josh did a U-turn and headed south. He wanted to call Jaden, but that would break the connection with Ms. Trung. Through the phone, he heard threats and an occasional crash. He pressed the accelerator harder and swerved his way through traffic, wondering if it was smart to not call 911. If something happened to the Trungs, he'd feel responsible.

Fifteen minutes later, Josh turned into the strip mall and parked in front of the Trung's store. Expecting someone inside to be watching, he took his time about getting out, then walked to the rear of his car, popped the trunk, and leaned in. With his head and hands out of sight, he opened a compartment, took out a loaded Beretta 92FS, and placed it in a special briefcase he kept for such an occasion.

He disconnected his phone from Ms. Trung and dialed

Jaden's house, hoping to get the answering machine. At this point, he didn't have time to talk to Jaden direct. She wouldn't understand why he was in such a hurry and would demand answers. As he hoped, the answering machine picked up. "Jaden. It's Josh. Sorry, Sunshine. I can't make it tonight. I have a continuation of the situation from last night. Talk to you tomorrow. I love you."

After leaving the message, he stood, took the briefcase, and headed for the store, walking as if he were in no rush whatsoever.

He entered and saw Mr. Trung behind the counter, both hands in view, a trickle of blood oozing from a cut on his cheek. Ms. Trung stood at the rear of the store with two males, her cell phone in her hand. One of the extortionists looked to be in his late twenties, early thirties. The other was a teenager, or not much more. Hard to tell. Baggy shorts and a muscle shirt made them all look alike. Josh nodded to Mr. Trung as he moved toward the threesome.

When he got closer, he said, "Ms. Trung. I have what you asked me to bring. Where can I meet with these gentlemen in private?"

She pointed. "The storeroom. That all we have. That where I keep my desk."

"That'll work. Gentlemen, after you."

The older man glared at Josh, then turned and headed through a door behind him. Josh stepped forward, following, then stopped and spoke to Ms. Trung. "We won't need you for this transaction. Stay out here and take care of your husband." He turned to the younger man. "You go in front of me. I'm not sure I trust you behind me." He waited until the teenager complied.

They entered a room about eight by ten feet with a small desk shoved into one corner. Boxes of product were stacked along the walls. A door opened into the alley behind the grocery. Everything was clean and dust free, causing Josh to surmise that Ms. Trung believed in cleanliness—even in storerooms. There were no windows, for which Josh was thankful. Cut down on the *innocent bystander* syndrome.

Once Josh closed the door, the older man said, "Okay, give it to me. One thousand tonight. Another thou tomorrow. After that, it's two thou a week."

Josh stared at the younger until he moved beside the other. "That's a lot of money. I have the thousand Ms. Trung asked me to bring. But I'll have to check her books before I can promise any more. This little grocery is not part of the Publix chain, you know. You're acting as if Mr. and Ms. Trung are rolling in dough. Before we go on, though, what are your names? I have to know whom I'm handing a stack of cash to. There are records to be maintained, withdrawals to be documented. Plus, you'll have to sign a receipt. IRS will demand proof they donated it to a worthy cause."

A staring contest followed, one that Josh won. "Gerard. That's all you need to know."

"And your son?"

"He's not my son. His name is Raul."

Josh laid the briefcase on the edge of the desk and popped the latches. "Not your son," he said, stalling. "I'm glad to hear that." Reaching in, he gripped the Beretta, then brought it out with a jerk. "I'd hate to take two from the same family."

"Hey. What th—"

Josh punched the older in the gut, dropping him to the floor. "It's a Beretta 92FS. Fires a slug big enough to rip your heart out with one shot. I know. I've seen the results. Two quick squeezes and both of you are dead. I suggest you divest yourselves of any weapons you're carrying. Now."

"What the hell do you think you're doing?" Gerard said, wheezing. "Do you have any idea how big a mistake you're making? You'll be dead before daylight."

"Yep, same as last night. That one seemed to work out pretty good, so I'll take another chance. You did get a briefing before you came here, didn't you?" He looked at

Raul. "Junior, you're too young to play with guns. Lay it on the desk."

With a frown of fear, Raul took out a snub-nose revolver and put it down.

Josh picked it up and gave it a quick onceover, then dropped it in his briefcase. First, it needed a good cleaning. After that, it might be salvageable—or not. "You should thank me. I might have saved your life. That piece of junk could blow up in your face. Where'd you get it?"

Raul looked at Gerard who still held his gut.

"Oh. Okay, I get it. Pops, is yours any better?"

"I'm not carrying."

"Sure, and I'm Cinderella waiting for my crown prince to walk in with a glass slipper. Either produce it now, or I put you down for good, then search you at my leisure. Your choice." Josh waved the Beretta to emphasize his point.

"You'll pay for this."

"I expect to. But if you don't cooperate, you won't be around to enjoy it. You have three seconds."

Gerard straightened, pulled a revolver out of his rear waistband, and laid it on the desk. It appeared in better condition than Raul's, although not much.

"Now the switchblades. Both of them."

"What do you mean?" Gerard said. "We don't—"

"Oh, please," Josh said. "Do you think you're the first punk I've braced? You may as well have a tattoo of a switchblade on your forehead. You were knife fighting before you were twelve. I want it." He looked at Raul. "Both of you."

Gerard pulled a five-inch knife from his hip pocket, and Raul followed his example. The blades went into the briefcase with the revolvers.

"Wonderful," Josh said. "I love it when people cooperate. Raul, let me see your driver's license. Please move slow or my trigger finger could have a spasm. Make sure it's the real one, not your phony beer-drinking license."

He fished it out of his wallet and handed it to Josh.

"As I suspected," Josh said, returning the license. "Sixteen." He shook his head and frowned. "Let me explain what is going to happen. We'll walk through the store, and both of you will say a pleasant good evening to the Trungs. As part of that, you'll tell them you're sorry for any inconveniences you caused. Gerard, you leave a hundred dollars on the counter to pay for damages. When we get to the sidewalk, we'll split up.

"Raul, you're going to walk toward 441 without looking back. I promise if I ever see you again, you'd better be wearing a backpack filled with schoolbooks. Get your ass back in high school and graduate. After that, enroll in one of the community colleges. Make something of yourself. If you don't, you'll end up like this sleaze you're running around with. I won't appreciate that and will make sure you gain a full understanding of my opinion. Do I make myself clear?"

Raul nodded, fear sparkling in his eyes.

"One last thing," Josh said. "Here is my name and phone number." He handed Raul a card limited to that information. "If you ever need help, feel free to call me. However, let me warn you that if you decide to give that card to people who want to do me bad, I'll make them pay, then I'll hunt you down, and the results will not be pleasant. I can be a nasty sonnavabitch, as Gerard is going to find out. Do you comprehend what I mean? Just think of what happened to the three punks last night, and double, no, triple it. You won't be pretty when I'm finished with you."

Raul nodded.

"What about me?" Gerard said. "What did you mean?"

Josh smiled a wicked smile. "You're my special project."

"I ain't going with you."

"Gerard, I have a full night planned for you. My goal is to introduce you to experiences you've never known before. If you prefer, it can start here in this storage room. When was the last time you were pistol-whipped? Don't answer. Let me guess." He hesitated. "I'm thinking *never*. Well, I can tell you that a Beretta 92FS leaves some awful lumps on your head. Not to mention how it smashes cheekbones, the nose, and eye sockets. However, if that's what you want, I'll accommodate you."

"I ain't going."

Josh grimaced. "Fine by me. First, let me ask Ms. Trung for a bucket of hot water and some cleaning supplies. When we're finished, you'll have to clean up the blood, vomit, and other mess you make in here. After that, we'll leave together. I may be carrying you, but you'll leave with me."

Josh glanced at Raul and saw a face filled with confusion and fear. He appeared more than ready to leave.

"So, you still want to stay here?" Josh asked.

"Uh, maybe I'll go a ways with you," Gerard said. "I ain't got nothing better to do tonight."

NINE

Josh reached into his boot and came up with his single-action, five shot mini-revolver and pointed it at Gerard. He laid the Beretta 92FS in his briefcase. "Now, don't get all excited, thinking about jumping me. This .22 might only have a two-inch barrel, but if one of its magnum cartridges tears into you, the game will be over. In case you're wondering, I am good with it, and at this range, I'd have to practice to miss. Keep a close watch. You're about to learn one of the many Josh Hawkins' secrets."

Josh slid the Beretta under a holder in the upper left corner of the briefcase, then strapped it in. The end of the barrel rested in a slot in the liner. He ran a second strap through the trigger guard, securing it in place. Last, he placed a hook around the trigger and fastened it to a second hook just under where the handle attached. All this was done one-handed while he covered Gerard and Raul with his .22.

Josh said, "It's not fancy, but it works. All I have to do is point the case and squeeze the handle. Boom. No more Gerard. Of course, if you don't believe me and are ready to die. I'll be happy to oblige you."

"Cute toy," Gerard said. "Bet you're just full of tricks."

"Yep, that's what they call me—TJ, Tricky Josh. Stick your hands out." Josh slipped plastic ties around Gerard's wrists and drew them tight. "Now, the three of us are going to walk out of here. Once we get clear of the store, Raul, you have your instructions. Move fast and don't look back. Gerard, you and I will get into my car, then go for a little ride. Is everyone ready?"

* * *

Josh opened the passenger door to his convertible. "Get in, Gerard. Fasten your seatbelt." He ran a plastic strap through the wrist ties and snapped it to a ring on the right side of the firewall. "Turn your head this way." Josh slipped a black band around his head, blindfolding him. "Sit tight. I'll be right with you."

He stood and looked around the parking lot. No one seemed to be paying any attention. There were times when the indifference of South Florida was good.

As he pulled out of the parking lot, Josh activated his phone and said, "Chief Wasan." The voice activated call system sent its signal through and the phone on the other end rang. Chief was a Seminole Indian and an old Army buddy of Josh's. They served together in Special Forces and went on several operations together. Chief—as he was called, not named—had retired and returned to his ancestral home in the Everglades. His full name was Holata Wasanjua. Within a few days of joining the Army, his drill instructor stumbled over the name for the last time and christened him Chief Wasan. It stuck. He and Josh weren't blood brothers, but their friendship had been cemented on the fields of battle. Josh had used the Chief's facilities before.

"Josh Hawkins. About time you called. When are you coming for a visit?"

"Tonight, Chief, but not for social purposes. I'm due a few days off soon, though. Maybe we can get together for some fishing and beer drinking. I want you to meet my fiancée."

"Fiancée? You've been busy since the last time you were

here. The squaw and I would love to meet her. I have a few things I can fill her in on."

Josh chuckled. "I'll pay you well *not* to do that. She thinks I'm perfect. Speaking of which, how is Sandra?"

"Every man's dream. And, of course, she reminds me of that often."

Josh's laugh caused Gerard to jerk in his seat. "Hey, while you're bullshitting with your buddy, these ties are cutting into my wrists. When are you taking them off? And while you're at it, get this damn blindfold off."

"Excuse me, Chief. A bit of interference on the line." Josh smacked Gerard across the face, then addressed the phone again, "Like I said, I'd like to come out tonight. I have some business to conduct. Is Miss Allie in house?"

"Sounds like you have company. Should I prepare a picnic basket?"

"That would be nice. Just drop it at Miss Allie's quarters and leave the lights on. Then you and Sandra might want to visit some friends."

"Okay, I'll take care of it. Looking forward to your visit and meeting your fiancée."

A few minutes later, they said good-bye, and Josh continued traveling south on Route 441. When 441 intersected the Sawgrass Expressway, he turned, swinging west around the built-up areas of Broward County. He set his speed control at eighty and held in the center lane as traffic flowed past.

Opposite Fort Lauderdale, he took Interstate 75 west across the Everglades toward Naples. While the traffic around him increased its speed, Josh kept to eighty. "Okay, Gerard, here's the deal. I need to know who you answer to. Also, who you deliver to above you. Ready to share with me?"

"You can go straight to hell. I don't rat out my friends. Where the hell we going?"

"Somehow I expected that response. Things will be

much easier on you if you talk to me now. Plus, it'll save me the misery of watching you crash."

"In your dreams. Like I said, I don't rat out my friends."

Josh shrugged and checked his side mirrors, then his rear view mirror. "Looks like we have the night to ourselves. No one back there. Just the three of us—you, me, and the Everglades."

"Who's this Allie you asked about?"

"Oh, she's one of my friends," Josh said. "And, like you, I don't rat out my friends. However, you'll have a chance to meet her—up close and personal. I'm sure she'll like you."

"We'll see."

Josh squinted into the darkness beyond his headlights. "Our turnoff should be coming up soon. There it is." He decelerated, pulled into the exit lane that led into the Big Cypress Seminole Indian Reservation, then turned onto Florida Route 833. "Hang on. Lots of curves and potholes coming up."

Gerard's head moved, as if struggling to see through the blindfold. "Where are we going? Where are you taking me?"

"Patience. I'll let you see when we get there, and that'll be soon."

They drove in silence as Josh swerved left then right, dodging some ruts, but hitting others. After a few miles, he turned off onto an unmarked road, not much more than a path. Rounding a curve, a lighted area loomed in the distance. "Not much farther. Think you can walk out of here?"

Gerard's head stayed pointed straight ahead. "You gotta be kidding. How the hell would I know? All I know is you're hitting every pothole in South Florida. When do we stop this game? My ass is killing me."

"When we do, you might wish we'd kept going."

A few minutes and numerous potholes later, Josh pulled onto a side road that led into a compound. There were three poles about twenty feet tall with lights at the top. The lamps provided enough illumination to see, but nothing more. He stopped about twenty-five feet from a ten-foot tall chain-link fence, turning the car so it faced the way they'd come. "Okay, Gerard. You asked where you were going. This is it. Like it?"

"How would I know? Everything's black for me."

Josh flipped the blindfold off. "Take a look."

Gerard didn't answer, just blinked, gazing at the area. His face a huge question mark.

While Gerard was distracted, Josh leaned over and pushed against the left wall of the foot area. A door sprung open and he removed an object. "Sit tight. I'll be around to let you out."

He got out of the car and walked to the passenger side. Opening the door, Josh shot Gerard with a stun gun, giving him enough of a jolt to put him out. "Sorry friend, but I have work to do, and I'm sure you wouldn't choose to cooperate."

* * *

A half-hour later, Josh sat at a picnic table, sipping a beer. Gerard's right arm and right leg were attached to the chain-link fence separating them from a watery enclosure.

Josh had put on a long-sleeved shirt to protect himself from the many varieties of blood-sucking insects buzzing the area. Mosquitoes were in the majority, but they had enough cousins to make the area busier than a major airport on Thanksgiving Eve. Tape secured Josh's pants around his ankles and the shirtsleeves around his wrists. He had sprayed exposed skin—face, neck, and hands—with a heavy dose of repellent, and was unbitten, although hot and sweaty.

Other than mosquito repellent, there wasn't much he could do for Gerard. He wore long baggy shorts and a muscle shirt. His calves, ankles, shoulders, and arms were exposed. Josh draped a blanket around him, but didn't expect it to keep too many bugs away. They'd root under it. He rose and sprayed him again, wanting to keep him as untortured as possible until he was ready to expose him to the hordes—if he needed to. Gerard remained unconscious.

Josh looked inside the cooler sitting on the table. It was the *picnic basket* Chief had referenced. There were four frozen chickens and a six-pack of beer, Killian's of course, along with a supply of plastic ties—enough to accomplish what Josh needed. He and Chief had worked this way before, and four chickens were always more than enough to elicit answers.

"Ah, man, what'd you hit me with? I ache all over." Gerard was awake and squirming.

"Welcome back," Josh said. "I've missed your scintillating conversation."

"Hey, what th' hell?" Gerard squirmed under the blanket. "It's too hot for this. Get it off me. Then—" The fence jerked. He had discovered the ties around his wrist and ankle. "What's this bullshit?"

"Just something to protect you and keep you in place while we talk. If you do what I ask, you might get out in one piece."

"Crap. Who you trying to kid? I done told you I ain't telling you nothin'."

"Your choice, my friend. Your choice." Josh reached into the cooler and grabbed a frozen chicken. As he lifted it, a thought hit him, and he dropped the chicken back in place. He walked to his car and opened the trunk. There were the Publix bags containing his dinner—a dinner he'd never get to eat. He took the steak package out and moved back to Gerard.

"You might, or might not, have noticed the bugs in the air. In case you don't know, those are mosquitoes whining past your ears. The reason they're buzzing you like that is they're bloodsuckers. And they sense you're loaded with it. I sprayed you with repellent and covered you with that blanket. That's keeping them at bay right now. However, the stuff will wear off, and I can always remove the blanket. Then you'll become their dinner. Want to see what it will look like?"

Josh unwrapped the steaks and tossed one onto the ground near Gerard. In an instant, insects formed an outer layer. "Darn shame. I was looking forward to that tonight. Why don't you watch for a while?"

As they stared, the steaks shrunk, the juices being sucked out of them. The layer thickened as more and different types of insects found the meal.

Josh looked at Gerard, who appeared fascinated by the steak and the effect the bugs were having on it. "Imagine that happening to you. Not pleasant, is it? They'll suck the blood out of you just as effectively as they're taking it out of that steak. You're probably anxious to talk to me now, but before we start, I have something else to show you."

"Dream on, jerk. I ain't afraid of no bugs. I been bit before."

Josh took a chicken from the cooler and held it up. "See this. It's frozen—hard as a rock." He rapped on it to prove the point. "Now, keep your eye on the birdie." He tossed the chicken over the fence.

Water flew as a huge alligator leaped into the air and grabbed the chicken, crashing down with a splash that doused Gerard.

"What the hell was that?" Gerard said.

In the dim light, Josh saw that Gerard's eyes appeared to have doubled in size. He'd lost all interest in the steak.

"I've never seen anything like that," he said.

Josh studied the water where horrible crunching sounds could be heard. "You asked about Allie. You just met her. She goes thirteen feet and weighs in at almost eight-hundred pounds. She's the main attraction here. To render her proper respect, we call her *Miss* Allie. I suggest you do the same."

Gerard puffed himself up. "Big deal. So why are we here?"

"Like I told you earlier, I want to know who you report to and who he reports to. Not too much to tell, is it?"

Gerard frowned. "Enough to get me killed. That's all."

Josh scanned the area, taking his time before getting back to Gerard. "From what I can see, you're a dead man if you don't talk. Just how do you think you're getting out of here?"

"You wouldn't."

"No? Why not? No one knows where you are. No one knows you're with me, except Raul, and he's still running. Behind that fence is a powerful disposal unit that can take care of your body. Not a molecule of you will be identifiable. Even if Raul finds his courage and talks to the police, there'll be no corpus delicti to tie us together. Sounds like I have firm control of the wheel, and there is a clear road in front of me."

Gerard stared at the water, then at Josh. "You wouldn't. I've known touchy-feely types like you before. You're all talk and no action."

"Right," Josh said and ripped the blanket off Gerard.

TEN

Within minutes, the insects found Gerard's thin muscle shirt. His bare skin remained bug free under the effect of the repellent, but he squirmed as female mosquitoes found a good place to drive their proboscises. His free hand was busy sweeping his chest.

"Want I should spray your back?" Josh asked.

"Please. It's stinging bad."

Josh followed up, and the insects cleared away.

"How about my chest?" Gerard said.

"Nope. You're doing fine without my help."

"Can I have the blanket back?"

"Sure, if you're ready to start talking."

Gerard said nothing.

Josh walked to the cooler, took out another chicken, and tossed it over the fence. There was a surge and three alligators appeared. Allie captured the carcass, but the other two jumped on her. There was a brief struggle before the smaller gators gave up.

Gerard appeared to forget the bugs. "How many are in there?"

"Don't know. I've counted up to twenty, but that might not be all. It's a big pen, and they go and come on the back side."

"Oh."

"Ready to tell me what I want?"

"No. Not a chance. They'll kill me."

"Your call. Let me give you the ground rules. Now that you've seen what Miss Allie can do, we'll concentrate on the pests of the Everglades. First, I'm going to cut your shirt off and give the mosquitoes and their friends an unrestricted run at your back and chest. As the repellent I sprayed on you loses its potency on your other bare skin, I won't re-spray you. That'll open up fresh feeding areas. We'll see how long you tolerate it."

"I'll take it. At least I'll still be alive."

"Oh, don't take any heavy bets on that. You see, if the insects don't convince you to share with me, you'll visit Miss Allie."

"No way."

"Some way. If you don't talk, you're no use to me. As I intimated earlier, Miss Allie and her friends will solve the problem of disposing of your body. There will be nothing left to hide, not even any DNA to test. I'll drive away, my conscious clear because I gave you a choice. By the time I get back to the lights and music, I'll have forgotten you ever existed."

Gerard stared into the compound where the water had once again quieted. No motion and few sounds.

Josh followed Gerard's gaze. He saw what appeared to be several logs floating. Except, he knew they weren't logs. They were alligators.

Josh took out another chicken and tossed it over the fence, eliciting the same response as before. The *logs* moved with lightning speed. "They never seem to get enough to eat. I've never seen them when they weren't hungry."

He waited, watching Gerard whose eyes were glued to the action in the pool, until it quieted again. Then he got up, took a filet knife out of the cooler, and walked to Gerard.

"What's that for?" Gerard said, staring at the knife.

"Time to lose the shirt. I can't hang out here too long. I

have morning appointments." He slipped the blade under the neck of the shirt at the back and sliced downward. The thin cotton parted like whipped cream, leaving a small stream of blood behind. "Oops," Josh said. "Guess I got some skin."

Gerard flinched. "You damn right you did. Be careful with that thing."

Josh grabbed Gerard's free arm and ripped the shirt off his front. "There. Let's see how tough you are now."

He walked back to the picnic table and took a large slug of his beer, emptying the bottle. He dropped the empty into the cooler. Chief believed in recycling. Behind him, he heard the fence rattling as Gerard tried to protect himself from bites. Josh took another beer and sat down. "I'll give you ten minutes. Then you go face to snout with Miss Allie, and I head for Boca." He leaned back, pulled his hat over his eyes, and rested.

Sounds of swamp critters came at him from every direction. He found the calls fascinating, but knew little about their origin. Some evening he wanted to sit here with Chief and let him identify them. He considered how it would be to live surrounded by nature, none of the hubbub of society interfering. No sirens, no racing motors, no neighbors' televisions corrupting the night, no loud sounds from passers-by, no eighteen-wheelers grinding through their gears. Just the silence and isolation of the Everglades with its creatures in full voice. He'd listened to and marveled about the sounds from Chief's compound before, but this time, they were soon replaced.

A memory drifted in of the first operation he and Chief went on—just the two of them infiltrating into hostile territory. The environment was arid, opposite from tonight. Chief was the senior, struggling to teach a novice to survive in a real world. Their task was to kidnap a tribal sheik and deliver him to the interrogators at headquarters. Intelligence reported he'd be traveling a certain route at a certain time. All he and Chief had to do was sit on his trail and execute the op order. On paper, it was simple.

In such an environment, where places to hide were few and far between, the easiest approach was to hide in plain sight—sort of. They dug trenches, crawled in, spread camouflage covers over themselves, then pulled sand in to cover everything except their heads. A camouflaged scarf over the face blended into the landscape.

They reached the ambush site and prepared their hidey-holes. As planned, they were six hours early, so there was nothing to do but wait—and sweat. Chief appeared to zone out, putting himself into some kind of trance. Josh wished he could do the same, but his nervousness did not allow him to relax. Instead, he kept reminding himself of each step of the operation.

One, take out the sheik's bodyguards, up to four expected. Two, grab the sheik. Three, run like hell for the landing zone. Four, call in the pick-up chopper while expecting an attack. Their biggest fear, other than being wounded or killed in the kidnap attempt, was a sandstorm. If the wind kicked up, the whirly-bird would be unable to fly, leaving them stranded with a pissed-off band of cutthroats hot for their blood. In that case, their orders were to dig in and defend until the weather cleared. If the nasties overran them, the word was specific. *One, kill the prisoner. Two, don't get captured alive.*

Josh smiled as his memory reminded him of Chief's words at the embarkation point. "Piece of cake." Josh's nervousness must have showed because Chief looked up from sharpening his knife. "You must not be afraid, my brother. Fear takes the edge off your vigilance. If you are to die, it will happen no matter how scared you are. Do you want to meet your Maker smelling of fear? I think not. Better to go with blood on your blade, empty magazines in your guns, and bodies of your enemies around you."

Somehow, Chief's words gave him strength. As anticipated, the sheik and his entourage appeared, the bodyguards were dropped where they stood, and the surprised sheik was rushed off before he could sound an alarm. The mission was accomplished with a minimum of resistance and the helicopter appeared on schedule. The weather stayed perfect. In and out in twenty-two hours. *Piece of cake.*

Josh peeked at Gerard whose misery flooded his face, matching the tears from his eyes. His free hand was busy slapping every inch of his chest and back within reach. "Time's running out. Had enough yet?"

"You're a real bastard. You know that?"

"Yeah, I've heard it before. Your easy way out is to tell me what I want to know. But, if you prefer to protect people who wouldn't cross the street to help you, that's your prerogative. You have two more minutes, then the game changes. Do you need another Miss Allie demonstration?"

No response from Gerard.

Another minute passed before Gerard cracked. "Okay, okay, I'll tell you, but you gotta get these bugs off me first. I can't take it anymore."

Josh rose, picked up the spray and another cold beer, then took his time walking to Gerard's position. "Good. Glad you're wising up. I'll compromise with you. I'll spray your back, then you can keep swatting your chest while we talk. Deal?"

Gerard's face was flushed and feverish-looking. "Anything. Just get'm off me. Spray my back—please."

"While I do that, have a beer. You look thirsty." Josh applied a heavy covering of repellent, watching the bugs abandon Gerard's back in the hundreds. What they left was not pretty. Red welts rose from every pore. There would be several days of misery before Gerard felt like wearing any close-fitting clothing. Unknown, of course, was what diseases the various insects carried—malaria, yellow fever, even West Nile Virus. Josh remembered the preventive vaccinations he had prior to operations in certain parts of the world.

While Josh returned to the table and picked up a voice-activated recorder, Gerard turned the beer up and drank about half of it, then placed it on the ground and returned to swatting.

ELEVEN

Gerard swatted, then took another slug of the beer. "Thanks. Maybe you ain't as bad as I thought. The guy you're looking for is Tony Carrillo."

"Hold on." Josh checked the recorder, saying, "One, two, three, test." Satisfied that it was working, he turned toward Gerard. "Okay, start again."

Gerard took a deep breath, staring at the shirt pocket-sized machine. "Tony Carrillo. That's the guy you want. Everything I collect goes to him. He returns twenty percent to me at the end of the month. From what I hear, he pays up the line, but gets a ten percent commission for being the middle man."

"Who does this Carrillo pay?"

"I don't know. I don't even know who else is collecting. It's a tight operation. I get a job. I do it. I deliver. That's it."

"Who were the three from last night that you replaced?"

"Same answer. I don't know. Until the Trungs, or maybe you, said there were three guys from last night, I didn't know. Go back to what I said about a tight operation. I got a call from Tony today, and he told me to collect $1,000 from the Trungs. I grabbed Raul because I needed a backup. The guy I usually work with is on vacation in Las Vegas."

Josh stared at him, looking for the lie. If it was there, Gerard hid it well. He continued to swat and sweep his chest, his face giving off little except pain.

After letting Gerard think, or kill mosquitoes, Josh said, "Where does Carrillo do business? How do I find him?"

Swat. "I don't know. The way it works is he calls me with an assignment. I complete it, then contact him. He sends a man to pick up the money."

"How do you contact him?"

"Phone. He has a new one each time. He uses throwaways."

"What number do you call?"

"Same as he calls me on. One call. Then he gets rid of the phone—I think."

"Smart man. Who does he send to pick up the money?"

Swat, swat. "Most of the time, it's a guy named Diego Delacruz. He shows up, I hand him the cash, and he leaves. The only reason I know his name is because someone saw us together one day and asked me about him. He let the name slip, then asked me to forget it."

"What's Delacruz's phone?"

"Never had a number for him."

"The guy that saw you, was he another collector?"

"Mister, in this business, you learn not to be too curious. People who ask questions disappear. I heard about two bums who got too nosy. They started sniffing around, then weren't seen anymore. They either moved out of state or took a one-way ride. Me, I just do my job and survive." Swat, swat. Gerard finished the beer in a second long drink.

"What's the friend's name, and how do I find him?"

"Don't you ever give up?"

"Nope. The name?"

"Martino. I only know his first name."

"Don't mess with me, Gerard. Miss Allie is still hungry."

Gerard shuddered as his head spun toward the enclosure. "Mister. I'm not messing with you. I see Martino in the pool hall. We shoot a friendly game. That's it."

"What pool hall? Describe Martino."

"Ah, hell, I don't know." Gerard appeared to think. "Shorter than me. Maybe five-eight or so. About same build as me. Black hair. Second generation Cuban."

"Accent?"

"Don't know. We speak Spanish."

"Pool hall?"

"The Havana Pool Station in Fort Lauderdale."

"What else can you tell me? You may as well give me everything."

"Got another beer?"

Josh handed him one.

Gerard studied him. "You can do whatever you want with me, but I'll die knowing the last man I talked to is dead. These people don't mess around. Best thing I can tell you is forget you ever met me and ride away. Far away. If you don't . . ."

Josh stayed quiet, ignoring the threat and wondering if Gerard had any other info he could extract. After mulling what he'd heard, he decided he'd pushed enough, and turned off the recorder.

"So, what happens now?" Gerard asked.

Josh stood and walked around the area, deep in thought. Did he dare trust Gerard? He didn't want to kill him, but didn't want Gerard loose to finger him either. "We have a problem. Under normal circumstances, people I introduce to Miss Allie don't survive the night. She gets a meal, and I get rid of a witness. Would you like that to be your fate?"

Gerard looked at the enclosure again. "Are you nuts? You've done this before?"

"Not nuts, just thorough. But what difference can that make to you?"

"Uh . . . none, I guess." He appeared to think. "Look, I don't want to die out here—not for no lousy thousand dollars I didn't even collect. What's it going take for you to turn me lose? Money? Name it, and I'll get it."

"I don't need your money. You've already given me what

I wanted—names. So, here's what I'm thinking. If I leave you here as a main entrée, and you lied to me, I won't be able to drag you back out here and have the satisfaction of feeding Miss Allie. However, if I let you live, and you lied to me, I *will* find you, and bring you here. I'll shoot you up with enough stimulants to keep you conscious until Miss Allie takes her last bite of you. You'll die in more agony than your feeble brain can imagine."

Josh paused, studying Gerard's face. The terror he saw was real, of that he was sure. "Now, in case you're thinking you'll go to ground and hide away for a while, rest assured that I will track you down. And then there will be a trip with two coming out and only one returning—me. Miss Allie will get a live treat, and I'll laugh as she crunches your bones. You follow what I'm saying?"

"Yeah, I . . . I get it."

"Do you need to change your story, or change the names you gave me?"

"No. I gave you all I got."

"Okay, one last thing, and we'll get out of here. Give me a hundred bucks for the floorshow. Miss Allie has a hearty appetite."

After Gerard fumbled out five twenties, Josh tossed the steaks and the last chicken into the enclosure, then dropped the money into the cooler.

* * *

Josh drove to the shopping center where he'd grabbed Gerard. After giving him a final warning, Josh headed for home in Coral Lakes. It was pushing midnight, too late to go to Jaden's. She'd be sound asleep—he hoped—and she needed her rest. Also, Josh had work to do.

Once at home, he booted his computer and, while it ran its opening routines, took a Killian's from the fridge. By the time he returned, the intro screen was up and ready. After hooking up the recorder and transferring its contents to the hard drive, he listened. Gerard's voice came through loud and clear. Unfortunately, so did background noises, clearly identifying the Everglades.

Josh disconnected the recorder, then took it into the kitchen, erasing Gerard's words—twice. He laid it on the counter and attached a boom box. After loading a Rap CD, he pushed the record button. As the *music* began, he returned to the computer and began stripping out the background sounds around Gerard's admissions, the boom box *booming* in the kitchen.

Thirty minutes later, the rap music stopped, and Josh ran the erase program again. After satisfying himself the system was clean, he set it to record again, started the boom box, and returned to the computer.

He repeated the routine twice more, ending with what he hoped was a blank chip. He couldn't be sure he'd obliterated everything, but, at least, he had made it more difficult to recover.

By three a.m., he'd removed the background sounds from Gerard's story. Feeling satisfied with his night's work, he went to bed.

* * *

Josh slept late, then took his time with his shower and grooming. He had nothing on his schedule, however, he wanted to spend time in the courtroom where Jaden was prosecuting. He missed speaking to her the night before and receiving an update on how her day had been. He suspected not good.

But before that, he needed a large meal. There had been no time for dinner the previous night. Since there was a restaurant in the shopping center where the Trungs had their grocery, he decided to go there. He wanted to check if everything was okay with them.

Also, at some point, he had to talk to Newsome and establish ground rules, especially how much he'd be paid for tracking Blanc. It was obvious, even to him, he'd decided to take on the task. Meeting a nice couple like the Trungs had swung the pendulum. Their parents had sacrificed everything to escape the tyranny of communism so their children could be raised in freedom. Yet hoodlums threatened that very freedom through thuggery. That could not be allowed, not in the USA he'd fought to keep free. Too many heroes over the years had given their lives so people could live in peace. No, the Trungs and all others like them had to be protected. His gut agreed with Newsome. There might be a connection between the extortion scheme and Blanc. Several layers in between, but a connection.

At two, Josh slipped into the back row of the courtroom. His brief stop at the Trungs had proven uneventful. No one had bothered them. Josh planned to visit again during the early evening since that was the usual *collection* time.

Jaden strolled from the prosecution table toward the witness stand to cross-examine a defense witness. Today, she wore a navy blue pantsuit which looked great with her red, shoulder-length hair. Conservative black flats adorned her feet. She carried a folder in her left hand, gently slapping it against her thigh, sporting a demeanor that she hadn't a care in the world.

The witness had Latino features and was dressed in an ill-fitting suit. He kept shrugging his shoulders as if not comfortable in a jacket. As Jaden neared him, he ran a finger under his collar, then loosened the knot in his tie. From Josh's position, it appeared he wanted to appear cool, but was terribly nervous.

"So, Mr. Vasquez," Jaden said, "you testified you were in the living room with Mr. Rodriguez just before Ms. Rodriguez died?"

"Yes, ma'am."

"And, in your presence, Mr. Rodriguez did nothing

aggressive toward her?"

"That's right, ma'am."

Jaden placed her forefinger across her lips, appearing to think. "So that I'll be clear on what happened, would you be kind enough to tell us again."

Vasquez sighed and leaned back in his chair, a smirk playing around the corners of his mouth. "Well, ma'am, like I told Ms. Kennedy," he pointed to the defense table, "me'n Santiago was drinking some beers when Sophia come in. She acted mean, like she was mad about something. She said, 'While you and your buddy are getting drunk, maybe you can do some of these chores.' She stuck a paper in Santiago's face."

"How did Mr. Rodriguez react?" Jaden asked.

"He didn't. I mean, he just took the list and looked at it. Me, I'd a told her where she could shove that list."

"Thank you, Mr. Vasquez, for that insight, but it's not your reaction I'm interested in. What did Mr. Rodriguez do?"

Vasquez made a show of thinking. "Well, he didn't *do* nothing right then. He said, 'Sure, honey. I'll get right on it.' Then he got up and went into the garage. When he came back a minute later, he had his toolbox, and said, 'Honey, where's the picture you want me to hang, and where do you want it?' He was being as nice as could be."

Jaden held up her hand. "Where was Ms. Rodriguez then?"

"Not sure. Maybe the bedroom because she came from the back of the house carrying a picture. 'I want it right there on that wall,' she said, and she shoved the picture at him. And she didn't do it very nice."

"I see," Jaden said. "What did Mr. Rodriguez say?"

"Nothing that I remember. He just took the frame from her and went over to the wall. Then he opened his tool box and started rummaging through it."

"And Ms. Rodriguez?"

"She kinda glared at him, then went into the kitchen."

"Continue."

He shrugged. "Santiago took out a hammer, drove a nail in the wall, and hung the picture, just like she asked him to. Then he said, 'Honey, see if this is okay.' Well, she come through that kitchen door, acting mad as a wet cat. When she looked at the picture, she said, 'No, stupid. It's too low, and it ain't centered. You shoulda known it was too low and off to one side. Raise it about six inches and move it a bit to the right.' Then she stormed back into the kitchen. Her face was red, and she was stomping like them Nazi army people you see in the movies."

"What did Mr. Rodriguez do?"

"He gave me a look like, *what's a guy gonna do?* and took the picture down, then removed the nail. He raised it a few inches, shifted it to the right, and started to hammer in the nail again. That's when she came through the door throwing things."

"Throwing things?"

"Yes, ma'am. Stuff was crashin' all over."

TWELVE

Jaden took a few steps toward the jury box, then turned toward Vasquez. "What did you do when she began to throw things?"

He grinned. "First, I ducked. I was afraid I'd get hit by a pot or something."

"I can understand that," Jaden said, smiling. "Did you stay and watch?"

"Oh, no, ma'am. I headed for the door and got out of there as fast as I could. Just as I swung it closed behind me, I heard somethin' heavy like a frying pan hit the doorjamb. Too close for my blood."

Jaden looked at the jury as she addressed her question to Vasquez. "Let me recap, if I may. Ms. Rodriguez came out of the kitchen throwing things like pots and pans. Is that right?"

"Yes, ma'am."

"Plates?"

"Oh, yes, ma'am. They were crashing against the walls. Pieces bouncing all over."

"Cups?"

"Yes, ma'am."

"Saucers?"

"I think so, ma'am. Coulda been small plates."

"Bowls?"

"Gosh, ma'am, I can't be sure of every piece. Maybe

bowls."

"How many pieces would you say she threw in all before you ran?"

"Uh, before I ran? Uh, maybe ten."

Jaden walked to her prosecution table and leaned against it. "How tall was Ms. Rodriguez?"

Vasquez frowned. "Tall? I don't know. Maybe five-two, five-three."

"And how much would you say she weighed?"

He paused, looking mystified. "I don't know. I don't know nothin' about women's weight."

"Okay, that's fair," Jaden said. "Neither does my fiancé. So, let's try from a different angle. Was Ms. Rodriguez overweight?"

"No, I don't think so."

Jaden walked toward the jury box. "Was she underweight?"

"Objection, your honor," the defense counsel said. "Where is she going with this? Mr. Vasquez doesn't claim to be an expert on women's heights and weights."

The judge frowned. "Ms. Archer, I hope you're not simply stalling, and it sounds suspiciously like it. Are these questions going to add something worthwhile to this trial?"

"Yes, your honor. If you'll bear with me a few more minutes, you'll see why this line of inquiry is important."

"Okay. You've got two minutes. You'd better pull it together fast, though."

Jaden turned back to Vasquez. "Now, where were we? Oh yes. Was Ms. Rodriguez underweight?"

"Ma'am, I don't know. I thought she had a nice figger. You know, kinda like yours. She was 'bout your size."

She spun toward him. "So, if we say she had an average build, how did she carry all those kitchen things and have a hand free to throw? Did she have a little red wagon or something?"

"Objection, your honor." The defense counsel was on

her feet. "She's making fun of the witness. He's attempting to answer her questions as good as he can."

The judge studied his gavel. "Objection sustained. Ms. Archer, please leave the comedy routine at home. Confine yourself to asking straightforward questions."

Lowering her chin, Jaden said, "Yes, your honor. May I rephrase the question?"

"Yes, please do."

Jaden appeared to think for a moment. "Mr. Vasquez, please tell us how Ms. Rodriguez carried so many kitchen items and still had a free hand to throw."

Vasquez looked at the defense table, squirming in his chair. "I don't know. She just did. I wasn't studyin' her or nothin'. I was too busy ducking."

"Thank you," Jaden said. "No more questions at this time."

The judge excused Vasquez and the defense counsel called her next witness, giving Josh an opportunity to slip from the courtroom. He smiled, giving Jaden a mental pat on the back. If the jury was paying attention, she had shaken Vasquez's integrity. No one could carry an arsenal like he described in one arm, especially a woman the size of Sophia Rodriguez. However, he doubted it would be enough.

As he walked toward his car, his cell phone chimed its *anyone but Jaden* sounds. It was a number Josh didn't recognize.

"Hello," he said.

"Mr. Hawkins, this is Raul. Remember, from last night?"

"Yes, Raul. I hope you're calling from school." He glanced at his watch. "Or while you're walking home from school."

"You're in trouble, Mr. Hawkins. People grabbed me this morning and made me tell them." Raul's words were rushed. It seemed he was struggling to be coherent. "They just let me go. You gave me a chance. You better get out of town. They're some mean dudes."

"Thanks for the warning, Raul. I'm not worried. I'm always careful. Thanks for the call. And make sure you go to school tomorrow."

"Okay. I'm gonna do that."

Josh disconnected, his forehead creased. Word was moving fast. Apparently Gerard hadn't gotten the message. When time allowed, Josh would make good on his promises.

His phone rang again. "Hello."

"Hawkins," a gruff voice said. "You're in way over your head. Get out or get hurt—bad." The line went dead.

"Damn," Josh said. "Looks like Raul was right. I must have stepped on the right hill. The fire ants are swarming. That's good. The more they race around, the more obvious they'll become." He continued walking toward the parking lot where he'd left his car.

His phone rang a third time. "Hey, must be my day in the limelight." The number looked familiar, but not one he could put a name with. He punched the connect button. "Hello."

"Is this Mr. Hawkins?"

"Yes. Who is this?"

"Someone you met a couple of mornings ago in a small group. You promised to give me a call."

"Ah, yes," Josh said, recognizing Newsome's voice. "You were on my list for today. I've been rather busy."

"So I'm told," Newsome said. "Apparently, you've made some dear friends and continue to support them."

"Oh? And how do you know that?"

"Please, Mr. Hawkins. Let's not play games. You know I have many sources keeping me up to speed."

"Maybe we'd better meet," Josh said. "It appears we need to have a serious conversation."

"I agree—one hour in the room where we met before."

"No. A public place. At this point, you've given me no reason to trust you. In fact, quite the opposite. I'll meet you in Barney's Bar in the six-hundred block of South Federal

Highway—near the courthouse—in one hour."

"Too public. We need privacy."

"Not too public. And your definition of privacy and mine aren't the same. We'll have privacy by my definition. I'll pick the booth."

"You're a suspicious man."

"And very much alive. I intend to remain both. If any recordings are made of our meeting, I'll make them."

"Two hours."

Josh grinned, figuring Newsome was playing for time to get his people into the bar. "Forty-five minutes. I'll be there in ten, watching everyone who comes through the door. If I see anyone I don't trust, or if you're late, I leave, and you can find yourself another consultant."

Newsome chuckled. "As close to forty-five minutes as I can make it. I'm beginning to like you more every minute."

"Like or dislike doesn't enter the relationship. It's trust or distrust from this point forward."

"Agreed," Newsome said, "but I still like you."

The phone clicked in Josh's ear.

Josh left his car in the public parking lot and walked the few blocks to South Federal Highway, aka US 1. A smile played at his lips as he considered Newsome. He was a smart bureaucrat, of that there was no doubt. Probably didn't have much experience on the street, though. That could work in Josh's favor. Josh hoped he could trust him. He'd make a valuable ally—or a formidable adversary.

* * *

Josh settled into a booth in the right rear corner where he had a clear view of the doorway and the bar. He studied the few patrons. No one appeared to pay any attention to his entrance, as expected. It had only been seven minutes since he spoke with Newsome. He'd have had to have someone close by to get him there before Josh. Of course, Josh didn't fool himself. Anything was possible when you had Newsome's power.

The waitress came over, and Josh ordered a Killian's in a frosted mug, then settled back to wait. A couple of people paid their tabs and left. No one entered for the next twenty minutes. At the thirty-five minute mark, a burly man came in. He sauntered to the bar, concentrating on no one, as his eyes did a dance around the room. He wore a suit, not unusual this close to the courthouse. The man did not have the look of a lawyer, and the suit did not measure up to an attorney's wardrobe, more like a defendant's or cop's attire. He ran to about six-two with well-proportioned weight to match. And his walk said *Cop*, loud and clear. No doubt in Josh's mind.

Josh studied him as he took a seat at the bar and ordered a draft. When the barkeeper set the beer in front of him, he never glanced at it. He was too busy searching the room using the mirror behind the bar. When their eyes crossed, the cop looked away. Josh grinned, wondering if he was the only contact Newsome had brought in. Time would tell.

Eight more minutes passed, and another customer rushed through the door. This one wore shorts, tennis shoes, and a ratty T-shirt, but otherwise fit the description of the first man—except being flushed as if he'd been moving fast. He took a seat several stools away from the first policeman, and used the mirror to scan the room. He was obvious in ignoring the cop who'd arrived first.

Josh nodded. The pieces were in place. Newsome had managed to get two bodyguards in the room. He'd be coming along any minute.

In the fiftieth minute, Newsome walked in, stopped, took a moment to allow his eyes to adjust to the dimmed light, then walked to Josh's booth.

Josh found it interesting Newsome appeared to have known which booth to approach without making eye contact. One or both of the cops must be in radio contact with him. Not surprising, but it didn't enhance Josh's trust in him.

Newsome slid into the booth and looked around. "Not as bad as I expected. I figured you'd get me in some grungy place where you'd think I felt intimidated."

Josh sipped his beer. "Is that why you sent your two boys ahead of you—to make sure the décor was proper? They're a bit obvious, you know."

Newsome tilted his head and smiled. "You didn't give me much time. I had to take what I could get." He studied the two men. "Yeah, now that you say it, I have to agree with you. Definitely a police aura surrounding them."

"Bringing them in doesn't enhance my confidence in you. Whatever happened to liking me?" Josh asked, smiling.

"Oh, I do. But that doesn't mean I trust you so much I'd put my life in your hands. Not yet, anyway."

Josh waved the waitress over. "Bring my friend . . ." He left it dangling for Newsome to complete.

"A draft. Something light, please. I still have a busy afternoon and evening in front of me."

After the waitress delivered Newsome's beer, Josh said, "Give me the radio. I don't feel comfortable with your boys listening in. Also, if you're wired—and my guess is that you are—put it on the table."

"What makes you think—"

"We don't have time for games." Josh scowled. "I'm leaving in thirty minutes. We can spend it playing games or discussing business." He took off his watch and laid it on the table, then tapped it. "Your choice."

A quick frown ran across Newsome's face. "Josh, I'm not sure we'll be able to do business this way. I'm not accustomed to people who work for me telling me what to do. If you want—"

"Fine," Josh said. "First, I don't work for you, and second, I don't need your headaches." He stood, picked up his watch, took out his wallet, and dropped a twenty on the table. "Take your time. The beer's paid for. Maybe you'd like to invite your buddies over. Also, FYI, even if we work together, it'll be *together*, not I *for* you. I'm freelance and intend to stay that way."

As he began to walk away, he heard a clunk and Newsome said, "You'd really do it, wouldn't you?"

Josh stopped mid-stride, then turned back. "Do what?"

"Walk out on me."

Josh leaned in and whispered, "There seems to be some confusion here, and I think it's on your part. I'm not one of those assigned to you. I'm not even on the taxpayers' payroll like the two guys at the bar. I'm Joe Civilian, and I don't give a rat's ass who set up your task force. I used to work for his boss. You asked for my help, not vice-versa. So, we either play by my rules, or I don't play at all. And my rules say you don't broadcast our conversations, and you don't record them." He straightened up.

"Relax. There's the microphone." Newsome pointed to an object on the table. "And here's the recorder." He took a small plastic item from his pocket and put it beside the microphone. "Satisfied?"

Josh picked up both objects, dropped them to the floor, then crushed them with the heel of his boot. "Is that everything? Any more electronics?"

"I'm clean. If you glance at my escorts, you'll see they don't understand why they're not receiving a signal anymore."

Josh looked. The suited cop wore a funny look and was tapping his breast pocket. The other wore the same look and was feeling in his hip pocket with one hand and prodding his ear with the other. Josh nodded. "That's better. Now, let's go for a walk. We have some talking to do. As we leave, tell your flunkies to stay at least fifty yards behind."

THIRTEEN

When they cleared the front door of Barney's Bar, Josh crossed the street, then took a right, heading north. Newsome fell in beside him. Pedestrian traffic was light. People in South Florida parked as close as possible and walked as little as possible.

"So," Newsome said, "what's on your mind?"

"We'll wander a bit first," Josh said, "to see what your two hounds do—and to make sure they are the only two of your friends in the area."

"I told you they were."

"Uh-huh. Have I ever *told* you about the wonderful conversations I had with Abe Lincoln? I advised him on conduct of the Civil War. Both stories meet the same test of truth."

"As you say," Newsome said, grinning. "You know, I'm liking you more each moment."

"Save it for your fan club." Josh smiled to soften the words.

At the intersection of South Federal and North Rio Vista Boulevard, they crossed the street and headed east. A few yards past the intersection, Josh halted Newsome beside a hedge that lined the sidewalk. "Let's wait a few seconds." He did a slow count to ten. "Okay, back the way we came."

They rounded the corner onto South Federal, and Josh

94

saw the two policemen from the bar hurrying across the street. He whistled, and they almost tripped when they saw him, but then continued, acting as if they'd never hesitated. They made a strange looking pair—one in a suit and the other dressed for squash. Josh studied the few pedestrians. No one else appeared to be reacting to his and Newsome's double back.

"Tell'm to reposition fifty yards behind us," Josh said. "Then it'll be time to talk."

"I gather you thought I might have a third person out here?" Newsome said.

"And I'm sure you would have if you'd had time."

Newsome chuckled. "Of course I would." He waved the two over. "Mr. Hawkins prefers you not be too close. Says it's bad for his reputation. Give us at least half a block lead, then maintain that distance. I'll signal if I need you."

The cops glared at Josh, but backed away as ordered.

"Can we go now?" Newsome said. "My time is short. I have a meeting I need to attend."

"Let's do it." Josh led Newsome south. "First question. How much are you paying if I deliver this guy, Blanc?"

"Pay? Aren't you patriotic?"

"Sure. Just like you. I'm guessing you draw a paycheck, a fat one, from the government."

"Touché," Newsome said. "What do you think would be appropriate?"

Josh went a few yards farther before answering. "Well, I've given that some thought. Bin Laden was worth twenty-five million, dead or alive. I figure this guy must be worth at least a mill."

"And I'm thinking you overrate yourself."

Josh stopped and studied the two cops assigned to Newsome's detail. They were busy looking in a shop window. "If you thought there was someone better than me, you'd have brought him in. Since you didn't, I'm pretty sure you think I'm the best." He hesitated, watching Newsome's face.

"Of course, if I'm wrong, you're more than welcome to tell me you don't need my services." He finished with a grin and began walking south again.

"Remember what I said about liking you? Maybe I was a bit hasty."

"It's not a popularity contest. It's the death of a crime lord you admit you can't touch."

"Another point for you. Okay, no more games. I'll go a half-mill—five hundred thousand—if you produce absolute proof Blanc is out of the game."

"Tax free and no IRS snooping?"

"I can slide it under the table, if that's what you mean, But tax free if it's found? I'm sure you're aware no one controls the IRS—not even the President."

They covered another block, neither saying anything.

Josh said, "I don't like it. You hand me a half-mill, then the IRS swoops in and takes it back. While they're crowing about their coup, they put me in jail on a trumped-up tax charge. You get Blanc, and I get time with nasty people who'll let me know exactly what they think of me. Sounds like a win-win for the government and a lose-lose for Josh Hawkins."

"That's the best I can do. We're at the take-it-or-leave-it stage. I'm trying to meet you more than halfway, but if it's not to be, it's not to be. I'll find another operative. You're my first choice, but not my only choice. Make up your mind."

"The half-mill plus a written explanation from the Attorney General."

Newsome rubbed his cheek, appearing to think. "That might be possible—or not. But what is possible is a written explanation signed by me. You'll have my words to help if IRS targets you."

It was Josh's time to think, to consider the ramifications of the offer. Strange how they were cementing a contract between a government representative and an assassin that could lead to the deaths of several people, yet the primary worry was the IRS. It did not speak well for the current state of the country. Finally, Josh said, "Draw up the paper. If I like it, we have a deal, and Blanc will be all but finished."

"Great. When will you start?"

"As soon as you deliver everything you can find out about these two people. I want rap sheets, girlfriends, points of contact, friends and acquaintances, hangouts, everything." He handed Newsome a piece of paper with the names Tony Carrillo and Diego Delacruz written on it. "All I know about them is they're involved in an extortion ring and operate in Palm Beach County. Delacruz is a bagman for Carrillo. The sooner I have the info, the sooner I kick in the first door."

Newsome took the paper, glanced at it, then put it in his side pocket. "I'll call you tomorrow."

"Good. Now, you can rejoin your puppies. We're finished for today." Josh turned and moved across South Federal, leaving Newsome standing alone.

* * *

Josh retrieved his car from the public parking lot and drove north toward Boca Raton. He planned to check in with the Trungs, then duplicate his dinner purchases of the previous evening. All except the wine, that is. That was still in his car, probably boiling in the bottle, but there. On second thought, he'd get another one.

He worked his way west to US 441, then turned north. Forty-five minutes later, he parked across from the Trungs' Vietnamese grocery. He walked to the front door and looked in. The store appeared empty except for Ms. Trung and a customer—a lady about the same age with Asian features. They were in animated conversation. He waited a moment, and when the scene didn't change, made his way to Publix.

After completing his shopping—again—including fresh wine, he passed in front of the Trungs' grocery. The customer had left, and Ms. Trung stood behind the counter. He stuck his head in. "Everything okay here?"

"Oh, yes, Mr. Hawkins. Today quiet. No one come except friends who shop here. Things good for you?"

"Yes, all is well. Call if you need me." He went to his car, hoping for a quiet evening with Jaden.

* * *

Once at home, Josh put both bottles of wine in the fridge, hoping yesterday's buy wasn't ruined from a day of car-heat in South Florida. Then he wheeled his Weber grill into the backyard, scrubbed the cooking grate, and poured in the charcoal. He left it ready to douse and light as soon as Jaden got home.

In the kitchen again, he washed the salad makings and set them aside in a colander to drain along with the asparagus. Since he'd bought potatoes packaged for baking, there was nothing to do to them. He left the steaks in their wrappers on the counter. Pre-prep for dinner was as complete as he could make it.

He took a Killian's from the refrigerator, then settled onto the couch with the *Palm Beach Post*. It wasn't filled with news, but it was his local paper of choice. As usual, the sports section carried the woes of the Marlins, the local professional baseball team. Each season, they broke the hearts of their small group of loyal fans. Well, there had been the one year when they'd surprised everyone by winning the World Series. But the owner had responded by breaking up the team, and they'd been less than spectacular since.

At six o'clock, he prepared a scotch and water and placed it in the freezer. His plan was for it to have ice crystals floating when he handed it to Jaden. She loved them extra-cold.

At six-twenty, he heard the garage door going up, took the drink from the freezer, and headed toward the laundry room. As he walked in, the entry to the garage opened, and Jaden entered. "Your choice, Sunshine. An icy scotch and water—or me."

Jaden pretended to study the choices, then put one hand behind his head as her other took the drink. She kissed him, then took a sip. "I choose both. Hmm, that's good—both, I mean."

"Ah, you vixen, once again you have wrapped me around your little finger. Get changed, then prepare the salad and veggies. They're waiting for you. I'll light the charcoal. We can be eating in less than an hour. I'm starved."

"Me, too. You make fire, me make salad." She kissed him again and headed for the bedroom.

Almost true to his words, they sat down to eat in an hour and ten minutes. The steaks were grilled to their specifications—rare for Josh, medium rare for Jaden—the asparagus was steamed, the potatoes were baked to perfection with crisp peels, and Jaden had made Texas toast. Added to that were a glass of wine and his fiancée, making dinner as close to paradise as he ever expected to get.

They ate in silence for a few minutes, then Jaden said, "Okay, what was so important last night? What have you gotten yourself involved in?"

"Not until you bring me up to date on Rodriguez's trial."

Jaden sighed. "Not much to tell. I'm losing. Defense keeps herding in witnesses to say what an out-of-control woman Sophia was. About the best I can hope to do is put doubt in the jurors' minds about their veracity."

"Yes. I saw one such today. I thought you handled it well."

"Which one?"

"Uh . . . Vasquez, or something like that."

"Oh, yes, him. I didn't handle him good enough, I fear. I'm hoping the defense will overplay her hand, but it's a small hope, at best. Every piece of evidence we have against him is being turned into something logical to support his and his witnesses' stories. My gut says he'll walk again." She shook her head. "I guess I could say the good news is I'll probably get another crack at him down the road somewhere, sometime. He won't be able to stay out of trouble." She emptied her glass. "Refill, please."

Josh complied, then topped his up, wishing he could tell her Rodriguez might walk, but not far. He'd never appear in her courtroom again. Instead, he said, "What's your plan for tomorrow?"

"Uh-uh. You're stalling. Your turn to come clean. You've been gone the last two nights—last night, all night. If you don't come up with a good story, I'll assume you're messing around, and you'll have to sleep on the couch."

"No. You know I hang off the end of that thing."

"Tough. Spit it out."

FOURTEEN

Josh pushed his plate away and rested his elbows on the table. "We could—"

"The time has come, my dear," Jaden said. "I've let you stall as long as I intend to. Start talking."

Josh had considered how much to tell Jaden and how to present it. She was too sharp for him to blow a cover story passed her, but would never condone his signing on as an assassin. Somewhere in between would have to do. He loved her far too much to take a chance on losing her. It would be a fine line to walk, but, for the sake of their relationship, he had to do it. The question was could he pull it off.

He picked up his glass and sipped his wine as he looked into her eyes. He saw no give. In reply to her penetrating stare, he said, "The day after my trip to the police station with the Trungs—two days ago—I was approached by a federal agency to take on a specialized job for them. They said they needed someone with my unique qualifications. Maybe they were scratching my back—or maybe not. Anyway, it will entail a lot of research and time on the ground. I'll be gone for periods until the task is completed. I had to sign a secrecy oath so I can't say much more." Even as he heard his words, he wondered how many of them he'd believe if someone else uttered them. Not many he guessed—unless they came from Jaden, then maybe, just maybe, all.

"Periods until the task is completed? You made that so sufficiently vague you can be gone for a day, a month, or a year. I'm not buying it. Give me specifics."

"Okay, I'll do the best I can, but I really have no firm answers. I hope things will be wrapped up in a month, or not much longer. During that time, I'll have to react to the situation. There will be quiet time, I suppose, but it also could get pretty active." He stopped and thought about what else to say. He had nothing. "Sorry, Sunshine, but that's as close as I can get."

Jaden sipped her wine, staring over the top of it. She set the glass down and smiled. "That's the biggest bunch of malarkey I've heard in a while—even more unbelievable than the crap Rodriguez's witnesses are spinning in court. Stuff like that only happens in books and movies. Beside you, Rodriguez is a fount of reality. Want to try again?"

Josh wasn't surprised at her reaction. He had his answer. He probably wouldn't have believed it either. "Your skepticism pains me. However, it is misplaced. What I told you is true. Strange as it may sound, that is exactly what happened. And I am committed to do the job."

"Uh-huh. Two nights ago, you called me, surrounded by the police after you'd pounded three *thugs*, or that's what you told me. The police hauled you into the police station along with the *elderly* couple you said you defended. The police supposedly lost interest in you and released you and the Trungs. Now—after being AWOL last night—you trot out a story about being a government agent. You, who is over-endowed with brawn and under-endowed with common sense when it comes to your own safety—and, at times like this, I'm not sure about brain." She shook here head. "Like I said, want to try again?"

Trouble. Josh knew he'd lost the argument, but had nowhere else to go. His story might be incomplete, but it was true. It was time to stick with the old axiom, truth will set you free. "Last try. Two nights ago, I stopped a Vietnamese couple, the Trungs, from being extorted by three thugs. The police showed up and took us in. As I left the station, I received a message to return in the morning, reason not given. I figured it would be smart to do what they said—plus, I admit I was curious. That was yesterday. I met with representatives of a federal agency who recruited me for a specific task—not dangerous, simply a specific job. They stroked me by saying I was the best-qualified candidate to do it. They demanded I sign a secrecy oath. Didn't surprise me. The government always covers its butt. I even told them I needed to brief the love of my life, but they denied permission. Last night, I did research in preparation for getting started. And tonight," he raised his glass in salute, "I dine with the woman I adore." He leaned back in his chair. "That's it. That's all I can say. And, you may find it strange, but it is the truth."

"Damn you, Hawkins. Okay, but if you kill someone— or someones—make sure the remains are never found, and there is no trace back to you. Rest assured I'll prosecute you just as hard as I do Rodriguez if you're arrested."

"I believe you. In your world, there are only the guilty and the victims. Mine has shades of gray." Josh stood and began to clear the table. "However, I'm hoping I'll never have the opportunity to face you from the other side of the courtroom. Do you want me to save the rest of your steak for lunch tomorrow?"

"Not for lunch, but, maybe I'll have it for dinner with a salad. I'm sure you'll be off somewhere *researching*."

"That works," Josh said, smiling.

* * *

The rest of the evening, they kept their limited conversation away from either of their assignments. For Josh, it wasn't intentional. He had simply said all he could about it.

Jaden dug into her briefcase, dragged out some files, and

immersed herself in them. She only looked up once in a while, mostly to shake her head. Josh assumed the papers were the Rodriguez case.

He opened a book he'd started a few nights previous. It was a thin plot, but the hero was a strong character who walked through trouble as if wearing a magic cloak. At one point, the protagonist was in a room surrounded by four armed bad guys intent on killing him. Josh stopped reading, hoping it wasn't a forecast of his future. When he returned to the story, he learned that the hero fought his way out without a scratch, leaving devastation behind him. Josh could handle that as a harbinger.

Josh's cell phone rang. He checked and saw the name, Phil Summers. Frowning, he stood and walked into the kitchen. No need to disturb Jaden.

"Phil. What's up?"

"I'm at my desk, waiting for that phone call you promised. You said you had to face the cops again. When do I get to assault your character? Oops, I mean give you a sterling character reference."

Josh's conscience slapped him. "Sorry. I meant to call you back, but things kinda got out of hand. The police lost interest and returned me to the street. Said don't come back."

"What about your meeting the next morning with them?"

Oops, Josh thought. "Ah, they offered me a medal, but I told them it wasn't necessary. Just doing what any good citizen would do."

"Sure. Have you ever considered writing fairy tales?"

"Does that mean you don't believe me?"

"It means exactly that. However, I accept that whatever it was is not intended for my ears. You could have called though."

Josh chuckled. "You're right. I do owe you an apology. Maybe I can buy lunch one day."

"What? Be seen with you in public? You want Richards

to put me in uniform? I don't do well on foot patrol."

"Is he still on my case?"

There was a moment of silence. "Not really. We've been too busy chasing real bad people. But I know my lieut. He has a long memory—and you did kind of make him look bad."

"Not intentionally, I assure you. I just happen to guess right that time." A thought popped into Josh's head. "Have you heard of a man named Henri Blanc? What can you tell me about him?"

Wariness wrapped Phil's response. "Why do you want to know?"

Uh-oh, Josh thought. Sounds like I'd better tread with a light touch. "No specific reason. I just happened to hear his name. Rich French-Canadian. Spends a lot of time here in South Florida. Throws his money around—or so I heard."

"Yeah, sure, and I expect a visit from my Fairy Godmother tonight. She's bringing me a carriage to take me to the ball. Look, I only know one Henri Blanc. If it's the same guy, stay clear. Leave him to the pros. I know your ego, but tone it down. You won't win against him. He eats bums like you for breakfast."

"C'mon, Phil. You know I'm all gristle. Tell me what you know."

"Know? I know he's slippery—never been arrested even. But his name comes up often, always as a mystery figure who may—or may not—be involved. I also know there are some big agencies interested . . . Whoa, Josh. You haven't signed on with the big boys, have you?"

Ouch, Josh thought. I shouldn't have started this. No wonder he's such a great cop. Gotta get out of here fast. "Me? Phil, you know I'm retired. The only Feds I'm interested in is IRS, and that's because I don't want them auditing me. Anything else, I'm pure civilian."

"Okay," Phil said. "I'll pretend to believe you. But I'm telling you, be careful. You're out of your league with Blanc.

No one can touch that guy—local police, FDLE, feds, nobody. And, while I can't prove it, don't even have a sniff of a clue, my gut says he's responsible for several unidentifiable bodies turning up in the Everglades and washing up on the beaches. Don't add yours to his collection."

"Not my intent. I'm quite satisfied with staying alive. First thing in the morning, I'm calling and cancelling my lunch date with him." Josh forced a chuckle. "He wants to introduce me to his sister. Said I'd make a good brother-in-law."

"Laugh while you can." Phil's voice had lost all traces of levity. "You cross paths with him, and laughter might be a thing in your past. Gotta run. Call if you need a character witness." He paused. "And stay clear of Blanc."

The phone went silent. Josh stared at it. Phil had told him more than he realized. Blanc was indeed a formidable opponent who needed to be brought down. It would take patience and would involve risk, but when it was over, the country would be a better place to live—at least until another Blanc became the cream of the crap.

Later, as Josh and Jaden lay in bed, she rolled over and said, "This Vietnamese couple. Are they worth it? My woman's intuition says you're headed into some heavy stuff. I also know you won't tell me, but you are my fiancé, and I'd like to keep you around long enough for the ceremony. Convince me they're worth risking our future together. Convince me this whole thing you're in is worth making be a widow before I become a bride."

Josh hesitated, remembering the story Ms. Trung told him. How their parents had helped the Americans, how they'd been abandoned in the US rush to pull out of Vietnam, how they'd hidden from communist death squads, and then, in desperation, pushed off into the vastness of the South China Sea in a leaky round boat, rescue only a remote dream. Freedom meant more to them than their lives, something forgotten by many generations of Americans. Back then, when the US deserted them, they went through hell. Now, a ring of extortionists wanted to take them back to those days. It couldn't be allowed. They had paid their dues. He cuddled Jaden and whispered, "Yes, my love. They are worth it." *They are oh so worth it.*

As Jaden's breathing settled into the pattern of sleep, Josh lay awake, thinking. He had agreed to do something the power of the government couldn't do. How stupid could a person's decision be? Had he let Newsome's praise lead him into a deathtrap? It was times like this he missed the military the most. Throughout Josh's career, he'd had contemporaries he could discuss situations with. Whenever Josh needed a dose of reality, someone was there to give it to him—with words or fists, whichever worked. But Josh was on his own this time. Those friends were far behind him. As he'd told Summers, he was Joe Civilian.

Even though his military career was behind him, facts didn't change. The task was too big for one man. He needed partners, allies, someone to cover his back as he charged into the unknown. If it were a military operation, he'd have time for reconnaissance, perhaps on the ground, perhaps by air. Worst case would be studying terrain maps, videos, and pictures. But there would be intelligence. There would be *red teams* scrutinizing the operation, ripping it apart, then another team rewriting it, making it stronger. It would be massaged, rewritten, practiced, and rewritten again until it was as perfect as it could be. Not today though. He stood alone, no allies in any direction. Going after Blanc was like diving into an alligator infested canal. Josh knew the danger was there, but didn't know from whence the attack would come, or how strong it would be.

No, nothing was ideal about this situation. He drifted off to sleep as he considered the people he might be able to recruit. The list was short.

FIFTEEN

Sometime during the night, Josh's subconscious took over and gave him the answer. A dream showed Josh, accompanied by Chief Wasan, detaining a faceless man and telling him he was out of business. Although Josh ran over six feet, Chief towered above him. He had his neck bowed and his arms hung out from his side. He wore a muscle shirt which barely came to his waist, displaying the bottom of his rock-hard abs. His arms resembled something you'd expect to see on Popeye, except the bulges covered the biceps, too, not just the forearms. A coal-black braid hung over one shoulder.

Josh awakened, smiling. Yes. There was the partner he needed backing him on this case. With Chief by his side, Blanc was already a footnote to history. When he returned to sleep, his dreams became normal—videos of Jaden.

In the morning, Josh kept things as natural as possible while his mind raced with thoughts of recruiting Chief to assist him. After kissing Jaden at the door as she left for work, Josh sat with a cup of coffee, considering his options. Chief was the obvious choice, obvious to Josh anyway. The question was would Chief agree to work with him.

Josh took out his phone and punched in Chief's number.

"Again, so soon," Chief said, answering. "We haven't talked in six months and now twice in as many days."

"I miss your smiling voice—and your classic Indian face.

108

If you have time today, I'd like to ride out. I have a business proposition to discuss with you."

"Another one. You left a hundred bucks the other night. Miss Allie says thanks. She'll have fresh chicken for quite a while. We both appreciate your generosity—or did you encourage someone else to contribute?"

"No comment. Tell her she was the star of the show, just as I expected. But this new project is massive. It'll earn us a big payday—or make us dead. Not so different from the old days, except we'll get paid better."

"In that case, come out right now. My day is yours. I'll ask Sandra to chill the beer."

* * *

Josh and Chief sat at a picnic table under palm trees, sipping iced tea in Chief's front yard, well away from the alligator compound. From the Everglades came a variety of sounds and calls Josh could never identify.

"That's the deal," Josh said. "I'm promised half-a-mil if I make a certain crime lord disappear." He had briefed Chief on his recruitment and the operation without giving specifics. "I'd like to tell you more, but I signed a non-disclosure agreement. I'm sure you remember those pesky NDAs. Some things in the government never change. Come in with me, and I'll tell you everything. We'll split the payoff fifty-fifty."

"Hell, I'm tempted to do it for free. Do you know how boring it gets out here? Yeah, there are tourists groups that come through, but it's the same questions over and over, and the same marveling at Miss Allie's size. *Boring.* On the days Miss Allie visits her relatives, the mosquitoes are the most excitement I see. But my ancestors learned to take what they could from the white man, so I continue to smile for them. Now you're talking real money. Two-hundred-fifty-thou works. Of course, like our days in the Army, I'll expect an insurance package to be paid to Sandra if I don't make it back."

"Agreed. And, if neither of us comes out alive, both Sandra and Jaden are young enough and lovely enough to start over with better men."

"Yeah, but they won't be snake-eaters."

Laughter filled the humid air as Josh remembered the classic nickname for Special Forces operatives.

"Okay, here's the deal," Josh said. He filled Chief in on the details as he knew them. "Later today, or so I hope, I'll have info on a possible keyway into the Blanc empire. How soon can you break away and join me? I think things would work better if you moved in with me until we finish. Once we start, things might move faster than we can control. Too fast for you to be an hour or so away."

"I see your point. How about a week? I have a few things in progress, plus I need to find someone to take care of the compound. My brother probably has the time, but I need to check with him." He paused, stroking his chin. "Yeah, a week should do it. Does that work for you?"

"I'll give you four days. The trail might get too cold if we wait any longer." Josh stuck out his hand, and he and Chief shook on it.

* * *

As Josh drove toward Coral Lakes, his phone rang. Newsome with the info on Carrillo and Delacruz, he thought. But when he answered, he heard Robert Irving's voice.

Irving was a partner in Irving and Irwin, the law firm from which Josh drew a small retainer as an on-call investigator. He made himself available when they needed him, otherwise they left him alone. And best of all, they didn't try to tell him how to live his life.

"Yes, Robert. What can I do for you?" Josh said.

"I have an assignment for you—if you have the time."

Josh thought about it. Four days before Chief could join

him. "Sure. Always time for you. What's up?"

"Well, it's a bit on the weird side."

"Let fly. I'm always up for weird." Josh chuckled.

"I have an aunt who lives in an over-55 community in Coral Lakes. She plays mah-jongg at the synagogue. One of her friends is telling the strangest story, yet she's convinced it's true." He paused.

"Uh-huh. You have my curiosity up now. Give."

"Well, according to Ms. Goldstein, someone is taking her car for a joyride in the middle of the night, then returning it to the same parking space before she gets up."

"Is that possible?"

"As you know so well, it's South Florida. Anything can happen."

"Yeah. Okay, tell me about it."

"Well, basically, she says it wasn't parked the way she left it. Also, she believes the fuel gauge is not the same when she goes out in the morning. In fact—get ready for this—she says sometimes it has more gas than when she left it. Other than that, there's nothing to show it's been moved."

"How about mileage? Is it different?"

"Unknown. My aunt didn't mention it."

"I shouldn't ask, but is this lady all there? I mean, does she see little green men?"

"Yes . . . I mean, no. My aunt says she's sharp and has the memory of an elephant when it comes to mah-jongg. She believes her."

"Then I'll believe her, too. Tell her to call the cops."

"She did. A uniform came by and took a statement. Ms. Goldstein says he didn't believe a word she said. He couldn't wait to get out the door, fidgeted the whole time. The police haven't been in touch since. She called the station a couple of times and, according to her, got the *runaround*. Nobody wants to talk to her."

"I'm sure you'll get there someday, but can we speed it up a bit. What does your story have to do with me?"

Irving chuckled. "You sure know how to wreck a good setup. I'd hate to have you on a jury. My aunt told her I have a hotshot investigator on staff. Ms. Goldstein wants you to find out who is driving her car. Do you have time to handle it?"

Josh shook his head. "Wait a minute. I need to make sure I understand. Your aunt's friend, a Ms. Goldstein, thinks someone is joyriding her car and wants to hire a lawyer so he can assign a private investigator to check it out. Does she know how much it will cost?"

"Uh . . . my aunt might have told her I'd do it for free."

"Oh, that's even better," Josh said, chuckling. "So . . . you're paying my rates?"

There was a moment of silence. "Since you put it that way, I guess I am."

"Good, as long as I'm paid. Give me her name and address, and I'll stop by and talk to her in the next couple of days. Be sure and let her know I'm coming. Don't want to be met with a blast through the door. If this lady is astute enough to notice the position of her car and a minor difference in the fuel gauge, she might have a shotgun."

"Sylvia Goldstein. She lives in Unit 1006, 952 South Trample Avenue, Coral Lakes. I'll get the word to her. When's the best time for you?"

"Can't say, but it'll be soon."

"Excellent. Thanks, Josh. When you pull this one off, expect more business from my aunt. She runs in a tight circle."

Josh heard laughter as the line went dead.

* * *

Henri Blanc sat in a recliner, a biography of General Dwight D. Eisenhower open in his lap. His wife, Collette, sat across from him, doing needlepoint.

Blanc leaned his head back and stared at the ceiling.

"This is such an interesting country. General Eisenhower grew up in Abilene, Kansas. He qualified academically for both the Naval Academy and West Point, but went to the latter because he was too old for the Naval Academy. Lucky for the U.S. he did. During World War One, he volunteered for overseas assignments several times, but luck—I'd say good luck—kept him stateside. In spite of that, during World War II, he rose to the rank of General of the Army, five stars, and Supreme Allied Commander of the Allied Expeditionary Force responsible for wresting Europe from the Nazis. Next stop, President of the United States for eight years. Quite a life for a boy born in the little town of Denison, Texas."

Collette smiled. "I sometimes wonder why you don't apply for citizenship here. You have such respect for this country."

"Yes, I do. It's been the world leader longer than I've been alive, and the world is better off for it. How would you like—"

A knock on the doorframe interrupted him. "Yes, Gustave. What is it?"

"Can we talk, sir . . . in private?"

"Go ahead, dear," Collette said. "I've lost you for the afternoon whether you go with Gustave or not."

Gustave moved aside and followed Blanc into Blanc's spacious office.

"What is it? You know I don't like to be interrupted during afternoons with my wife."

"Yes sir, I'm aware of that. You've told me before. But I heard from forty-three again and decided you need to be briefed."

"Forty-three? Our source near Newsome?"

"Yes sir. The report says Newsome met with the assassin he hired, that guy Hawkins. Hawkins tricked him into a public meeting, then stripped him of recorder and microphone. He handled Newsome like a pro. Other than that, all forty-three knows for sure is Newsome came back with the names Tony Carrillo and Diego Delacruz. He wants a full report on them so he can pass it to Hawkins."

"Do we know these people?"

"Yes sir. Carrillo is one of our middle-level people. He pools money from the collectors on the street and passes it up the line. He's also responsible for paying the lower level. Delacruz is one of his bagmen. I've had contact with Carrillo from time to time. He's okay, but it's bothersome that Hawkins has his name."

Blanc chuckled. "We have obviously underestimated Hawkins. He appears to be gaining ground faster than we expected. Probably time to start throwing up some barricades. Don't take action against him yet. We can learn more by having forty-three keep us informed of his actions. I'll have his records pulled. In the meantime, sever the connection with Carrillo and Delacruz. I'm sure we have replacements, don't we?"

"Yes sir."

SIXTEEN

At seven p.m., Josh knocked on Ms. Goldstein's door, hoping she'd be back from her early bird dinner.

"Yes. Who's there?"

"It's Josh Hawkins, ma'am. I've come about your car."

The door opened, and a well-coiffed woman of indeterminate age stood in the doorway. Even at a glance, Josh could see she wore far more jewelry than the modern world called for. Obviously, she was from a different generation. Although her clothing was dated, no one would mistake it as being secondhand. His guess was her weight hadn't changed more than a few pounds in the last twenty years. The gems she wore looked real to his eyes. He hoped they were paste. She was a walking invitation to every mugger in the area.

"Oh, yes. You're that young man who works for Ms. Irving's nephew. She said you'd be around."

"Yes, ma'am. May I come in so we can talk?"

"Of course." She opened the door wider, and Josh entered. "Have a seat. I'll make tea."

Before Josh could refuse, she disappeared toward the rear of the unit. He smiled. It was nice to see that the civilities which had once ruled society were still in vogue with the older generation. Not having anything better to do, he walked around, looking at the furnishings, noticing that it seemed warm in the unit. The furniture was out of date and well worn, but spotless. Pictures of individuals—he supposed family—covered most open spaces. Josh dropped onto an uncomfortable couch and waited.

A few minutes later, Ms. Goldstein entered, carrying a tray. Josh jumped to his feet to help her.

"Oh, sit down, you silly boy. I might be old, but I'm not helpless. Now, sugar or lemon?" She placed the tray on the coffee table.

"Uh, sugar," Josh said, daring not tell her he seldom drank tea.

After the tea was served, stirred, and sipped, Josh said, "Please tell me why you think someone is messing with your car."

Ms. Goldstein set her cup down. "My, you are direct. You young people are always in such a hurry. I often wonder if you ever slow down and enjoy the beauty around you. When was the last time you stopped and listened to a bird sing? They have such gorgeous tunes. And the flowers? We live in a floral paradise. Have you smelled a bloom recently?"

Josh lowered his head. "Guilty as charged. I guess I do rush hither and yon without paying attention to what's in between. Thank you for reminding me."

"You're welcome, young man. When you're looking back at life, as I am, you see so many things you missed. Since I can't get a redo, I'd like to help younger people enjoy every minute of every day." She picked up her cup and sipped, then set the cup on the tray. "Now. What was that question you asked?"

Josh put his cup on the tray also. "Why do you think someone is messing with your car?"

She pursed her lips. "I first noticed something last week, on Monday or Tuesday. I decided to drive to Publix to get some groceries. I don't keep much in the house. It's easier to eat out. But I needed milk and those chocolate chip cookies they sell in the bakery. Nothing much better than dipping one of them into a glass of cold milk. Yes, even an old woman has her vanities. But, you didn't come here for that. You want to know about the car.

"As I walked past the front of it, I noticed the hood seemed to be dirtier than the rest of the car. And there were handprints on it. Some of my neighbors need to lean on things as they walk down the sidewalk. Even I need help occasionally. So that, by itself, didn't mean anything, but when I got in, the gas tank was a bit above half. It had been more than a month since I gassed up, and I thought it should be less than a half-tank. Anyway, I topped it off, ran it through a car wash, got my groceries, and then drove back here, and parked it in my reserved spot."

"You're saying the tank was full then, and it was clean?" Josh said.

"Yes on both counts. Of course, I knew it wouldn't stay clean. There's so much dirt in the air here. Anyway, I parked and didn't think much more about it. Last Sunday, I took it to the park. I like to feed the squirrels, and it's so peaceful there."

"Didn't you drive it between Monday or Tuesday and Sunday?"

"No."

"Why not?"

"I don't drive very often—just enough to keep the battery charged. My husband taught me that. Mostly, I take the bus and leave the driving to others. At my age, I'm not comfortable out there with all the crazies."

"Perfectly logical," Josh said. "This might sound too basic, but I need to know. Did you lock the car, and if yes, are you sure?"

Ms. Goldstein chuckled. "I'd have been disappointed if you hadn't asked. And yes, I did. And yes, I not only did, but I double-checked to make sure. I don't have much faith in those electric things. My husband taught me that, too."

"Your husband sounds like a smart man. Wish I could

have met him."

"He was," she said, a smile splitting her face. "My Bernie was a brilliant man in his own way. Something that has been lost in our modern world is respect for those endowed with common sense. My Bernie had more common sense than anyone I've ever met. Show him a problem, and then give him an hour, he'd bring you the answer. It might not be solved by the book, but he'd have it right. I think he'd have liked you."

Josh hunched forward. "I'm sure I would have liked him. What happened on Sunday?"

"Again, something didn't seem right. The seat was fine, but the mirrors weren't quite set for me. Just a little off, but off. The gas gauge read full, but it dropped off the full mark on the way to the park."

She hesitated as if reflecting on what to say next. "It wasn't right. I know it wasn't. Someone had been in the car. I called the police, and they sent a uniformed officer around. Now, Mr. Hawkins, I want you to know I have the utmost respect for the police. They have a terrible job, and sometimes it seems they aren't as responsive as we'd like them to be. But without them, where would we be? If I had my way, we'd double their salaries. But this particular young man . . . Well, he made it pretty obvious he thought I was a senile old woman telling stories because I was bored—or something. He looked at the car, made a few notes, and left in about five minutes. His attitude said I shouldn't expect to hear from him again. I called the station a couple of times, but no one had any information for me."

"How did you end up asking about me?"

"I didn't. I was telling my friends at mah-jongg about my suspicions, and Ms. Irving talked about her nephew, the lawyer. Next thing I knew she said she was going to contact him and have his ace investigator take the case. Guess that's you."

Josh chuckled and scratched his cheek, feeling a blush

rising. "Ace investigator might be a bit strong, but I'll do what I can. One more question, then I'd like to see the car."

"Of course. What is it?"

"Do you keep up with the mileage? Did you notice how much the odometer changed?"

Ms. Goldstein frowned. "No. I never thought of that. In fact, I pay no attention to it. The dealer calls when I need service, and I take it in. I have no idea how many miles are on the car."

Josh smiled. "I understand. Now for the car." He stood.

"Let's go." She bounced up from her chair, leaving Josh hoping he would be half that agile when he reached her age. "Give me a moment to get my sweater." She left the room.

Sweater, Josh thought. It's still over eighty degrees out there.

A moment later, she returned, slipping her arms into an ornate sweater that matched her dress. "It's no fun being old. Seems like I'm cold all the time. I take a sweater wherever I go."

They rode the elevator to the first floor, then walked outside. Ms. Goldstein stopped before the third handicapped space. Josh halted beside her, looking around at the cars near them. Several expensive sedans and one sports car.

"Which is yours?" he asked.

"This one," she said. "We stopped in front of it. Here's the key."

Josh did a double take. Never would he have expected a little old lady to own a red Mercedes SL550 hard top convertible. "Ah . . . this one?"

Ms. Goldstein laughed. "I can see how surprised you are. I understand. It was my husband's final dream. All his life he wanted something like this, but always settled for what was best for family transportation. He'd say, 'Next time. Next time, I'm going to get a special high-end sports car. We'll ride in style.' So, eight years ago, I said, 'Do it. This might be your last chance.' I didn't know how well I had predicted the future."

She wiped a finger under her eye, then sighed. "Anyway, he did. Two years later, he died. But during those two years, he was more alive than I'd seen him in at least ten years. Every day he was washing or polishing or vacuuming or something to keep it looking new. He loved this car. On his deathbed, he asked me to take care of it for him. Other than me and the kids, it was his most precious possession."

"That's quite a story," Josh said. "It's a beautiful machine. Maybe someday, I can follow in your husband's footsteps and own something like that."

"I hope you do," she said. "Every man should touch his dream. Can you catch the person who is messing with it?"

"Perhaps," Josh said. "I plan to give it my best. May I see inside?"

After she gave him the key, he unlocked the door and sat in the driver's seat, careful not to touch anything. The interior was immaculate. He wondered if it was worth the effort of looking for fingerprints. It would be a shame to leave powder all over everything, and he suspected someone had wiped it down, probably Ms. Goldstein. There wasn't a speck of dust to be seen. After mulling it over, he decided not at this time. Instead, he would do a stakeout. If someone was bothering it, Josh would be there to disrupt him. No one should interfere with an old woman's memories.

Josh accompanied Ms. Goldstein back to her apartment.

"Thank you for showing me your car. It was a pleasure to be near something as nice as that. You probably won't see me again for a few days, but that doesn't mean I won't be looking out for you. I work best when I stay out of sight. When it's over, I'll let you know how it came out."

"I trust you, Mr. Hawkins. You do what you need to do. Ms. Irving says you're an *ace investigator*." She chuckled. "That's good enough for me. When you visit again, let me know you're coming. I bake the best chocolate chip cookies in the state." She sighed. "My husband branded them, not me. I don't do it as often I used to when he was here. It's easier to duck out to Publix now."

"Yes, ma'am," Josh said, opening the door. "I'll be in touch."

Once he reached the parking lot, Josh stopped and examined the area, breaking it into quadrants and searching it as he would a potential ambush site. That's what it would become if he were successful. He'd use it to ambush a car thief.

It was a narrow rectangle with a row of parking on each long side. All the spaces near Ms. Goldstein's Mercedes were handicapped and reserved—unit numbers painted on the concrete. The ones on the opposite side were also reserved and each occupied. No place to park nearby.

He walked around, scoping out fields of fire, or more accurately for the civilian world, angles of vision. He wanted a spot where he could park and then get out quickly, if necessary.

Toward the end, he found himself at the *visitor* spots where he'd parked when he arrived. He looked toward Ms. Goldstein's car and shook his head. He could park in a *visitor* place, maybe, and not attract attention, but he couldn't see well enough for surveillance. As he continued his examination, he noted the lack of hedges and other large vegetation. The groundskeepers kept all bushes cut back to non-hiding height. He supposed it was a security measure meant to keep undesirables away from the complex. About the only place he could conceal himself was in the shadows of the building itself. Not good. Any curious resident or passerby could spot him and call the police. Josh kept searching.

Growing in the swale, across from the entrance to the building, was a live oak about thirty feet tall. The trunk wasn't thick enough to hide a man, but there was a bench for the bus stop under its overhang. He wondered if the homeless ever slept on that bench. Josh smiled and nodded. Yep, any homeless person might choose to sleep there—problem solved.

Next, he considered the timeframe he needed to cover. Anyone messing with the car would have to wait until he was sure the residents were in bed. Since they were mostly retirees—probably all—that could present a problem. Some would go to bed early, but others would suffer from various forms of insomnia and be up late. The parking lot could have cars in and out until midnight as visitors left and residents returned from visiting others. Josh figured the thief would wait until two or three in the morning. That meant Josh would need to be on site earlier, stretched out on the bench by one a.m., at the latest. Now, he had to hope no other homeless person would see it as better than sleeping on the grass and beat him to it. If so, he'd convince him to move on. In the meantime, he should get some rest.

He was in his car, preparing to leave when his phone rang. Unknown caller.

"Hello," Josh said, "who's calling?"

"Isaac Newsome here. I have the information you wanted. Can we meet?"

So much for resting. Ms. Goldstein could wait until tomorrow. "Of course. Want me to pick the place again?"

"I think not. The info I have is in hard copy. Police headquarters will work much better. I can show it to you without worrying about who's watching from the next booth. Plus, I feel more comfortable talking there."

"No cameras, no recorders?"

"None. I promise. Mr. Hawkins, you're going to have to learn to be more trusting."

"Sure, then I'll trust in Santa Claus, too. I'll just keep chugging along the way I've been doing. It's kept me alive so far."

"Okay. How long before you can be here?"

Josh did a quick calculation against his current location and the expected traffic. "Forty-five minutes to an hour."

"Fine. Same conference room we used before. I'll let them know out front."

Josh hung up, satisfied that Newsome had come through with the information so quickly. He hoped the files would contain something useful in opening the door to Blanc's operation. Blanc had to be brought down from the inside. If any kind of an outside attack would work, Newsome's task force would have already found it.

* * *

Josh's escort left him at the conference room, saying, "They're waiting for you."

When Josh opened the door, he was surprised to see all five members of the task force gathered around the table. He walked in, and then stopped short. "What's this? I thought we'd meet alone."

Newsome smiled. "I prefer to keep the entire team in the loop. No secrets makes for a more cohesive unit."

"And a better chance of compromise," Josh said. "Since it's my butt on the line, I'd prefer to lessen those chances to the lowest possible level."

"I assure you," Newsome said, a hint of frustration in his voice, "this team is air tight. These people have been scrutinized at the highest levels of government and found to be beyond reproach. I trust them. You'll have to do the same."

Josh stared at Sutherland, who sat, glaring at him, a smug smile on his face. "I suppose the good news is I'll know where to look if there is a leak. But I warn you, Mr. Newsome, I am not a forgiving type. If I go down, it had better be all the way, or I'll rise up and strike hard—very hard."

"Enough with the threats," Newsome said, irritation showing. "Let's discuss the information we gathered on Carillo and Delacruz. Please have a seat."

Josh pulled out a chair beside Roz, the DEA representative. "No offense intended," he said.

"None taken," Roz said. "In your shoes, I'd probably be more paranoid."

Newsome slid two folders to Josh. "Here are the details of what we found. It comes from different agencies. That's what's blacked out. Didn't figure you needed to know who collected what. Not a lot, I fear, because they're pretty small potatoes. I assigned the job to Roz, and she came through for us." He acknowledged her with a nod. "If you'll open the folders and follow along, I'll summarize. Then you'll have time to study the information and ask questions. Memorize the parts that interest you. The hard copy must stay here."

"And if we'd met in a bar?" Josh said.

"I'd have given you a limited briefing only."

"Picky, isn't he?" Josh said to Roz.

She laid her hand on Josh's arm. "I suspect you faced these types of restrictions before. How often did you carry folders of data into a military operation?"

"Touché," Josh said. He nodded at Kelly and Randolph on the other side of the table. "I haven't heard from you. What do you think?"

Randolph answered first. "I go along with Mr. Newsome. If the paperwork stays in a controlled environment, there is less chance of the wrong people seeing it. There are methods and sources of collection that are highly classified which can be discerned from the info."

"Not to mention costing people their lives," Kelly added. "I, too, approve of Mr. Newsome's M.O. If my butt was on the line, I'd sure want it handled this way."

"Guess that makes it unanimous," Josh said. "Let's get to work."

"What about me?" Sutherland said. "Don't you want my opinion?"

"Nope. I already know it. You go where the big dogs go, sniffing every bush and fire hydrant they use."

"I resent that."

"Good." Josh looked at Newsome. "Can we get started? I do have a life outside this room."

Newsome struggled with a straight face. "Yes. First, we'll look at Diego Delacruz. He's small peanuts. Basically, a bagman. Goes where he's told to go, does what he's told to do. We have him connected with several operations over the years, but nothing extreme. His worth comes from his honesty—or fear. He's afraid to skim, so he delivers every penny. We've identified several larger fish he worked for by tracking him to their front doors. Right now, as you thought, he works for Tony Carrillo. Want to tell us how you came by that information?"

Josh thought for a moment. "Let's just say a little bird told me—and he swore me to secrecy—sensitive sources, you know."

"I'm not surprised with that answer. I'd have said the same thing, only a bit more tactfully." Newsome opened the second file. "Carrillo is a different situation. Not a brain, but the kind of man the brains want on their team. He's what I call mid-level management. He's given a job to do and does it. He finds the people he needs to get it done—no matter what it is—handles the pay-offs, and keeps the secrets of those above him. A good man to have around—if you're a criminal mastermind. We believe it possible he has direct access to Blanc. But we could be wrong. There might be another level between them, maybe more than one. If you go after him, I hope you will answer that question." He paused, as if searching his memory. "Questions?"

"Addresses, contacts, strengths, weaknesses, security? How many more subjects would you like?"

"Everything we know in that vein is in this file. Now, I have to go, but the others will stay in case you have questions or need clarifications. Take your time with the records, but make sure everything stays here. Anything else for me?"

Josh looked around Roz. "Take Sutherland with you. I

won't have any questions for the feebie."

"I resent that." Sutherland rose, his cheeks turning red.

"And I say again, good. Now, act like a good puppy and follow your boss out of here." Josh pulled the file toward him in a final dismissal of Sutherland.

Sutherland turned toward Newsome. "Are you going to let him—"

"Let's go, Brad. I get the impression Mr. Hawkins doesn't like you." He took Sutherland by the arm and led him toward the door.

"We're not finished with this," Sutherland said, looking over his shoulder at Josh. "You'll get yours."

Josh laughed. "Any time, any place. But if you expect to win, you'd better bring your badge."

When the door closed behind them, Roz said, "You shouldn't be so hard on him. He's young. He'll learn."

Josh looked at her, then at Kelly and Randolph. "Forgive me if I say, *been there, done that*. I saw too many people like him placed in positions of authority. Usually, it cost someone his career, or worse yet, his life. A few of them did learn and became competent leaders. Most never improved a whit. But, in both cases, they left a lot of pain behind them. I was fortunate then. They'd wash out and be gone before they could do any real damage. But, this outfit is different. The fact he's still here proves nothing is going to happen to him. I don't intend to become a notch on his badge. The less I see of him, the more comfortable I'll be."

Roz, Kelly, and Randolph stared at the table. Whatever they were thinking was not for Josh's consumption.

They spent the next two hours digging through the files. Josh asked question after question. All of them were answered. More often than not, though, the answer was *we don't know*.

At eleven o'clock, Josh closed the folders. "I've had it. If I haven't learned it by now, chances are I won't. Your files are decent, filled with cold facts, but what's missing is the essence of the men. How will either of them react if pressured? Who will they call if threatened? Where will they hide if they think they're in danger? Those are some of the things I need to know. Guess I'll have to find those answers for myself."

"I agree," Kelly said "Bottom line is we don't know. Surveillance can tell you a lot, but it can't get into a man's head. I don't envy you your task. But at least you know more than you did."

Josh slid the files into the middle of the table. "Thanks for your help. Please make sure Newsome knows I took no notes. I don't mean to come off as an ass, but I'm the one stepping into the crosshairs. And, if I might be so forward, watch yourselves around Sutherland. I have a gut feeling he's not trustworthy. Whether from intent or incompetence doesn't matter. Before this is over, I suspect he'll be standing on someone's back, reaching for a promotion. That someone may well be one of you." He stood, shook hands with the three of them, then left the room.

SEVENTEEN

Josh arrived home at eleven-thirty, too wired to sleep. He popped the top of a Killian's and sat at his kitchen table. Sipping the beer, he attempted to compartmentalize the operations in which he was involved. Blanc would have to wait. While Carrillo made an interesting target, Josh wasn't about to try him without backup. He wouldn't have that until Chief came on-board.

As for Rodriguez, nothing could be done until he was acquitted of the murder of his wife. Then Josh would have to tread lightly to keep from incurring Jaden's wrath. The planning on that couldn't start for a while.

That left the joy rider who was messing with Ms. Goldstein's car. Josh needed to stop him before it happened again. That slid into the number one slot, and he'd be on it tomorrow night.

He finished the beer and headed for the bedroom. It was time to will himself to sleep. He'd done it before. He could do it again. It was a trick Chief taught him to get through the boring hours of drawn-out operations. Tomorrow would be a day of preparation.

* * *

The following day, Josh took care of chores that had piled up over the past week—dropped off and picked up from the cleaners, paid a couple of bills, and had the oil changed in his convertible. On the way home, he stopped at Publix to stock the refrigerator for Chief's visit. As he walked the aisles, he felt challenged to get one of everything, remembering Chief's appetite.

By early evening, he was ready for a nap, knowing the night would probably be long. He kicked back in his recliner and set his alarm for eleven-thirty.

* * *

On time, Josh woke to the chiming of his clock. He shook his head, trying to dump the hangover of sleep, then walked into the bathroom where he washed his face with cold water several times. That finished his waking process. After drinking a glass of ice water, he prepared to leave the house.

He checked his weapons—the Beretta 92FS; his ankle weapon, the single-action, five shot mini-revolver; and his pride and joy, the special knife he designed while in Special Forces. It was black with a nine-inch stainless steel blade and a hollow, leather-covered handle. The cutting edge was hair-splitting sharp while the back was a marvel. It swept upward from the point with a cutting edge, Bowie knife style, for three inches before straightening. The next three inches were a standard saw blade that changed into a hacksaw the rest of the length. He hoped he wouldn't need any of the weapons, but he'd learned in previous operations that you couldn't be too well armed—only underarmed.

He changed into dark jeans, a long-sleeved burgundy shirt, black tennis shoes, and popped a navy baseball cap on his head. At twelve-fifteen, he walked out the front door. Thirty minutes later, he pulled into Ms. Goldstein's parking lot, drove through to assure himself her car was there, then backed into a visitor's space. He got out and walked to the swale, finding the bench unoccupied. Unfolding the ragged blanket he brought, he lay down. He hoped he looked like any of the numerous homeless who slept in similar situations across South Florida. Now, his task was to keep his eyes open.

Fortunately, it was a windy night with temperatures in the high sixties. He angled himself so the breeze hit him in the face, helping to keep him alert and the mosquitoes away. But, even then, staying awake wasn't easy. He cursed himself for getting soft. What he needed was some hardcore Special Forces training to toughen him up again. He'd assign that to Chief once they teamed up.

At one-thirty, an SUV came along the street, turned its headlights off, and pulled into the parking lot. It stopped behind Ms. Goldstein's car, then did a U-turn and left. A single figure stood, looking around, then moved alongside her Mercedes.

Josh threw his blanket off and hurried through the shadows. He made it to the first line of vehicles without alerting the person, then dashed across the open area, jumping between two cars. The man looked around, appearing to search the area. He walked to the end of the Mercedes, scanned left and right, hesitated, then returned to his task. It appeared he was trying to open the door.

Josh scooted from shadow to shadow until he was in front of the car beside Ms. Goldstein's. He knelt and waited. A moment later, he heard a click, like a door lock opening, then saw a flash of light. Stepping into the open space, he saw a man getting into the Mercedes. As the man twisted to drop onto the seat, one hand on top the car and one leg on the ground, Josh rushed forward and pushed the door closed, clamping arm and leg where they were.

"Good morning," Josh said. "May I see your driver's license and registration?"

"Huh," the thief said, his head spinning toward Josh. It moved so fast his hoodie fell off. "Who're you? You're hurting my leg—and my arm. Get off that door."

Josh realized the man wasn't a man. It was a teenage boy. Josh opened the door and said in a brusque voice, "Get out and tell me what the hell you're doing here."

The boy crawled out, looking around, fear dominating his face. "I . . . wasn't doing nothing. Just gonna take it for a little spin. Wouldn't hurt it. I know how to drive."

"And who gave you permission to do that?"

"Uh. No one. I just do it. It's okay, ain't it?"

"I see," Josh said. "How old are you?"

"Ain't gonna tell you."

"Wanna bet?" Josh took out his knife and held it so the light reflected off the edge. He grabbed the boy by the T-shirt and jerked him over. He slipped the blade into the material and let the blade slide upward. "This says you're going to tell me whatever I want to know. Or, I'll let you choose where I start cutting."

The boy's eyes grew large as he felt his shirt and stared at the knife. "Fourteen," he mumbled, "I'm fourteen."

"Fourteen? And you're stealing cars already? Son, that's sad. You're heading toward a lifetime in jail."

"Not stealing. Just ridin' around, havin' a little fun."

Josh shook his head. "I'm afraid your buddies have neglected your education. When you take another person's property without permission, that's stealing. And stealing gets you before a judge who sends you to jail. And jail is not a place you want to be. Don't you know that?"

"Yes sir, I mean, no sir, I mean . . ."

"That's what I thought," Josh said. "You don't know a damn thing. Where'd you get the key?"

"Key? What key?"

"Son, don't play stupid with me. I'm not a patient man. The one in your hand. The one you unlocked the door with. The one you were about to use in the ignition. Where'd you get it? I'm sure the owner didn't give it to you."

The teen stared at the key as if he'd never seen it before. "A friend of mine. He got it from his brother who works at the dealership. He's the chief mechanic."

"Okay, I get the picture," Josh said. "That's enough for now. Walk over here while I call the police."

He led the boy to the ramp by the front door and, using plastic ties, secured him to the railing. He called 911.

When he got the requisite answer, he said, "This is Josh Hawkins. I'm at 952 South Trample Avenue in Coral Lakes. I interrupted a car theft and am holding the thief. Send a patrol, please. Oh, you'd better have someone from juvie come along. He's fourteen." He paused. "Also, you might need detectives. I suspect this might be only one tine on this fork."

Josh was surprised when the second car on the scene carried Lt. Jim Richards and Detective Phil Summers. "What brings you out in the middle of the night?" Josh asked. "Thought you were nine to five guys."

Richards gave him a look of disdain. "We were on a stakeout, trying to break a car theft ring. Looks like we could have slept in and called you in the morning. Why is it you're always a step ahead of us? Seems funny to me. Maybe you're one of the gang."

"Oops. Sorry," Josh said. "Didn't mean to solve another case for you. I keep doing that, don't I? Not intentional, I assure you. Do you think this ties to whatever you're investigating?"

Richards looked at Summers. "Phil, share with Mr. Hawkins. You're the one who thinks he walks on water. I have work to do." He stomped away.

Josh watched him go. "I guess he won't be inviting me to Thanksgiving dinner any time soon."

Summers chuckled. "No, I think not. Well, not unless he can serve you as *the* turkey. You still aren't one of his favorite people."

"I noticed. So, what's up? What's your case, and how does this call fit into it?"

Summers stared at Josh a moment as if deciding what to

say or how much he should tell him. "We don't know much. What we do know is someone is stealing high-end cars. No one sees anything. No one hears anything. The cars disappear during the night. Seems like black magic. Seven cars have been taken and not one clue—until tonight."

"Meaning me?"

"Meaning you—maybe. This could be just a kid joyriding, or it could be the break we've been hoping for. If the juvies get him to talk, we might hear some answers." He paused and looked Josh over. "That's it. I spilled my guts. Now, you. What're you doing here?"

Josh gave Summers the nickel version of his surveillance. When he finished, he said, "That's it. Contrary to what we read and hear in the media, a little old lady might be the key to your case. Guess they're not as helpless as we're lead to believe. When you interview her, ask for one of her chocolate chip cookies. I hear they're the best in Florida."

Summers grinned. "I learned a long time ago not to discount our senior citizens. Their eyes are always wide open, and their hearing aids are turned to high. Plus, their collective knowledge is far too valuable to ignore. I believe you." He paused. "Does she really make great cookies?"

"That's what I heard. Will you keep me in the loop on what you find out?"

"For sure." He glanced over his shoulder at where Lt. Richards talked with a uniform. "Well, as much as I can. Thanks." Summers held out his hand in friendship.

Josh shook it.

* * *

The next day, mid-morning, Josh's phone rang. It was Summers.

"Your catch last night was anxious to talk, especially after his mother began twisting his ear. I was afraid it might come off in her hand."

"Yeah, what's his name?"

"You know better than that, Josh. He's only fourteen. However, here's what I can tell you. He ran with three others—sixteen, sixteen, and eighteen." Summers chuckled. "He was quite proud that the older kids befriended him. Or he was until his mother gave him *the* glare. Anyway, the eighteen-year-old has a brother who works in the biggest foreign car dealership in the area. He's a valet driver. His function is to pick up the car in the drop-off area and drive it into the bay. When the work is complete, he takes it through the car wash, then returns it to the owner. That's what he's paid for. What he isn't paid for is duplicating keys while the car is serviced. The kid wasn't sure, but he'd heard the brother sold the keys to guys who stole the cars and sold them to a third party who got them out of the country within twenty-four hours. A classic case of grab and ship."

"Think it's the gang you've been chasing?"

"Could be. But, whether it is or not, we have a foot in the door of a theft ring. That's the plus. And, while the lieut will never say it, he's thankful to you."

Josh chuckled. "That would really ruin my day to think Richards appreciates anything I do. But, you haven't told me why the kid was stealing my client's car."

"Not exactly stealing. He says the valet keeps a few keys for his own use, singling out older drivers, women when possible. It was those keys he shared with his little brother and his friends. The kids would take the cars out, joyride all night, then return them to their parking places. They were supposed to add enough gas to bring the gauge back to where it was when they took it. They believed the elderly owners would never notice. Your interference was the first time their fun was disrupted."

Josh laughed. "Sounds like they had quite a system going—until they picked on the wrong person. Can I assume it's okay to tell my client her car is safe now?"

"Judging from the kid's mother's attitude, I don't think

your client will ever have another problem with that one. And, as soon as we close a couple of loops, a major ring should be off the street. Gotta run now. The lieut will be along any moment."

"Thanks for calling," Josh said as the phone went dead. He shook his head, marveling at the simplicity of the crime and the audaciousness of the so-called valet. If that approach to stealing a car caught on, no one in South Florida would be safe. Life involved using valet parking, whether it was a restaurant, doctor's office, hospital, bowling alley, or the local pool hall.

He checked his watch, then called Robert Irving and gave him a report. He closed by saying, "Tell Ms. Goldstein she might want to have her doors and ignition re-keyed. Or better yet, install a keyless entry and ignition. The car is worth it. If there's no rush on a written report, I'll get it to you in a few days. Okay?"

"Fine by me. And thanks. I'm sure my aunt and her friends will be thrilled and spread your reputation as a miracle worker. Expect more work." He chuckled. "How are you at finding lost keys and spectacles?"

"Better than being the class clown, I guess."

Laughter sounded on the line as he hung up.

Josh stared at his phone a moment, a warm glow making him feel good. Sometimes the simple things in life were the most fulfilling. He headed for the kitchen. He needed coffee.

While the coffee brewed, he leaned against the counter, deep in thought. As always, when relaxed, his thoughts drifted to Jaden—how much he loved her, how much he cherished her. Then a frown creased his forehead. The Rodriguez case. The possibility that a murderer would walk free. The very real possibility that the justice system would fail. It didn't make sense that the guilty could get away so easily.

He filled a cup with coffee and went into the bedroom. Once there, he picked up the small notebook he'd used the previous day, where he'd written notes after leaving the police station and Newsome's secret files. He studied the addresses and personality traits he'd recorded. While he didn't intend to go after Carrillo until he had Chief at his back, it would be time well spent to do some basic reconnaissance. No matter what the operation, it was impossible to have too much intelligence on the enemy.

Of course, a more enjoyable option was to visit the courthouse and watch Jaden in action. After thinking a moment, he accepted that he couldn't help her. But an afternoon surveilling Carrillo might make a difference. He chose Carrillo.

Three hours later, Josh sat across the street from an unassuming house on a quiet street in east Coral Lakes. From the looks of where Carrillo lived, he didn't appear to be getting rich through his larcenous behavior. Doing okay, perhaps, but not rich.

Josh looked around. The neighborhood was middleclass with houses built on zero lot line parcels with about ten feet separating them. From what he could see, many of the back yards were fenced, meaning the owners probably had dogs or small children. Not the best kind of neighborhood for what he had in mind. He didn't want to get involved with anyone's pet and certainly did not wish to have a child hurt. He'd have to find another place to grab Carrillo, which meant flushing him out.

Josh started his car and drove away. While he fully expected that Gerard had outed him, he didn't need to make things worse by hanging around and being obvious. He needed to keep his head down until Chief was behind him.

EIGHTEEN

Two days later, Josh and Chief sat at Josh's kitchen table, sipping coffee. "Sure glad you made it," Josh said. "It's a tough op, but I have some ideas on how we can play our way in."

"Whatever you need," Chief said. "You didn't earn a direct commission by being stupid. I'm with you."

"Great. Now, here's what I'm thinking—"

"Before we start, something I've never asked you. You'd don't have to tell me if you don't want to."

"Ask. Hard to keep secrets from a partner."

"What the hell happened? I thought you were on your way to a general's star, then I heard they caught you in a reduction in force when the budget was cut. With your record, I'd have thought you'd be the last guy singled out by a RIF. Anybody ever explain it to you?"

"Yeah. The group commander and the regimental commander both went to bat for me—wrote letters, made phone calls, did all they could. It didn't do any good. The final word was only officers holding at least a bachelor's degree were exempted from release. And a master's was preferred. If I'd been smarter when I was younger, I'd have taken advantage of my opportunities and done night school. Then I might have been spared. As *they* say, hindsight is always twenty-twenty. I missed the service for a while—the civilian world seemed so strange. I'm happy now. Plus, you gotta admit, I'd have never met Jaden if I'd stayed in."

"True," Chief said. "I just wondered. You were the best officer I ever worked with. Hell, you were even a passable NCO." He laughed and punched Josh in the arm. "It was a pleasure to serve with you."

"Thanks, Chief. The feeling's mutual. Now, back to our current case. It's legit, or I'm told it is. Simply stated, we have to climb a slippery slope and take out the guy sitting on top. Our first problem is not a lot is known about him. We'll have to develop intell on the fly." He hesitated. "I fear that hill is well-greased and out in the open with his people all around its base.

"Nothing new there. We've faced that before. We can do it again. Where do we start?"

"There is a keyhole into his operation, and I think I've come up with a way to use it. It's as risky as a frontal assault into the heart of an ambush, but if it works, we'll be in. That's where you fit in. You're the reserve force who will rush to the rescue if I need it."

"So, you're leaving me in the wings while you're the front man?"

"Basically, yes. I need my back covered more than someone by my side. Will you do it?"

"Whatever the op plan calls for. That's why I'm here. Where do I start?"

* * *

At eight o'clock that night, Josh took out a throwaway cell phone. "Okay, Chief, here we go. Let's see if his conscience is as guilty as I expect it to be—and how well he handles it."

He dialed.

"Hello," a female voice said.

"Mr. Carrillo, please."

"Yeah? Who are you?"

"Tell him to get on the phone. I'm calling to save his life."

There was a gasp, then a clunk as the phone was apparently laid down. A moment later, a male voice said, "Who is this? Is this some kind of joke?"

"Joke? Not unless you have a morbid sense of humor. I'm calling for Mr. Blanc. He wants to let you know he's well aware of your skimming operation, and he won't tolerate it. He—"

"What? Who?"

Josh hesitated, wondering if there were enough layers between Carrillo and Blanc that he didn't know Blanc's name. Not likely. Not unless Carrillo was dumb enough to carry beer to a keg party. "Mr. Carrillo, people who play games with Mr. Blanc only make more trouble for themselves. In fact, they have been known to take long trips to places unknown. As I said, Mr. Blanc is aware you've been withholding funds. Here's what—"

"No, no, I haven't. I've—"

"Shut up, Mr. Carrillo. If you close your mouth, open your ears, and obey, you may live to enjoy your family. You're trying my patience with your interruptions. You're acting stupid, and I have a low tolerance for stupid people. I'm closing this conversation in a few seconds. You can either listen . . . or you can die. Your choice."

Josh sensed a hesitancy on the line, then Carrillo said, "I'll listen, but I don't know—"

"You're gaining in intelligence. Mr. Blanc said you weren't the dumbest on his payroll, but you were slow. Sounds like you're beginning to pick up speed."

"I am not—"

"Enough. Mr. Blanc's records show you skimmed fifty thousand since you joined the operation—"

"What? Fifty . . . You think I'd still be here if I had that much money? I'da skipped town long ago."

Josh smiled. He was weakening, no longer denying the

skimming. "Not my job to determine what you do with the money. Just to make sure it's repaid—or take fifty K out of your hide."

"Look, let's work together. Maybe not everything went to Mr. Blanc, but it couldn't be that much. I'd never steal fifty thousand from a man like him."

"So how much did you take? Maybe I can help you with the boss. I'll let him know it's only forty, forty-five thou."

No, not that much. Honest, I haven't stolen that much. No more than . . . maybe thirty. Yeah, thirty. That's all."

Josh laughed into the phone. "Mr. Carrillo, you're a lousy liar." He'd scored, as he expected to. Anyone foul enough to be a collector for an operation like Blanc's wouldn't resist the urge to shave a bit off the sides, confident in his ignorance that his plan was not foolproof. "As I said—and don't interrupt again—Mr. Blanc's records show fifty thousand has not been delivered. If you didn't do it, you let those working for you hold out. In Mr. Blanc's world, that is the same thing. To square the records, you owe one-hundred thousand. You have until tomorrow night to produce it."

"I can't. I need more time. My money is tied up. It's scattered in different places. A week, at least a week."

"Mr. Carrillo, I'm just the messenger. If you have a beef with the timeline, you'll have to speak with Mr. Blanc. However, before you do, I should tell you that each day adds to the debt. Therefore, two nights from now, it'll be one-hundred-fifty thousand, three nights, two-hundred thousand, etc. Do you understand what I'm saying?"

"That's not fair. I can't possibly—"

"Fair?" Josh said. "Sounds very fair to me. The last man I worked for doubled the payment each day. Would you be happier if it went one-hundred, two-hundred, four-hundred, eight . . . Get my drift? Mr. Blanc is a very reasonable man. Don't you agree?"

Josh looked at Chief who had his hand over his mouth while his huge body jiggled in silent laughter. He turned away lest Chief's merriment destroy his tough-guy charade.

"Ah . . . yes, I suppose so," Carrillo said.

"Fine. Now we can decide on the payoff. You get the money together. I'll call you at seven tomorrow night and give you the time and place. Expect to move fast when you get the info."

"Why don't you tell me now?"

Josh chuckled. "Mr. Carrillo, you insult me. Have I impressed you as an amateur during our conversation? In case you have developed that opinion, let me assure you of several non-negotiable points. One, you *will* have minimum time to get to the meeting place. If you're late, I'm gone and will report to Mr. Blanc that you were uncooperative. Two, you *will* be alone. If I see anyone suspicious—even if it's only a curious bystander—I abort and report to Mr. Blanc that you were uncooperative. Three, you *will* be unarmed. If I even sense a weapon, much less see one, I abort and report to Mr. Blanc that you were uncooperative. Four, the money *will* be in a standard-sized briefcase. A nice leather will do. Did I leave anything out?"

"I . . . I don't think so." All bluster had disappeared from Carrillo's voice. He appeared to accept his fate. "Uh . . . suppose I can't get the money that fast?"

Josh dropped his voice a notch, making it sound more ominous. "You don't want to know. The end will not be pleasant. Your wife will be a widow, but will have to wait seven years to collect on your life insurance."

There was silence on the line.

It was time for Josh to drive home the last nail. "It's your lucky day, Mr. Carrillo. Anyone else would collect from you, then feed you to the fishes. However, Mr. Blanc is a fair man. For this one time only, he will allow you to repay the money. If there is another instance, your family will not have a body to mourn. Same thing if you disappoint me tomorrow night. Do you understand?"

"Like you, I am not stupid. Of course, I get it. Are we

finished?" There was the ring of false bravado in his words.

Josh laughed into the phone. "Sounds like you've decided to whistle through the graveyard. Make sure it's not *your* grave you're treading on. Good night, Mr. Carrillo." Josh hit the off button without waiting for a reply, took a deep breath, and turned toward Chief. "How'd I do?"

"Man, I hope you never get a case of the jaws at me. You had me shaking in my boots, and you weren't even talking to me. My bet is he'll bring more than a hundred-thou. He'll try to buy his way back into the good graces of this guy, Blanc. Where're we meeting him?"

"Details, details," Josh said through a grin. "I'm working on that. I have all day tomorrow to check out a few places."

"Want I should find a nice spot?" Chief asked.

"No, I'm more familiar with this urban area. Here's what I'm thinking, though. If you can add anything, I'm all for it. We need a quiet out-of-the-way place, preferably with only one, maximum two, ways in and out. It should have enough concealment for you to hide and neutralize any backup he might bring—and I do expect he'll have someone along. Innocent looking so he won't expect us to grab him, yet secure, so we don't have to worry about bystanders. Other than that, any place will do." Josh smiled to let Chief know he knew his requirements were difficult, but not impossible.

Chief appeared to think for a moment. "Sounds complete, but let me mull it over tonight. Shouldn't be too tough."

Josh examined his watch. "Eight-thirty-five. If you don't mind, I'm going to call Jaden, and if she's still speaking to me, head her way. I haven't seen her for a couple of days, and that's two days too long."

"Go. I'll watch a little TV, then hit the sack."

NINETEEN

Jaden curled on the couch, her head resting against Josh's shoulder. "Once we're married, you won't be allowed to stay away so long. I'm writing into the ceremony that one night every six months is the maximum. After one, I miss you too much."

"Oh, sure," Josh said, rubbing her back. "You were so busy reading briefs you didn't know I wasn't here. Speaking of which, where is the Rodriguez trial?"

"You had to remind me."

"Sorry. If you'd rather not talk about it, we don't have to," Josh said while his brain looked for ways to ensure she did.

Jaden sat up. "No, it's okay. It's number two in my mind anyway. We did summations today, then the judge addressed the jury and dismissed them for the day. They start deliberations first thing in the morning. I don't have much hope, though. After listening to Samantha Kennedy, his defense counsel, I'd be more inclined to vote Rodriguez for Pope than find him guilty. She's good and did a wonderful job of making Sophia Rodriguez an out-of-control shrew."

"Yeah, but I've heard you. You're better."

"Not today. I felt outmatched. Samantha mixed in the emotion of a loving husband tormented by an unpredictable wife, backed up with anecdotes from several witnesses.

Sophia Rodriguez treated her husband horribly, flying into fits of rage and attacking him. His friends were afraid to spend much time at their house, fearing she would come after them—like she sometimes did. All the while, Santiago tolerated her outbursts because he loved her so much. It was a stunning performance."

"And you? What did you counter with? I know you anticipated and were prepared."

"I wish. All I had were cold, hard medical facts. Bruises on the body. Evidence of past abuse, or in Samantha's vernacular, self-abuse. The hammer blow to her temple, which killed her. I couldn't even bring up the case we had against him before. I was pathetic."

Josh pulled her closer. "Maybe this was one you weren't meant to win. Sometimes it happens—it has to. As you've said, the system isn't perfect, but it's the best thing we have, and most of the time, it gets it right."

"Now I *know* you have an ulterior motive. I'm well aware of your real opinion of the justice system." She kissed him. "Why don't we go to bed now, and I'll prove that buttering me up earns a payoff."

* * *

Josh lay in bed thinking, Jaden breathing deeply beside him. Occasionally, a soft snore came from her, causing Josh to smile. His beautiful Jaden. He remembered the song, *Something Good*, from *Sound of Music*, specifically the lyric: *So somewhere in my youth or childhood, I must have done something good.* He didn't know what he'd done, but it must have been a real humdinger. What else explained Jaden loving him?

He shook his head, throwing aside the thoughts of what he and Jaden shared. His job was to protect her. If she was right, and he trusted her intuition, Santiago Rodriguez would be on the street in a few days. When that happened, there was nothing to keep him from returning to his old tricks. One of those was to harass Jaden by turning up wherever she was. His appearances would appear coincidental, but Josh believed otherwise. He knew Rodriguez was stalking her.

Jaden pretended to pass it off as nothing, but Josh saw through it. She was afraid of Rodriguez. Yet, there was nothing to prevent him from resuming his *innocent* acts of revenge. In fact, he'd probably be more confident of his invincibility. And why not? Twice, he'd been charged. Twice, he beat it.

Josh could not allow him to harass Jaden. Plus, justice needed to be served. Sophia's death must be avenged. Rodriguez was a spouse abuser who, after years of beating on his wife, killed her. Of that, he had no doubts. The justice system had made two attempts and, if Jaden's judgment was valid, failed both times. Josh would not fail. Rodriguez would disappear, would die, and society would be better off without him.

There were several ways to do it. As Newsome had reminded him during their first meeting, living in South Florida provided many ways to dispose of a body—the Everglades, the Atlantic Ocean, numerous canals, the foundations of the many condominiums and office buildings rising on seemingly every street corner. Getting rid of the body was not the problem. His dilemma was to do it in a way that kept Jaden from suspecting him. If she did, she might well reject him, and he'd never risk that.

However, he had to find a way. Santiago Rodriguez must die.

He lay there, considering one alibi after another, then discarding each. He had no idea how to be in two places at once, and that's what would be required.

After another half-hour, he was no closer to a solution, so he closed his mind and slept—the trick Chief taught him during his Special Forces days.

* * *

In the morning, he saw Jaden off to work, then sat with a cup of coffee and dialed his house. When Chief answered, Josh said, "Anything happening there?"

"Nope. All is quiet. Did you find a meeting place for tonight?"

"Not yet. I do have ideas though. I'm going to run a perimeter surveillance, then I'll swing by. Do you have anything to do today?"

"Just cover your back."

"Fine. I have a couple of errands to run, then I'll give you a call and pick you up. We can have a close look at them together. I'd like your input."

"Sounds good. I'll just laze around and eat your food. Let me know when to lace my boots."

Josh hit the off button, his forehead crinkled in thought. The more Josh considered his proposed locations, the more he liked them.

* * *

At midnight, Josh stood behind Trung's Vietnamese Grocery. The area was wide enough for reserved parking for owners and delivery vans to offload their products. On the other side, a ten-foot wall separated the strip mall from a housing development. Josh examined the setting. It wasn't perfect, but the alley was disarming enough that Carrillo accepted his cash delivery instructions without obvious alarm. There were several businesses that backed up to the lane. Carrillo would have to scan each since Josh hadn't given him a specific address.

Josh grinned, remembering the Trungs' reaction when he and Chief stopped by during the afternoon. After Josh asked about using their storage room, Ms. Trung, who stood under five-feet tall looked up at Chief, smiled, and agreed. "My, he big one," she added. "He keep you safe."

Mr. Trung had nodded his agreement.

The headlights of a car turning the corner snapped Josh back to the present. He retreated into the shadowed doorway. As the vehicle came closer, hesitating at each doorway, he identified it as a late model Cadillac like the one he'd seen in Carrillo's driveway. When it came abreast of him, Josh stepped out and waved with his left hand. His right held his Beretta by his leg. He wanted it ready, but not threatening—yet. The Cadillac pulled into a parking space, and Carrillo stepped out, tugging a briefcase after him.

"In there," Josh said, pointing at the open door.

Carrillo looked around, then followed Josh's instructions. "This is a stupid place to meet. The cops patrol this area."

"That's why we're going inside. I assure you we won't be interrupted." He led Carrillo into the combination storage room and office. It had changed little since he was last there. The shelves along three walls held restaurant supplies. The fourth wall had the entry to the grocery and a desk with a computer. The major difference was a recliner beside the desk. Apparently, someone had decided he needed to rest during the day. The room was clean and dust free, making Josh wonder if Ms. Trung had gone to a special effort for him.

Josh pointed to the desk chair. "Have a seat and hand me the briefcase. I want to count the money. Mr. Blanc will not be happy if it is short." He settled onto the front edge of the recliner.

Carrillo sat and let out a deep sigh, but instead of following directions, opened the case. As the lid came up, he reached in and took out a pistol. "Game's over. Whoever you are, I know you don't work for Mr. Blanc. I checked with my contact. He got back to me and was thankful I alerted him. Said it saved him a lot of effort finding you. A couple of his people will be arriving soon, then we'll be on our way. It's a shame your loved ones will never know what happened to you."

Josh had placed his automatic under his leg when he sat, and his hand rested alongside it. "Interesting. Sounds like you think I was naïve enough to trust you. You're under the impression I'm alone here, aren't you? Now I understand why there are so many job openings in your business. Stupid people don't last long."

Carrillo laughed. "Keep talking. You think I don't recognize a bluff when I hear one?"

"Apparently not," Chief said. "You probably want to give that peashooter to my friend. My gun's a lot bigger than yours."

Carrillo's head whipped around, and his eyes grew large. Chief stood in the inside doorway holding a Mossberg 590 pump-action shotgun.

"Nice weapon," Josh said. "Mr. Carrillo, I suggest you do what he says. You might—if you're lucky—get off a round, but unless you're a crack shot and hit me square in the heart, the best you can expect is a minor wound. On the other hand, if your finger even begins to tighten on that trigger, you'll be blown through the wall. You don't want to leave a mess for us to clean up, do you?"

Carrillo groaned, lowered his pistol, then dropped it. "Enjoy while you can. The night's young."

Josh spoke to Chief. "Any problems with his backup?"

"No, they're getting a good night's sleep. When they awaken, their memories will be a muddle. In fact, I figure they'll wake up in jail after the police search their car and find drugs. I put in a call, reporting a stolen car with two guys sleeping in it."

"See." Josh turned to Carrillo as he took the Beretta from under his leg. "Hope you've learned a lesson here. It pays to travel with reliable friends. Now kick your weapon toward my backup."

Carrillo frowned, but complied.

Chief picked up the gun. In his huge hand, it looked like a toy. "Is this what he brought, a .32?" He chuckled.

"Yeah. Guess he missed the *effective weapons* class. Of course, he looks like a wuss, so a lady's weapon suits him. Let's get ready to roll. Hogtie him and put him in the trunk of his Caddy. Then drive it to the place we picked this afternoon. I'll follow you. Mr. Carrillo has a story to tell, and it will be best told where his screams won't be overheard."

"Wilco," Chief said, loosening ropes hanging from his belt. "I haven't done this since my last boar hunt in the Everglades. I need the practice."

"But first, Mr. Carrillo," Josh said, "open the briefcase. I'm curious whether you brought the money with you. It will make a nice bonus."

Carrillo stared at Chief, a look of fear and defeat on his face as he opened the empty case.

* * *

An hour later, Chief and Josh stood behind Carrillo's Cadillac. Josh looked around the area. "Looks even better than it did this afternoon. We have the place to ourselves—just us and the critters."

"Yeah," Chief said. "Pretty close to perfect."

"Pop the trunk."

Chief pressed the electronic key and the trunk lid to the Caddy lifted. Inside, Carrillo was trussed like a calf at a rodeo, a handkerchief covering his mouth.

"Mr. Carrillo," Josh said. "Hope you weren't bounced too much during our trip here. If you'll be patient a bit longer, we'll have you out in a few seconds. But first, a couple of comments. We are alongside a canal in the middle of nowhere. Listen and you'll hear the sounds of Florida as it was before humans showed up to chase the local creatures into the Everglades. If you feel like yelling, calling for help, or saying your prayers, please feel free to do so. For the first two, no one except my friend and me will hear you. In the third, I suspect your words will fall on deaf ears. I can't imagine you have a good relationship with our Maker. However, as I said, feel free. Understand?"

Carrillo nodded, his eyes large with fear.

"Take off the gag," Josh said. "Free his ankles and set him on his feet. We'll give him a moment to vent."

Chief complied and stepped away.

Carrillo looked around, then turned his gaze on Josh. "Where are we?" His words were muffled, like his mouth was filled with cotton.

"Not important. All you need to know is what you see and hear. You're fortunate we have a full moon tonight. I assume your hearing is good."

Josh paused and the night denizens of the area seemed to accept his silence as their cue. Night bird calls and other sounds filled the air. A large splash came from the canal, perhaps a fish feeding—perhaps something larger.

"I love the Everglades at night," Josh said. "How about you, Mr. Carrillo?"

"You're a funny man. You'll need that sense of humor when I send you straight to hell."

TWENTY

Leaning against the Cadillac, Josh allowed Carrillo's curses to swirl past him, almost unheard. Instead, his mind raced, hoping Carrillo would give him the wedge he needed to break into Blanc's world. He needed to wrap this up quickly so he had time to prepare for Rodriguez's release. No, he had to put that away for the future. He pushed Rodriguez from his thoughts. Based on Carrillo's words, he realized he'd interfered with Blanc's operations enough to attract attention. Blanc was his physical threat, not Rodriguez. If he didn't take Blanc out, there would probably be no Josh to handle Jaden's foe. And now, he had Chief to take care of also. Chief's well-being was uppermost. Military training taught officers to protect their men.

Josh looked around. It was a bright night and his vision improved each second. Clouds skittered across the sky, allowing the moon to play peek-a-boo. Under different circumstances, one might say it was perfect for romance.

Weeds, wild flowers, and tropical plants overgrew the canal bank, sloping into the water. Collectively, they put an engaging scent into the air, kind of a minty aroma. A few yards away was an area of crushed grass and other vegetation. Possibly a parking spot for couples seeking privacy. He smiled, choosing not to look for evidence.

After a few minutes, Carrillo appeared to run out of

energy. The expletives slowed, then stopped. Only a fierce glare remained.

"Finished?" Josh said, pushing off the car. "If so, we can get to work. It's already two o'clock, and there is a lot of information I intend to have before the sun comes up."

"Go to hell."

"Most likely I will," Josh said. "I've never expected much else. But that's not why we're here enjoying this beautiful evening with nature. We have a much more specific reason. Follow me to my car." Josh walked toward his convertible, parked in front of the Cadillac.

"Why?" Carrillo asked, not moving.

Josh stopped and looked at Chief. "Explain it to him."

Chief slapped Carrillo on the back of his head, knocking him forward several steps. "Because he said so. You had your time to spout off. Now, do what you're told." He took out a sheath knife and prodded Carrillo in the back with the haft. "Don't make me turn this around. The way your ears stick out, they'd be easy to slice off."

Carrillo hesitated, then followed Josh. He tripped once, his head swiveling left then right as he tried to watch Chief rather than the ground in front of him.

Upon reaching his car, Josh waited for Carrillo to catch up. "Kneel here, facing the canal. I want you to enjoy the view."

"What? Are you—"

Chief chopped him behind the knees, dropping him to the ground. Carrillo rolled over and stared at Chief, hate streaming from his eyes.

"Do what he says," Chief said. "No discussion."

Josh lifted Carrillo's head by grasping his hair and jerking. "Mr. Carrillo, I'm a patient man, however, my friend does not share my patience. I suggest you move and move fast when I tell you to do something. It will save you several bruises and, probably, some blood. Now. On your knees."

Glaring at Josh, Carrillo raised himself to a kneeling

position. "I still say you can go to hell."

Chief slammed the back of Carrillo's head, knocking him onto his face.

"Get up," Josh said. "Are you learning yet?"

"I can't with my hands tied behind me," Carrillo said, spitting dirt.

Josh nodded, and Chief grabbed the collar of Carrillo's shirt and dragged him back to a kneeling position.

"I repeat my question," Josh said. "Are you learning yet?"

Carrillo nodded, his shoulders hunching as if expecting a blow.

"Good. This will go much faster if you don't make my friend expend unnecessary energy." Josh looked at Chief. "Would you please get the cooler? It's in my trunk."

Chief walked to the rear of Josh's car, opened the lid, and removed a white container. He carried it to Josh, setting it on the ground, and taking off the top.

"Any alligators around?" Josh asked.

Chief surveyed the banks, then cupped his ears to listen better. "Don't see any movement or hear any. Too dark to see'm if they're sleeping. Coupla big floaters down that way. Could be logs or could be gators."

"Let's find out." Josh opened the cooler, reached in, brought out a package of chicken halves, and popped it open. He tossed one into the canal. There was a splash when it hit the water.

Josh listened. No unusual noises.

"Don't hear anything," Chief said. "Carrillo might be lucky, and they're logs."

"Yeah. It seems a quiet night," Josh said. "You might be fortunate, Mr. Carrillo."

"What do you—"

A slap sent Carrillo onto his face again.

"Patience, my friend," Josh said. "Pick him up."

Chief restored Carrillo to his kneeling position.

"Here's the deal." Josh leaned against his car, fighting a smile caused by Carrillo's dirt and grass-stained face. He looked like a bad makeup job in a B movie. "I want everything you know about Henri Blanc. Who he is, what he is, where he is, his headquarters, how he operates . . . use your imagination to come up with any topics I didn't mention. He and I have a rendezvous, and I intend to be armed with information. You start talking, and I'll interrupt when I need something expanded. After you think you've finished, I'll have lots more questions."

"Go to hell."

Slap.

"Pick him up." Josh rubbed his chin. "Mr. Carrillo, I refuse to believe your vocabulary is that limited. Now, we can play this game all night, but, quite frankly, I find it boring. Watching you smash face first into the embankment is entertainment for only the first few times. However, I assure you, my friend can keep it up all night. He's made that way—like a robot—never tires. Maybe I should add a little more, so you have a better understanding of the possible outcomes tonight. You know what I'm after, so I won't re-visit that right now. The rest of it is this. We're in an isolated part of the state, far from help for you. I happen to know there are numerous vehicles at the bottom of this section of the canal. They've been accumulating for years. Probably some real collector items. Some are empty and some hold bodies in various stages of decomposition. I know because I submerged a few, and acquaintances are responsible for others."

A guttural sound came from their left, long and low. It sounded like a lion with laryngitis, establishing his domain.

Josh tossed a chicken half into the canal. The splash was followed by a sliding sound and an entry into the water. "Ah, one woke up." He turned his attention back to Carrillo. "I also happen to know this area is infested with alligators—big'uns, litl'uns, and in-between'uns. The sound you just heard was one of them getting curious about the racket we're making. Keep an eye peeled in case he decides to investigate. He might round up a posse to check us out. Like humans, they believe there's safety in numbers."

He threw another half of chicken, noting that Carrillo's head was jerking from side to side. The ruckus that followed was bigger than the previous. "Guess he's ready for a post-midnight snack."

"Mighta been a second one," Chief said. "Where there's one, there's gotta be more."

"Get to the point," Carrillo said, his head still swiveling.

"Don't hit him," Josh said to Chief who had his had raised. "It's a good comment. Shows he's in a hurry. My point is this. When the sun comes up, my friend and I will be gone. Your car will be at the bottom of the canal. The question is where will you be. One way or the other, you'll be in the canal—unless a gator has dragged your remains onto the bank. You can be in your car with the windows up, safe from the predators that live around here . . . or, you can be in the belly of an alligator. Note that neither of those options has you walking away—and there are no others."

"Why do you want to kill me?"

"Not *want* to kill you. Believe it or not, I'd prefer to deliver you home alive. I have no choice, though. You've already checked me out with Blanc and learned that I don't work for him. You have two henchmen back in civilization who probably know too much about me. I doubt you were discreet enough not to tell them whom you were meeting. And I have every confidence you'll run to Blanc as fast as you can if we set you free. So you see, my choices are limited because of your actions. I can't let you live. And the opposite is . . ." Josh let his words drift off.

Carrillo appeared to think for a moment. "Why should I talk to you if I'm going to die anyway? The way I see it, it's a win for you, but a loss for me. Let's make a deal."

Josh held up his hand to stop Chief. "I guess I left out a

couple of details. The first is—no deals."

"But—"

"Let me continue," Josh said, cutting in. "If you tell me what I want to know, I'll shoot you through the heart and put you in your car before pushing it into the canal. We'll leave the windows down about an inch so the Caddy fills and sinks all the way to the bottom. You won't feel a thing and death from the bullet will be instantaneous. If you don't talk to me, Chief will break your arms and your legs, then we'll throw you into the canal. You'll be helpless in the water, able only to flop about and drown. I'll leave it to you to imagine the pain—and that's before a gator grabs you and drags you under. Are you familiar with how they kill their prey? They grab a big mouthful, then go into a death roll, holding them underwater until they drown or die from loss of blood. After that, the eating frenzy begins."

Carrillo cringed. "You're crazy."

"Yes, it's been said before. But those who said it would also tell you I do what I say. Do you need a few minutes to think about it?"

Carrillo nodded.

Josh threw the rest of the chicken halves into the water. Several guttural sounds echoed in the night, followed by splashes. He walked a few steps away and waved Chief over. "Let's give him some privacy. I want him to study the canal and consider his choices. Maybe he'll see something to help speed his decision along."

"Think he believes you?"

"If not, I want you to break his left forearm. Can you do it?" Josh spoke loud enough for Carrillo to hear.

Chief chuckled and looked at Carrillo. "Piece of cake. Simple or compound?"

Josh smiled. "You're too eager. Simple—at first."

"Hey," Carrillo said. "Let's talk."

"Sure," Josh said, walking to where Carrillo knelt. "Ready to answer my questions?"

"You promise not to feed me to the alligators? You promise I'll be dead before you shove my car off the bank?"

"If you tell me what I want, you have my word."

"Okay. Ask your questions."

* * *

Two hours later, Josh and Chief drove away in Josh's car. Carrillo's Cadillac rested on the bottom of the canal with Carrillo's body floating against the headliner. As promised, there was an entry wound over his heart.

"Did we get enough?" Chief asked.

"He didn't know as much as I hoped, but I think we got everything he knew. Blanc is as smart as I feared he might be. You heard Carrillo say his contact was a phone number and a voice at the other end. Even when he checked on me, he could only call the number and wait for someone to get back to him. The worst part, though, is he didn't have information on any of Blanc's hideaways, or whether he's even in Florida. The phone number might help—if it's not a throwaway that has already been ditched. Best case, we gained an inch. Worst case, we gained nothing. We'll have to keep looking for the crease in his defensive zone."

"Yeah, I got the same thing out of what he said." Chief scooted down in his seat and rested his chin on his chest. A moment later, he was asleep.

Once they arrived at Josh's house, Josh sent Chief to bed, then sat at his computer. He took out his recorder and uploaded Carrillo's answers to his hard drive. Then he moved into the kitchen where he ran an erasure and set it to recording rap music. A few iterations of that and the chip would be cleansed.

Back at the computer, he began his process of eliminating identifying data from the transferred information. Once he'd stripped it of background noises, he listened to Carrillo's words. There were a couple of points that brought a pucker to Josh's forehead. Josh asked when Carrillo had last spoken to Gerard and the response was at least two days previous. If true, it meant Gerard had not given Josh away. However, later Carrillo also said, "When I talked to my contact about you, he said Mr. Blanc wasn't surprised. It was like he knew you'd come after me." Follow-up questions elicited no further information. Carrillo continued to say Blanc hadn't seemed surprised.

Josh pondered the comment. When he added the two henchmen Blanc had sent along with Carrillo, it appeared Josh was in more danger than he'd anticipated. There could only be one reason for Blanc's lack of surprise—he expected Josh. However, Josh reminded himself of a lesson he learned in the Army, *forewarned is forearmed*. Plus, knowing about Josh didn't mean he knew about Chief. If true, Chief was Josh's opportunity to deal from the bottom of the deck. From now on, they couldn't be seen together, but they shouldn't be far apart either.

Josh yawned. It had been a long night and morning. Time for a nap. When he awoke, he and Chief would kick around the best way to bring down Blanc—while staying alive.

TWENTY-ONE

Blanc stared at Gustave. He was angry, and he knew it showed, something he seldom allowed. "What do you mean? How did our people end up in jail? What kind of idiots are you hiring? And where is this punk, Carrillo?" He slammed each word at Gustave.

Gustave flinched, then leaned forward. "I have our lawyer working on getting them released. He said it'll take most of the day because they have to appear in court. Bond will be set, and he'll bail them out. Several baggies of cocaine were found in the car."

"You didn't answer my question. How did the police zero in on them, and where did the drugs come from? If you hired somebody stupid enough to—"

"No, boss. They claim someone planted the drugs. They say it had to be the man who knocked them unconscious. I believe them. They're too smart to get caught like that."

"But not so smart they couldn't be overpowered and not know how it happened?"

"I'm afraid there is a limit to their IQs."

"Okay, they're history. Make sure they are no threat to us. Enough about them. What happened to Carrillo?"

"I'm on it. I have people scouring the area, looking for him. Right now, he's invisible. It looks like Hawkins might have grabbed him."

Blanc spun his chair and gazed out the window. The view was gorgeous, the Atlantic Ocean lapping at the shoreline, licking at the feet of the beachgoers. Several boats bobbed in the waves far enough offshore to present no hazard to swimmers. Puffy clouds skittered across the sky casting quick shadows on the palm trees below. A perfect *wish you were here* scene.

When Blanc turned back, his face had relaxed as if the view calmed him. "Hawkins. Interesting case. He might be more than I anticipated. You keep looking for Carrillo. I'll do some research on Hawkins. I shouldn't have jumped to the conclusion he was another government flunky. That might have been a mistake."

* * *

It was mid-afternoon, and Josh and Chief sat in the breakfast nook, sipping coffee. Josh had brought Chief up to date on his computer work earlier in the day. Chief agreed there was a missing piece to the puzzle. The logical assumption was that Carrillo did not know Josh's true identify when Josh contacted him. But, if that was true, why wasn't Blanc surprised that someone was scamming Carrillo? It didn't make sense. If not Carrillo or Gerard, who could have alerted Blanc? Not the three punks from the first night. Their lawyer had their lips sealed, hoping to beat the extortion and battery charges. Not Raul. Even if he wanted to get the word to Blanc, Josh doubted he would know how. Gerard? Carrillo had sworn he hadn't seen him in several days, and Josh believed him. Nope, not someone whose path Josh had crossed—or maybe it was.

Josh stared at Chief. "Could Blanc have someone in Newsome's operation? Newsome says they're loyal, trustworthy, and hold the highest security clearances. But we have to accept that somebody's talking somewhere."

Chief took a sip from his cup while gazing out the

window. "Have you forgotten who our best sources were? Those closest to the top? There are weaknesses in every operation—and almost one-hundred percent of the time, it's a human. My money says there's a leak. Maybe not in those you met, but somewhere close enough to Newsome to know who you are."

Josh rubbed his chin. "Anything's possible, but I hate to think so. Each of them was handpicked because of their skills and integrity." Even as he said it, a picture of Sutherland popped into his head. Without a doubt, he was an obnoxious, butt-kissing jerk. But was he also a traitor? He considered the others. Had he missed a clue? How about Newsome himself? But, if Newsome were dirty, would he bring Josh in? Nothing made sense.

"Chief, right now, it doesn't matter who Blanc turned. We have to assume he's onto us. With that, we have to be more cautious than we've ever been before. We're deep behind enemy lines, and there's no chopper swooping in to lift us. The only way out is to complete the mission."

"That's how I see it, too. But we've been in worse situations. Remember Op 331?"

"Oh, yeah," Josh said, his memory taking him to the Landing Zone where he, Chief, and Ron Latanga were dropped off. It was one of his first operations after receiving his direct commission. He, a Second Lieutenant, Chief, a Sergeant First Class, and Latanga, a three-striper, a Sergeant.

Their mission was straightforward. Work their way into an enemy encampment ten miles away, capture the warlord who ruled there, get back to the LZ, and wait for pick up. They had twenty-four hours to get it done. Simple and straightforward. In Chief's vernacular, *piece of cake*.

Much discussion had revolved around the size of the force. The light colonels and colonels responsible for writing the operations plan wanted to send in a big force. Josh, once selected as team leader, argued that a small group would be less likely to be compromised before they hit the target's compound. A large contingent moving through the jungle would alert the locals, both animal and human. The word would race through the area.

His superiors stared at the gold bar on Josh's collar and questioned why they should listen to a Second Lieutenant. The argument disappeared when Josh's captain produced a list of Josh's commendations and the citations supporting them.

The threesome came in before daybreak and had to clear the LZ before the sun illuminated the area. Scrambling and keeping low, they made their way almost halfway to the encampment before hunkering down in the shadows for the rest of the day.

Everything went fine from an operational standpoint. They dug in, made sure they were well camouflaged, had a meal of MREs, and slept in shifts. At ten that night, they moved out, working their way toward the target. The closer they got, the more careful they were. They reached the edge of the compound at two in the morning. Examining it through night vision goggles, they saw the accuracy of the reconnaissance photos, right down to the automatic weapons pits featuring crisscrossing fire. However, those same pictures revealed a weakness in the perimeter. It was in the latrine area. No gun emplacements and no sentries. Josh supposed no one wanted guard duty in such an unappetizing spot.

As commander, Josh had assigned himself the job of hitting the warlord's hooch while Chief and Ron laid down covering fire. Chief protested, but when Josh reiterated the roles, backed down, saluted, and said, "Yes sir, *Lieutenant* Hawkins." The grin on Chief's face as he said it showed he approved.

They watched the compound for thirty minutes, noting little activity, then began their infiltration. Fifteen minutes was the maximum time they allotted themselves to set up defensive positions, grab the warlord, and get out. Not one of them thought it could happen without a ruckus.

Ten yards inside, Ron hit a trip wire, a flare lit up the night, and a siren sounded. Nothing to do but run like hell.

Josh arrived as the warlord rushed out, pulling on his pants. Josh shot the bodyguards and grabbed the leader, wrestled him to the ground, and injected him with a special sedative. A moment later, he was unconscious. Josh used plastic ties to secure his wrists and legs, threw him over his shoulder, and headed back the way he'd come. In the courtyard, confusion reigned. The terrorists ran in circles, firing in every direction, then dropped from the accurate firepower coming from Chief and Ron.

Bursting through the latrine area into the forest surrounding the camp, Josh gave the signal through his radio, indicating he was clear. He dumped his prisoner, then turned back to provide cover while Chief and Ron exfiltrated. Chief joined him a moment later, but Ron's weapon continued shooting from inside the compound.

Josh sent the signal again. Ron's position didn't change. His radio was either not working, or he was hit.

"Watch the prisoner," Josh said. "I'll get Ron." He dashed into the compound to where Ron lay, zigzagging his way through the inaccurate fire. Ron had been hit and couldn't walk. Josh put him in a fireman's carry and began backing out of the camp, firing as he went. Behind him, Chief continued to lay down a concentrated barrage.

Once in the trees, Josh signaled Chief to move out. Chief grabbed the warlord, tossed him over his shoulder, and they began a dash through the forest. They had to outdistance the pursuit and get back to the LZ by first light. But sometime soon, they would have to stop and check Ron's wounds. Josh looked at his watch—three o'clock. They were only a few minutes behind schedule.

For the next hour, they wound their way through the dense growth, returning fire when they had to, but otherwise moving as stealthily as possible. They were safest when their pursuers weren't sure where they were. After an hour, they appeared to have created enough space to take a breather.

Josh lay Ron down, sliced open his uniform, and examined his wounds. Not good. Blood still flowed. Josh treated and bandaged them. "Do you need a painkiller?"

"No," Ron said through clenched teeth. "Just get me the hell out of here."

Chief stepped up. "I'll carry him. You take care of our guest."

Josh turned to the warlord, who had regained consciousness. "Listen. I'm only going to say this once. Our orders are to bring you in. They don't say dead or alive. If you don't cooperate, you're dead. If your boys get too close, you're dead. If you open your mouth or do anything other than agree with me, you're dead. If you drag your feet, you're dead. Now get your ass up, we're moving out."

They maneuvered as quietly and quickly as they could for two more hours. Whenever they stopped, they could hear their pursuers thrashing about behind them. They sounded methodical, taking no chances of bypassing their leader.

They reached the edge of the forest alongside the LZ at five-thirty. Josh tied the prisoner to a tree and gagged him, positioning him so he faced into the woods. If they came under attack, Josh wanted the warlord to catch the first rounds. Ron had lost strength as they made their dash through the woods. Some of his wounds still bled. Josh changed the dressings, not liking what he saw. Then he stretched out about ten feet from Chief, establishing a two-man defensive perimeter.

Josh scanned the trees. Every moving shadow could be a terrorist, or a branch swinging in the slight breeze. He wiped his forehead and came away with a bloody hand. Racing through the brush and tree limbs had taken their due. Scratches and gouges covered every inch of uncovered skin.

Ten minutes before the helo was due. Which would arrive first—the enemy or rescue? They waited, hearing the pursuing party move closer. They were being thorough, apparently searching every place a small group could hide.

Josh heard the whop-whop-whop of the chopper's blades. Chief threw out a red smoke grenade, their predesignated signal for letting the pilot know the LZ was hot, then he and Chief prepared to run for it.

Josh cut the warlord loose from the tree and pushed him ahead as he ran for the center of the LZ. Chief was right behind him, carrying Ron. Shots sang out from the trees, kicking up dirt around their ankles.

Josh glanced behind and saw two men in full view taking careful aim. Ron raised himself and fired a burst. Both dropped and other heads disappeared.

With the chopper hovering a few feet off the ground, Josh shoved the warlord in, then spun, and began shooting into the trees. Chief rolled Ron in and signaled for Josh to get aboard. When Josh was halfway in, he felt a bump from behind as Chief dived in beside him. The helo lifted with Josh and Chief peppering the edge of the tree line. The return fire was inaccurate, not striking any vital parts of man or chopper.

During the flight, Josh ministered to Ron, but it was too little too late. Ron bled out and died en route—too many wounds.

Operation 331 was declared a success, the three of them were commended, Ron posthumously. The warlord was turned over to the interrogators where his resolve melted under their relentless questions.

"Yeah," Josh said, his mind returning to the present. "I remember 331. Ron Latanga was a fine soldier. Damn shame we couldn't get him out in time."

"We did what we could," Chief said. "We knew the odds going in. It could have been any one of us—or all three of us. I'm sure he understood. And he'd agree that grabbing that warlord produced intell that saved a lot of lives."

Josh sighed. "Ron left a wife and two children. We were so young then, thought we were invincible. Not sure I could do it today."

"You do what you have to. I've watched you many times. When you go down, you'll be surrounded by the bodies of your enemies."

"You mean with blood on my blade and empty magazines in my weapons?"

Chief smiled. "You remember well. And yes, that's what I mean. You're a warrior, Josh. Nothing will change that."

They sat, sipping their coffees without speaking, Josh remembering the horrific dreams that once hounded him after operations—bullets flying, bodies dropping, each of them with his face.

He shook his head, clearing it of the memories. "You know, we've been lucky. We survived some hairy operations, then you found Sandra, and I met Jaden. We've had better luck than we ever deserved. Today's Friday. Let's take the weekend off and spend time with the women we love. Blanc will still be alive next week. Plenty of time for us to find him." He paused and smiled. "Get out of here. I'll see you Monday."

* * *

Josh watched Chief drive away, knowing he'd made the right decision. Some things were more important than bringing down a mobster. Mobsters could be replaced. Relationships couldn't.

He took out his cell phone and speed dialed Jaden.

"I was hoping you'd call," she said. "How's your day going?"

"Quiet—the way I like them. What's up with the jury? Since you answered, you obviously aren't in court."

"That's why I love you. You're so quick to pick up on the obvious." She chuckled. "The jury's still out. A few minutes ago, I had a message from the judge saying if they don't reach a decision in the next thirty minutes, he's sending them home for the weekend. They'll reconvene Monday."

"Good," Josh said. "That's my side of hoping."

"And what's that supposed to mean?"

"That means I want you to come home as early as possible. We'll go out to dinner, then you're to pack for a weekend on the beach."

"Which one? There are dozens around here—and why do I need to pack? We can drive over, then come home and sleep in our own bed."

"That's the problem with having a lawyer for a fiancée," Josh said. "Every comment is met with questions. For this once, do what I ask. And take that new, hot pink bikini. I can hardly wait to show you off."

"Show me off? Why don't I like the sound of that?"

"There you go with the questions again. Signing off. I love you."

"Love you, too."

Josh hit the off button and smiled. He knew what he wanted for the weekend. As they used to say in the old westerns, *get the hell out of Dodge*. He went into the house and sat down at the computer. After a few minutes, he had a reservation at a hotel in Naples for Saturday night. It was located within walking distance of the beach and downtown dining. He pushed away from the desk and smiled, mumbling, "I should have come up with this idea a long time ago. We both need a break." He thought a moment, then went back online and booked for Friday night, too. They'd leave as soon as she got home and packed. They could dine in Naples, then spend all day tomorrow doing whatever they chose.

* * *

The weekend was as wonderful as Josh had imagined it to be. They strolled the beach, took a trolley tour, and acted like young lovers. The hot pink bikini spent more time lying beside the bed than it did on Jaden's body.

TWENTY-TWO

Josh and Jaden arrived home Sunday evening, tired but relaxed—feeling better than either had in weeks. The weekend had refreshed them and their love for one another. But in so doing, it left Josh more confused than ever. Jaden was more important to him than anything—or was she? If he had to choose between her and his disgust for the justice system, which would he select? If he had to watch guilty people walk free in order to keep Jaden, could he? Could he renounce his values, his belief that miscreants must be punished? He loved her. He knew that. He wanted to spend the rest of his life with her. He knew that. The Rodriguez situation would spin down in the next few days, and he'd have to face himself in the mirror—unless he found a way to once again postpone the decision.

While driving to Naples on Friday night, they had agreed to turn off their cell phones and only turn them on in case of an emergency. Such an emergency did not occur, thankfully, and their weekend went uninterrupted. But while living in a make-believe world of no outside interference is a wonderful idea, it does not relate to reality. Life slipped back in soon after they entered the house.

As they cuddled on the couch, Jaden said, "Have to find out what we missed." She pushed the power button on her cell.

"You had to remind me," Josh said, thumbing on his phone. The screen illuminated with a message saying he'd missed twenty calls. He scanned through the numbers, writing off several as telemarketers. Another area where laws proved ineffective or worse. Both the state of Florida and the federal government had established Do Not Call lists, however when businesses discovered that the policing was listless, they ignored the prohibitions. Josh had reported several violators, only to have them continue to call, apparently without retribution.

Three numbers he didn't recognize appeared several times. He wondered who'd been so persistent in trying to reach him. He then checked for messages and saw there were nine. He rose, walked into the kitchen, and sat down with a pad and pen.

He punched up the first message and heard, "We need to talk. Call me."

No name, just a call me? He shook his head and frowned. Not likely he'd answer that one.

He listened to the second message. "I've been trying to reach you. You need to contact me as soon as you get this."

Another mystery without identification or phone number. Both voices were male and could have been the same person. Strange.

Message three was no more enlightening. Another demand from an unnamed person for a phone call.

There were four more similar calls before he hit number eight, a different voice this time. "Mr. Hawkins. I work for Mr. Blanc. It's in your best interest to return my call. I won't be asking again."

Ah-ha, Josh thought. Blanc has me on his *do-call* list. Not good. I'd hoped to stay out of his sight a bit longer.

Message nine, which came in at six-thirty that same evening, was a home run. It was from a blocked number. "Mr. Hawkins, this is Henri Blanc. My people have been trying to reach you all weekend. I shall assume you're out of pocket and not simply ducking me. I expect you to contact me at this number no later than Monday noon." He read off a phone number. "If not, I'll send people to find you. I think you know why." The voice was clear, expressive, educated, and carried a confidence that said the owner was accustomed to obedience.

He glanced into the living room, hoping Jaden hadn't heard Blanc's words. She was on the phone so chances were she hadn't. Good. What she didn't know, she couldn't ask about. It appeared Carrillo was right when he said Blanc wasn't surprised when contacted about Josh's *skimming* story. Clearly, he had previous knowledge of Josh's mission.

Josh put the call on his line-up of things to do in the morning. For tonight, he wanted nothing interfering with his time with Jaden.

Pushing it from his mind and rising, he returned to the living room.

Jaden lay her phone down. "Anything good on yours?"

"Not really. The usual telemarketers. How about you?"

"One of the messages was from my boss. He hoped I was having a memorable weekend. Per his gut feeling, tomorrow won't be near as pleasant."

"Rodriguez?"

"Yeah. He thinks the jury will find for the defense. He says I shouldn't blame myself, I did everything I could." She gave Josh a beseeching look. "I can't buy that. I know he's guilty, and I should have convinced the jury. There has to be something I missed."

"Easy, Sunshine. The fat lady hasn't sung yet. Maybe the jury will see through that BS his friends put out."

"In the words of my incredibly romantic fiancé, *fat chance.*" She stood and moved toward the bedroom. "If you don't mind, I need to get my head back in the game. I brought home the file for my next case. Maybe reviewing it will take my mind off Rodriguez."

"Good point," Josh said. "I have a couple of calls to

make. I'll join you in a bit and ensure you don't stay up too late."

She grinned as she walked out of the room. "I'm counting on it."

Josh returned to the kitchen where he opened the refrigerator and took out a Killian's. He called toward the bedroom, "I'll be on the patio."

He followed up on his words, then sat, enjoying the freshness of the evening. A cooling breeze blew across the yard, stirring the palm fronds. The sky was dotted with clouds with the wind controlling their movement. The moon appeared to be rushing in the opposite direction, ducking in and out of the scattered clouds in a cosmic game of peek-a-boo.

He glanced into the house, then took out his cell phone and called Chief. Once he had him, and they'd exchanged the requisite number of insults and innuendos, he told him about the messages from Blanc and his henchmen.

"What do you want to do?" Chief asked. "I assume you're going to contact him. I'd recommend against it, but I suspect I'd be wasting my time. Much better to initiate contact on your dime, not his."

"I have to follow up. It could well be the break we've been looking for—a doorway into his lair. If so, I'll be the first to get in. According to the task force, he's been harder to catch than Brer Rabbit in the briar patch."

"Watch how you use that word break. It has more than one definition. He might use the one having to do with bones."

Josh chuckled. "I get it. I'll stick with it meaning opportunity. Anyway, what time can you be here in the morning?"

"Name it. I'll be there."

"Great. Until I find out what Blanc knows, it's best if we aren't together in obvious places. If I need you to rescue me, you'll have better luck if they don't know you exist. Agreed?"

"Agreed," Chief said. "If I'm facing the same guns at the same time as you, it makes rescue more difficult—not impossible, but more difficult."

"You're so logical," Josh said through a smile. "Let's meet at nine at the Dixie Grill for breakfast. We'll be anonymous there—I hope."

"What, you think Blanc and his cronies don't eat country ham, red-eye gravy, buttermilk biscuits, and grits? Oh, damn, I shouldn't have said that. I'm getting hungry already."

"Like when aren't you hungry? However, that's what I'm counting on. Somehow, I don't believe a lot of Canadians line up for southern cooking."

"Probably not," Chief said. "Do you have anything else? Sandra is calling me to bed, and she's a lot more fun than talking to you. See you in the morning."

"Enjoy yourself tonight. Once we fire up tomorrow, it might be several days before you get home." Josh rang off, grinning, glad he'd recruited Chief. Now all he had to do was keep him alive—keep both of them alive—while bagging Blanc for the task force. That brought him back to the possibility of Blanc having a mole in the system. Maybe he could trick him into dropping a clue, something he could use to out the traitor.

* * *

On Monday morning, Josh kissed Jaden off to work, then drove to his house to retrieve his weapons. He'd stored them before he and Jaden left for the weekend. Once fully armed, Beretta 92FS, his single-action, five shot mini-revolver in an ankle holster, and his special knife in a calf sheath, he headed for the Dixie Grill to meet Chief. Along the way, he took a circuitous route, checking for surveillance. Either Blanc's boys were excellent at their trade, or there was no one on his tail.

In the strip mall that housed the Dixie Grill, he parked at

the end opposite the restaurant and walked through the parking lot. He went into Publix and positioned himself to watch the entry, but out of clear view. No one suspicious came in. Exiting Publix through the second door, he worked his way closer to his target. At a Dollar Store, he entered and spent ten minutes wandering the isles, marveling at how so much could be sold so cheaply. Again, it appeared he was free of surveillance. Finally, he entered the Dixie Grill, walked to the back, and slid into a booth across from Chief.

"'Bout time you got here," Chief said, setting his coffee mug down. "I been smelling that country ham for ten minutes. I might order the whole hog."

"Sorry I'm late, but I wanted to make sure I didn't bring anyone along."

"Are you clean?"

"As an old maid's datebook—or they have a cloak of invisibility."

"I'm convinced. Can we order now?"

Josh waved to the waitress, who came to the table with pen, pad, and a practiced smile.

"Ready?" she said.

Josh grinned. "My friend is starving. Don't stand too close or he might bite you."

"Oh, hon, he don't look so fearsome. You outta see some of the folks we get in here. What'll it be?"

Josh deferred to Chief.

Chief held up the menu. "I need a fresh pot of coffee first. Then I'll have two number fives. Make the eggs over easy."

"Okay, hon, that's six eggs over easy, a double order of ham with redeye gravy, double order of grits, four buttermilk biscuits, and coffee. Is that all?"

Chief frowned. "Better bring a side order of country ham and redeye gravy and a couple more biscuits. That ought to hold me till lunch."

Josh shrugged at the waitress and ordered a single

number five. He suggested she bring a second pot of coffee since he wasn't sure Chief would share.

The waitress patted Chief on the shoulder. "Hon, you just hang on awhile longer. I'll put the rush on your order." She giggled and walked away.

"You must have missed breakfast," Josh said. "Sorry to have gotten you out so early."

"Not a chance. Sandra insisted on fixing bacon, eggs, and toast. She never lets me leave the house hungry. That's what's enabled me to make it this long." He looked toward the kitchen. "Sure hope they get a move on."

Josh laughed. "I can see that having meals with you will once again be an experience. I'd forgotten that mean appetite of yours. Now I remember how the mess sergeants loved you. You were their best customer."

"Hey, I'm a big man. Takes lots of food to keep me going. You want me at full strength, don't you?"

TWENTY-THREE

Chief attacked his food with such rapture Josh decided not to talk business until he finished. Instead, he concentrated on his breakfast. Soon, he was lost in the flavors of the South.

Finally, Chief sopped the last of his redeye gravy with the final crumb of his sixth biscuit and leaned back in the booth. "Ah, man. That was worth the trip across Alligator Alley." He sipped his coffee. "So whatcha going to do?"

"I'll call Blanc, but I'll keep him waiting until five minutes before noon. Don't want him to think I'm intimidated. In the meantime, there's a stop we need to make for supplies."

"GPSs?"

"Good guess. I want you to be able to find me at any moment, no matter where I am. Then, you make the call as to whether I can be rescued. You are not—I say *not*—to risk yourself unnecessarily. I don't want Sandra trying to run your alligator farm without having you to handle the heavy stuff. My guess is Miss Allie can be very demanding."

"Hey, we got the same goals," Chief said, a smile splitting his face. "Hell, I'll leave your ass in a New York minute if there's too much danger."

Josh knew it would never happen and debated whether to call him on it. No, he'd let Chief's brag stand. "Okay, I trust your words. But remember this. If you get yourself killed, I'm going to kick your butt all over the Everglades."

"Ha. Even dead I'll be able to take you."

"Ready to head out?" Josh asked, laughing.

"Let's roll."

* * *

Josh drove to a shop he'd used before—Mo's. No fancy name required, and Mo never advertised. Those who needed to know knew, and promotion came from word of mouth by satisfied customers. It was a legitimate cop supply store, however Mo added a few odds and ends he sold through the back door to preferred customers. He also handled special orders. It was Mo who had replaced Josh's military specification Beretta 92FS with a clean one. An earlier case had mandated that Josh get a new one with no history. His old one was at the bottom of the Atlantic, about a mile offshore.

Josh had acquired the first one in Fayetteville, North Carolina while serving with Army Special Forces at Fort Bragg. Buying a special-order weapon in Fayetteville was no challenge. Soldiers' preferences were well known along Bragg Boulevard, whether in the strip joints or the gun shops. It was more difficult in South Florida, but Mo had come through for him. He had the kind of contacts Josh needed, and Josh had a reputation Mo admired. They weren't close friends, but they had closed a bar or two.

Walking in, Josh said, "Mo, you old dog, how are you?" He looked around, not sure why. Nothing ever changed in Mo's. The place was set up like an auto parts store, except on a smaller basis. The front of the one-room shop held a counter, cash register, and a computer. The rear two-thirds had floor-to-ceiling shelves. Boxes of various sizes filled each shelf. Mo kept a tight inventory with locations on the computer. Nothing was ever out of place in Mo's.

"Based on the word on the street, a lot better than you,"

Mo said. "I figured you'd be along sooner or later—if you lived that long. Anytime one of you guys gets in trouble, you come running to Uncle Mo. But I like that. I double the prices." He chuckled and slapped Josh on the shoulder.

"Oh," Josh said, "what have you heard?"

Mo looked at Chief, then raised an eyebrow in Josh's direction.

Josh smiled. "Meet Chief. He's a white hat. We were SF together and now he has a place in the Everglades. Full-blooded Indian who claims he has taken many scalps."

"Nice to meet you," Mo said, fingering his baldpate. "No problem here. Someone already beat him to it." He stuck out his hand. "If Josh vouches for you, you're alright in my book. What can I get you guys?"

Chief said, "Paleface also got pale head," and shook Mo's hand.

Josh laughed. "Now that you two have bonded, tell me what you hear on the street."

"Nothing much. Just that you grabbed a tiger by the tail. Some folks are saying you met your match and will soon disappear."

Josh pondered that a moment. Was the word out he was hunting Blanc? If so, how did it happen? "Anything more specific?"

"Not really. Only a bunch of glowing generalities. Seems you rescued a Vietnamese couple from some people who resent your meddling. Rumor says they're looking for a hitman who'll take you on."

Josh took a deep breath in relief. "Yeah, I did stick my nose in, and I'm glad I did. They're a nice couple and don't need a bunch of petty hoodlums bugging them. How about you keep your ears open and let me know when I should start to worry?"

"You got it. But it'll cost you a case of Killian's."

"You're on," Josh said. "But now for business. When are you going to spruce this place up a bit? A good cleaning and a coat of paint would do wonders for the ambiance."

Mo looked around. "Looks fine to me. You want *ambiance*, go to Macy's. Here, you find what you need with the most knowledgeable service in town."

Grinning, Josh said, "I can't disagree with you. Besides, the layer of dust gives it that *much loved* feeling."

"Did you come in to bust my chops, or do you want something?"

"I thought you'd never ask. Chief and I need some small GPS's. The tough one is a pair we can conceal that won't be found. Then two more sets—one for the cars and one for the body that look hidden, but can be found. Got anything fitting those descriptions?"

"Wait a minute. Let's make sure I understand. You want a pair you can put on your person that *will* be found if you're searched, am I right?"

"Yes. I expect a pat down, and I want them to think I'm clean after they strip off a GPS."

Mo stroked his chin. "No problem there. Then you want a pair for your cars. Correct?"

"Yep," Josh said. "Something that can be attached and not be easily located."

"Got it. Then you want a pair that *will* escape detection?"

"Yes."

"Where do those two ride?"

"Someplace in our clothing or attached to our skin."

"What? Wait, scratch that. I shouldn't be surprised at anything you ask for." Mo stared at his shelves, then scrunched up his face, his hand rubbing his upper lip. "Not impossible. How much time do I have? I'm thinking I saw something in a catalog that would be perfect. Give me a few seconds. I need to remember which catalog."

Josh made a production of looking at his watch. "I can give you fifteen minutes."

"What? Are you— No, again I should have known. You never plan in advance. What's the deal?"

"I have an hour to make a phone call to set up a meet," Josh said. "I expect the other party will want to get together soon, maybe today. So, I need to be wired before it happens."

"Okay. Let's check the inventory." Mo punched up his computer, inviting Josh and Chief to watch.

* * *

Twenty minutes later, Josh and Chief left Mo's with the best of his equipment. Josh wasn't satisfied his *hidden* GPS would escape detection, but it was all Mo could do on short notice.

"When you gonna call this guy?" Chief asked. "Time's getting short."

"As soon as we get to the car and find a quiet spot. I'm waiting until the last minute so he'll know he doesn't have me quaking in my boots. Of course, I don't want any of his strong arms out looking for me either. He set noon as the deadline, so I'm honoring it."

They reached Josh's car and got in. He had parked on a side street where traffic was light. It was as quiet as it was going to get, so he took out his cell phone and called Blanc.

When he heard, "Hello," Josh said, "Mr. Blanc, please."

"This is Henri Blanc, Mr. Hawkins. My watch says it's three minutes before twelve. I'm glad you didn't wait until the last second."

Josh chuckled. "Obviously, you have a sense of humor."

"Perhaps, but I suggest you not push it. I hear distressing things about you. That does not please me. It's time we have a discussion."

Josh hesitated. "What have you heard?"

"I'm sure you know. And rest assured, I check my sources. They dare not lie to me. It costs too much."

"Do you provide life insurance to take care of the survivors?"

"You're living up to your reputation, Captain Hawkins. My choice is to meet this evening. Does that comply with

179

your schedule?"

"Captain? Should I assume you've been checking on me? You have people in places who reveal info they shouldn't?"

"You may make any assumptions you like. But be careful. I'm sure in at least one of your military classes the word assume was explained to you."

"Many times," Josh said, nodding. "Many times."

"Back to my question. Are you available for a meeting this evening? The correct answer is yes."

"I'll go with possibly. Where do you have in mind?"

"A friend owns a warehouse on River Street. He says it has a nice office and is very private. We'll meet there."

"Mr. Blanc, I appreciate your chutzpah, but I don't think so. Here's the deal. You pick the time, and I'll pick the place. Somehow, it doesn't seem healthy to let you select both. Like you said, I do have a reputation to uphold."

The phone went quiet, although there was a noise in the background that could have been whispering. After a moment, Blanc came back on the line. "No. We'll do it my way."

"In that case," Josh said, "bring your own entertainment to the meeting. I won't be there." He punched the off button.

Chief, whose head was against Josh's so he could hear Blanc's end of the conversation, said, "Pretty abrupt. Suppose he doesn't call back? I thought the whole idea was to go face-to-face with him."

Josh dropped his phone into a cup holder. "He'll either contact me or he'll send his boys after me. We'll see which he chooses. He wants to meet, and he's accustomed to getting his way. Are you hungry yet?"

Chief grinned. "You always were a hardheaded SOB. I'm starving. It's been hours since breakfast."

"Yeah. At least two. There's a deli down the block that serves the biggest subs in South Florida. A couple of those might satisfy you."

Chief appeared to reflect on it. "A couple of subs. Yeah,

that might work if they have a big variety of meats and cheeses."

They walked to the deli, entered, placed their orders, then sat in a rear corner. The restaurant was small, five booths and three tables.

Josh had a simple pastrami on rye with hot mustard while Chief had a foot long submarine with everything the counterman could load on it. Chips and sodas completed their meals.

Meats, cheeses, peppers, pickles, mustard, mayonnaise, and greenery protruded as Chief attempted to shove the full width and height of the sub into his mouth. Not happening. He finally compromised and bit from the top half.

Josh's smile was mischievous as he said, "Think that'll hold you for a while, or should I order a couple to go?"

Chief stopped chewing. "I won't know until I finish this one. I'll tell you then."

"How the hell do you keep your weight under three-hundred—or do you?"

"Hey, I'm a growing boy," Chief said through a mouthful. "If I ever develop a weight problem, Sandra will tell me and put me on a diet."

"Yeah? I want to be there when it happens. I'd love to see Sandra padlock the fridge on you."

Josh's cell phone rang. The caller ID said *unknown*, but the number was Henri Blanc's.

"Hello," Josh said.

"Is this Josh Hawkins?"

The voice came through loud enough to force Josh to hold the phone away from his ear. It wasn't Blanc's. "Who wants to know?"

"Call me Mr. Blanc's booking secretary. He told me to find out where you want to meet."

Josh noticed that Chief had leaned forward and his mouth was not moving. "Depends on his choice of time. Obviously, the location will be affected by the hour. What's his choice?"

"Eleven tonight."

"That sounds good," Josh said. "I'll call this number between ten and ten-thirty with a location."

"Ridiculous. Mr. Blanc will never agree. Give me the place now."

"Be near the phone when I said. For now, my lunch is getting cold. Goodbye, Mr. Booking Secretary." Josh hit the off button, grinning.

"Can you back up the tough guy approach you're using?" Chief said. "Suppose he decides to hell with a meeting and sends his goons to blow you away?"

"No. If that were an option, he'd never have contacted me. By doing so, he's given me a small window into his world. The phone is probably a throwaway, but it's still tied to him. Plus, he's let me know how important it is that he talk to me. I don't know what he wants, but he wants it *before* he eliminates me. Whatever it is, we can handle it."

"Where you get that *we stuff*, white man?" Chief's grin gave away the gibe as he took another huge bite.

TWENTY-FOUR

Josh and Chief ate quietly for a couple of minutes before Chief said, "What about the intell Blanc has on you? Do you think he got access to your military files? Somehow he knew you were a captain. Obviously, he knows you're digging into his operations."

Josh rubbed his chin, then took a bite of his sandwich, chewed, and swallowed. "I don't know. It is worrisome, though. Someone somewhere is not shooting straight. I've been debating whether I should talk to Newsome."

"Why wouldn't you? Blanc doesn't care that you know. Do you think he'll care if Newsome knows he knows?"

"Suppose Newsome is the mole."

Chief leaned forward. "Not like you, Josh. I'm beginning to wonder if you have your head fully in this operation. You're not thinking straight. Don't let Jaden's problems distract you."

"What do you mean?"

"If Newsome is the mole, you won't be telling him anything he's not already privy to. And, if he's not the mole, you'll be alerting him to a big hole in his operation."

Josh blinked, then shook his head. "Damn. You are right-on. I'll call him. Finish your sub, and let's find someplace we won't be overheard."

"While you're at it, figure out where you're meeting

Blanc and his boys tonight."

"Yeah," Josh said, "that too."

* * *

Once they were in Josh's car, he dialed Newsome's private number.

"Hello, Josh. Do you have news for me?"

"Yes, but you might not like it. In case you haven't figured it out, your operation is burned. Blanc knows as much about me and our relationship as you do."

"How can that be?" Newsome sounded incredulous.

"Start by looking around you. Someone is feeding him. And, for now, I'm the *entree du jour*. Not something I appreciate. I suggest you discover who your traitor is and take appropriate measures. I don't want a backstabber behind me."

"Are you sure? I mean, really *sure*? You're making a powerful accusation against handpicked people."

Josh frowned and took a deep breath. "Mr. Newsome, I wouldn't have said it if I was not *absolutely sure*. And the more you hesitate, the more I wonder if it might be you."

Silence filled the line, then, "I'll assume that was a poor attempt at humor. I'll unearth the infiltrator, if there is one. How are things going otherwise?"

"I'm working it. Until you find the mole, that's all you need to know. Just make sure you have that half-mill ready when I wrap this up."

"I like your optimism."

"We'll see," Josh said. "Now, I have to get back to harassing Blanc." He hit the off button.

Josh turned to Chief. "Okay, that's that. It's his problem now."

"Well done. What about tonight? How about the lobby of the police station? That'll keep his strong-arms under control."

Josh grinned. "Great idea. That's exactly the kind of place we need. And I know the perfect place. Here's how we do it."

* * *

As Josh finished briefing Chief, his phone trilled its special ring. Jaden.

"Hello, Sunshine. Any word yet?"

"No," she said, "and the suspense is killing me."

"Quit emoting and look in the opposite direction."

"Yes, my dear shrink, and what will I see on that horizon?"

"Oh, did I get a promotion? No, don't respond to that. But, to answer your question, you'll see a half-full glass. You have jurors who didn't buy into the claptrap the defense and her *witnesses* put out. They are locked in that room working to convince the others of Rodriguez's guilt. The game isn't over yet. Plus, don't make me trot out the cliché again about the fat lady singing."

"Please don't. Makes me want to diet and never sing again. You're right, though. As long as they're talking, we have a chance. Now, I have to ignore that for every half-full glass, there is a half-empty one. Scratch that. I didn't say it. I didn't even think it." She chuckled, enjoying her joke. "I have to get back to work now. I simply wanted to hear your voice. I knew you'd come up with something optimistic to lift my spirits."

"That's why you keep me around," Josh said. "I'm such a positive person. Call me the moment you learn anything."

"I will. I love you."

"Love you, too."

Josh closed his phone, smiling. "Well, Chief. Hope isn't lost for the Rodriguez case. Jaden says the jury is still deliberating. Maybe they'll put that SOB away yet."

"And if they don't, you will?"

"Yeah. I will."

They sat quiet for a few moments, then Josh said. "Time to call Summers. Keep your fingers crossed."

Chief said, "Before you call, explain this guy to me again, and why you think he'll jump to help you."

"He's a detective in the Coral Lakes department with a sense of humor and an insatiable curiosity. We have some history together. I busted a case he and his Lieutenant were the leads on. Pissed off his L T, but Summers thought it was pretty neat. My guess is he'll leap at this. Make sure you pay for the beer."

"Correction. *You* pay for the beer. Summers and I will take on the task of drinking it."

Grinning, Josh dialed Summers' cell number.

"Phil, it's Josh Hawkins. I'm calling to pay my debt."

"Debt? You recognize a debt? Why don't I like the sound of this? I'm already getting twinges about the ass-chewing I'll get from Lt. Richards."

"You're so insecure. Would I do anything to get you in Dutch with your honorable boss?"

"In a word, *yes*. And that's without my asking which debt. However, you've piqued my curiosity. How do you intend to make a payment?"

"Here I thought you'd never ask. The beer is on me tonight."

"Uh-huh. Keep talking. I know there's a lot more to this fairytale. And the part you so carefully omitted is where I get in trouble. Spit it out."

"Okay. Can you make it to the Blue Line about ten-thirty? I have a friend in town I'd like you to meet. Plus, you might see something that will make your day."

"Damn you, Hawkins. That's below the belt."

"What? Oh, Phil. I just want you to meet my friend, drink a few beers, and bond a bit. It's been awhile since we had the opportunity."

"Ha," Summers said. "We've never had that *opportunity*.

I've stayed too busy defending you from Richards' long arms."

"Yes, you have. That's why I owe you. What say? Ten-thirty? Blue Line Bar? I promise you an enlightening evening."

Summers laughed. "You're on. Tell'm to clean the tap lines."

They hung up, both chuckling.

Josh turned to Chief. "You'll like this guy. He's a straight shooter, but he works for a lieutenant who hates PIs, so he has to walk a fine line when dealing with me. A couple of times his boss had me in his sights, but I managed to escape. I suspect Phil was a major reason I didn't get more heat. I wasn't kidding. I do owe him."

"What's your plan? Am I entertaining Summers while you spend time with Blanc?"

"That's about it. I want you close enough to step in if necessary. If you're sitting alone, you'll stick out like an oversized Seminole with a long braid in a cop bar. And having another friendly face in the place won't hurt."

Chief laughed and punched Josh on the arm. "That's why I like working with you. You're full of surprises. Let's get it on."

* * *

At 10:20, Josh and Chief entered the Blue Line Bar, conveniently located a block from Coral Lakes police headquarters. Anytime the bar was open, a majority of the patrons were cops. If they were on duty, the bartenders knew to serve only coffee, soda, or juices—nothing alcoholic. If off-duty, the inventory was open.

Josh slid into a booth near the back, taking the bench facing the front, and Chief sat across from him. Josh smiled as he looked around the room. Framed pictures of Coral Lakes officers, from the chief down to new academy graduates, covered one wall. Occasionally, among the photos, there was a blank spot, representing someone who drew an undercover assignment.

Replicas of badges from across the country, grouped by state, filled another wall. Florida had the most representatives—no surprise since the bar was in Florida. The third wall held pictures of officers who fell in the line of duty. The frames were more expensive and each had a black ribbon across a bottom corner. Management of the Blue Line admired the police and wanted everyone to know it.

Josh smiled and let out a satisfied sigh. "We'll wait until ten-thirty to call Blanc. That'll give Phil time to arrive before Blanc shows up. Once Phil is in house and I brief him, you two can move to another table and slurp beer while I meet with the boss criminal. Make sure you pick a chair where you can see me and the rest of the room. Don't be obvious, but keep a sharp eye out."

"Oh, gee, boss. You're so full of expertise. I'd have never thought of any of that." Chief's grin was as sparkling as wampum.

Josh laughed. "Sorry. You're right. Do what comes naturally. The key thing here is to bring Phil into the loop. If something should happen to us, he'll have a place to start looking."

The minutes ticked by and at ten-thirty, Phil entered. He hesitated, looking around the room. Several patrons called greetings to him, which he returned with a wave. When he spotted Josh, he headed for the booth.

After introductions and Phil had settled in with a beer, Josh said, "Want the secondary reason for the invite?"

"As if the first was to pay your debts to me?"

"Absolutely," Josh said. "After tonight, we'll be even again."

"Not a chance—unless the secondary reason is extraordinary."

"I'll let you decide." Josh looked around to see if anyone was paying undue attention to Phil and him. He leaned forward and lowered his voice. "I'm about to call Henri Blanc and have him come over for a *tête-à-tête*. I thought you might be interested."

Summers' surprise was almost tangible. "You have contact with Blanc? Not a chance. He's a ghost. No one is able to get a handle on him."

"Listen and learn." Josh punched Blanc's number into his cell.

"Mr. Blanc? Josh Hawkins here. I trust your secretary gave you my message about the meeting."

"Yes, he did. I can't say I'm happy with your attitude. I offered my hand in peace, and you slapped it down. I am unaccustomed to such a response."

"Not intended that way. But I learned to grab control and hold it. I suspect you took the same class. Here's the deal. Go to the Blue Line Bar on Eisenhower. I'll meet you there. I'll be alone and expect the same from you." He held the phone so Chief and Phil could hear Blanc's response.

"You're rather presumptuous, aren't you? Suppose I don't agree with what you say."

Josh brought the phone back in. "Fine with me. You're the one who wanted a face-to-face."

Phone out. "True. But I could accomplish the same thing by staking out your home and grabbing you."

Phone in. "Mr. Blanc. I'm assuming you had a reason for contacting me. Now I'm thinking you might have been playacting. In other words, you wasted my time, and I don't appreciate it. I'll just go back to what I was doing."

Phone out. "Easy, Mr. Hawkins." There was a pause on the line. "Okay, I'll be at the Blue Line within the half-hour." The phone clicked.

Josh looked at Phil. "So? What do you think?"

"I'm too steeped in awe to think. You realize that man could have you killed in such a way you'd never forget it. Yet you treated him like an errant school kid. Not smart, Hawkins. Not smart."

"A way I'd never . . . Don't bother. I wouldn't understand."

Josh explained how Blanc contacted him and requested a get-together. Then he said, "I had to live up to my reputation. You've heard the cliché, fight fire with fire. Well, I happen to believe you fight a bully by bullying him. Now, you guys need to move. Chief knows what to do."

"C'mon, kemo sabe, the Lone Ranger wants us to hide in the rocks."

Phil looked at Chief. "Is that braid for real?" He slid out of the booth, followed by Chief.

"Yes, but you don't get to pull it. We'll sit over there." Chief pointed toward a table located alongside the *fallen heroes* wall. It offered a full view of the room.

TWENTY-FIVE

At five after eleven, the front door to the Blue Line opened and a bodyguard walked in. Even to an amateur, the word *bodyguard* would have come to mind. While many policemen work out with weights and bulge their uniforms, this man's black T-shirt appeared filled with nothing except muscles. His hair was long and braided into dreadlocks, and he wore black, mid-thigh shorts. His quads rippled with each step, straining the fabric. A pair of black tennis shoes completed his ensemble. He stood somewhere north of six feet, perhaps not as tall as Chief, but at least Josh's height or better. He carried himself with the assurance of one accustomed to winning.

He stopped inside the door and scanned the room. When his gaze found Josh, he nodded and left the bar. A moment later, he was back with a second man who could have been his clone. They took up positions on each side of the entrance, apparently not caring that they attracted the attention of everyone in the place.

After another couple of minutes of their eyes sweeping the room, the man on the left opened the door and a third person entered. His dress was more conservative, a pair of tan slacks and a dark blue pullover. Tassel loafers adorned his feet. Bodyguard number one whispered to him and pointed toward Josh.

The third person weaved his way through the tables,

ignoring the stares he collected, and approached Josh. "Mr. Hawkins, I presume."

Josh stood and stuck out his hand. "Yes, and I'm guessing you're Mr. Blanc. You make quite an entrance."

"Henri, to you," he said, looking around the bar, then shaking Josh's hand. With a last glance at the other patrons, he slid into the booth, across from where Josh dropped down. "I appreciate your meeting me. Although this isn't the place I would have chosen."

"Yeah, I suspected it might not be your first choice. However, these are the type people I identify with best. I assume you know almost every one here is now or has been a policeman."

"Of course. The Blue Line is well known as a cop bar. I have no reason to care. I respect the police."

A waiter came to their table. "Can I get you something to drink?" he said to Blanc. "Another Killian's?" He directed the second question to Josh.

"I'll have one of those," Blanc said, pointing to Josh's beer. "I'm not surprised he has a taste for the Irish."

The waiter turned away, then came back. "Would you ask your friends to move away from the doorway and take a table? Our customers seem to find them more interesting than their drinks."

Josh looked at the two bodyguards, then scanned the bar. No one appeared to be paying attention to them. He assumed the waiter was simply asserting the bar's authority.

Blanc followed the waiter's gaze and nodded. "I'll take care of it."

Josh said, "They might want to wait in the car. Having a roomful of cops studying their faces could be a threat to their freedom. You might not have a rap sheet, but I suspect those two do."

Blanc appeared to think. "Good point." He gave a hand signal, and the two bodyguards exited.

The waiter returned with their beers. "Thank you, sir.

The air already seems fresher." He placed the drinks on the table and moved to another booth, busy being unobtrusive and giving the customers their privacy.

Josh held up his beer. "*À votre santé.*"

Blanc smiled and returned the toast. "I should have known you would be multi-lingual."

"Yes, but my skills have eroded since I left the Army. Not much use for them in my civilian world—except for Spanish, of course."

"That, I understand."

They sipped from their bottles as the other customers lost interest in them. Josh glanced at Chief and Summers. They weren't staring, but seemed to find Josh and Blanc fascinating as their eyes flicked back and forth between the two.

Finally, Josh said, "At the risk of rushing things, why did you want to meet?"

Blanc settled into the back cushion and studied the room. His eyes lingered on the fallen heroes wall, then he leaned forward. "Mr. Hawkins, I've learned a great deal about you in the last few days. You're a formidable adversary with an incredible record behind you. I admire what you've accomplished."

"Mr. Blanc, I don't mean to be rude, but you're beating around the bush, and I don't have time for that. We're both professionals. We can shit-can the cocktail party crap and get to the point."

Blanc studied Josh. "Okay, but first some background. I was in the Royal Canadian Air Force, the RCAF as we called it, and served in the first Gulf War. I flew sorties with the American Air Force and learned to respect their expertise. At the air base, we often partied together. During the ground phase of the war, I flew close air support and saw what a wonderfully brave military you have."

"So, you came home and built a criminal empire in the U.S. because you have so much respect for us?"

"Let me finish," Blanc said, clearly not appreciating the interruption. "I'll address your so-called criminal empire later. Where was I? Oh, yes. Naturally, when I saw your record, that respect transferred to you. After all, you went farther than any of the brave men and women I knew. Farther than any I've ever heard of."

"How did you get access to my 201 file?"

"Is that what your personnel records are called? If so, the answer is the same as with most things—money. Lay down enough of it, and the strongest principles crumble. The cliché that every man has his price did not become a cliché because it's not true. *Au contraire.* Every man does have his price, some much less than what it could be. Your records were cheap."

"Uh-huh." Josh sipped his beer. "You were going to tell me about your criminal enterprise."

"Yes, I am anxious for you to understand. I do nothing criminal—well, nothing more than cheat on my taxes a bit here and there. But, that's a popular pastime for most citizens worldwide, as well as businesses. Even your politicians are found to be wanting in this area."

"Especially our politicians," Josh said. "If it's not a criminal effort, what do you call it?"

"I sell confidence. I run a legitimate single-owner insurance operation. People pay my premiums, and I guarantee them financial support if they need it."

"Bullshit," Josh said. "You take money from petty crooks of all ilks. You call them legitimate?"

"No, I do not and never said they were. I only sell them insurance."

"Okay, I'll bite. Tell me about this insurance."

"Simple. They pay me, and I provide legal representation if they are caught by the police. I pay their attorney fees and, if they go to jail, a small stipend to the family, if they have one. Quite simple, quite legal."

Josh stared at Blanc, trying to see behind his façade. "I'm

not buying it. Why would a bunch of lowlifes pay you when they can get legal help for free?"

"You'll have to ask them. They have every right to do things their way and ignore my services. Many do—for a while. However, when they see the life expectancy of their comrades' efforts, they usually decide to avail themselves of my policy."

"Meaning."

"It appears that those who do not buy get caught more often and spend longer periods in jail. Not something I understand, but statistics bear me out. For example, a second story man who sees his friends carted off to prison might become convinced he needs me. He might even contact my people and beg for a policy."

Josh grinned. "I see. The old protection racket using the police to do your dirty work. Pretty slick. How much does this cost your . . . uh . . . clients?"

"I keep it simple so everyone can afford me. A percentage of their take. They all pay the same level and receive the same benefits. Kind of like the flat tax many of your politicians ascribe to. Simply stated, those who have a larger income pay more in fees. By basing everything on the size of their *income*, those who are more successful pay a higher premium. *Liberté, Égalité, Fraternité.* That's what I offer. I ask you. What is so criminal about that?"

"I'm sure you're leaving out a few details. What about those who have disappeared with or without your insurance?"

"Casualties of business. That's all. Compare it to the hundreds of thousands who died building your great railroads. Compare it to the thousands who die every year commuting to and from work. Or die in the workplace. No great enterprise has ever been built without unfortunate deaths. You, of all people, should understand that."

"Oh, and why me?" The statement intrigued Josh.

"Your most recent assignment is to track me down. To do that, you've been through some of my clients. Three in the hospital and two disappeared. Wouldn't you call them *casualties of your business?*"

Josh shook his head. "You're good, Mr. Blanc, very good. But I hardly consider that the same. My goal is to take criminals out of circulation. Yours is the opposite. If I break a nose, it's to show the person the error of his ways. If you do the same thing, it's to convince him to pay up."

"Aw, my good man," Blanc said, "you're equivocating. How about Tony Carrillo? Word is you are the last to see him. I understand Tony was a good man—weak, but trustworthy. I feel certain he would be in touch with my people if he were alive."

"Sorry, I don't know the name," Josh said.

"Whatever you say."

Josh took another slug of his beer. "Let's say I buy your story. You're as pure as the Pope and the Dali Lama combined. I still don't know why you called this meeting."

"Simple. I want you out of my life, to forget I exist. Tell Isaac Newsome you changed your mind."

"Just like that. I'm supposed to walk away."

"Not exactly all of it. I don't know what Newsome is paying, but I'm sure I can offer more."

"Yeah? How much?"

"A hundred thou for you and fifty for your friend with the braid who is sitting over there. I don't recognize the other man, but I assume he's part of your team. I'll throw in fifty g's for him, also."

Josh considered the offer. "So, all I have to do for the money is leave you alone?"

Blanc smiled. "Yes. I'll pay cash or transfer the money to any account you name."

Josh waived the waiter over and ordered another round of Killian's. When the waiter was out of hearing range, Josh said, "Let's suppose for a moment I'm interested in your proposition, although the paltry amount you're offering is an insult. There would have to be one other ingredient to the settlement."

Blanc rubbed his chin. "Yeah? What is that?"

The waiter sat fresh beers in front of them.

TWENTY-SIX

Josh drained his first bottle, then set it aside. Blanc followed suit.

The waiter took the empties and moved to service another table.

"So," Blanc said, "what would you want other than more money?"

Staring into Blanc's eyes, Josh said, "I want to know which of Newsome's *friends* is on your payroll. I have no love for people who put my life in danger."

"What makes you think I have someone birddogging Newsome?"

Josh laughed. "So far, my impression is you're playing straight with me—well, only minor twists along the way. Now, you've crossed into fantasyland. I haven't lived to my ripe old age by believing in fairy tales. You and I both know you have someone feeding you information on every step Newsome makes, and consequently, everything I report to him. I want him . . . or her. It's part of the price."

"Even as you ask, you know if it were true, I would never tell you. Would you give away an undercover operative you were running? If so, I badly misjudged you. Sorry, if there were such a person, the identity would not be open to negotiation." Blanc sipped from his fresh Killian's. "You said my offer was insulting. How much would it take to make it a compliment?"

Josh steepled his fingers in front of his chin. "I'm thinking a mill for me and a half-mill for each of my friends—and there might be more than the two you see."

Blanc shook his head while chuckling. "At the risk of attacking your ego, you're not worth that much . . . and neither are your friends."

"You miss the point, Mr. Blanc. It's not about how much I'm worth. It's about what you're worth. Do you have such low self-esteem you think your value is less than a few million? Especially, when you have so many of them squirrelled away in offshore accounts? Think about it."

"No, I fear it is you who doesn't understand. Were I to meet your demands, every con artist between here and the Canadian border would be trying to cut in. My insurance program would soon be lacking for customers. Part of my persona has to be playing hardball with everyone. One sign of softness, and my venture crumbles. I'll raise my offer to two-hundred thou for you and a hundred for your accomplices. And no, I will not give up any imaginary sources. That's it. I will go no farther."

Josh shook his head. "I'm glad to hear you say that. If you'd offered the mill, I'd have lost respect for you. Mr. Blanc, the bottom line is you do not have enough of anything to buy me. I might die a pauper, but I will die true to myself. We have nothing further to discuss. I'm glad you gave me a chance to learn a bit more about you. It's nice to know you're not just a piece of gutter flotsam. Too bad you aren't using your talents to improve society, rather than taking advantage of its flaws. I may actually suffer a moment of regret when I stand over your body."

"Don't get overconfident. I don't intend to fall. You're not that good."

Josh leaned forward. "The fact you're here says you're worried I *am* that good. And, rest assured, I am. You think it can't happen to you—to other people, but not to you. It would be less of a challenge to go against someone who didn't believe he was invincible. But your greed establishes your vulnerability. Eventually, it will give me the opening I need, and you will be no more."

"Or, the opposite might happen. This isn't a movie script. The *white hat* could lose."

Josh stared at Blanc as he sipped his beer. "I've faced tougher men with nastier friends hiding behind stronger fortifications. I'm still here. They're not."

"This is all too bad," Blanc said. "In a different world, we might have become friends. We have a lot in common. I think I would have liked that. However, as the old saying goes, let the best man win."

"So be it."

"So be it." Blanc laid two twenties on the table. "It's been a pleasure meeting and talking with you. I assume I'm free to walk out of here."

"Of course," Josh said. "You're under a flag of truce. If you decide to reconsider your position, you have my number. I've enjoyed our chat. Thanks for the beer."

"I understand. Don't try to reach me. The number you have is already dead." Blanc slid out of the booth, stood, squared his shoulders, and walked out of the Blue Line without looking back—a proud man showing his disdain for the world.

When Blanc cleared the door, Josh waited a couple of minutes, then waved Chief and Summers over. They joined him in the booth, bringing their beers with them.

He briefed them on the conversation with Blanc and confessed that he found Blanc to be likeable.

"Easy," Chief said. "That might have been part of the reason for his request to meet. You can't afford to let feelings enter the picture. They can cause you to hesitate, and hesitation leads to death."

"I understand," Josh said. "Blanc still needs to go out of business." He turned to Summers. "I suppose you'll be briefing Richards first thing in the morning."

"You know I will," Summers said. "And he'll give me hell for not putting the collar on Blanc. It'll take me ten minutes to remind him we have no outstanding warrants." He hesitated, sipping his beer. "Josh, you're fishing in some treacherous waters here. I know you're good, but Blanc is an enigma no one has been able to solve. Some well-protected people have disappeared after crossing swords with him."

"So I've heard. But they didn't have Chief guarding their rears. I do."

"As my daddy used to say," Summers said, "Better the enemy you know than some sonnavabitch slipping around behind you. I suggest you two walk back-to-back and both carry mirrors."

"Glad to know you care. However, I still have the same problem. I need the combination to Blanc's vault, how to get inside his operation."

"One thing I don't understand," Summers said. "What's your interest? Why are you dogging Blanc?"

Josh considered how much he should share with Summers. If he expected cooperation, shouldn't he reciprocate? And, since he was getting zilch from Newsome, he needed info from somewhere. After rolling things around in his mind for a moment, he realized he must come down on the side of slippery. The Non-Disclosure Agreement with the Government had to take precedence. Violating it carried a jail term. "Sorry, Phil, I can't answer that question with any kind of specificity. Here's what I can tell you. I've been brought on board by a reputable organization to help put Blanc out of business. This outfit considers him a threat to national security."

"Oh, that's enlightening. What you're saying is someone, somewhere thinks you can do what no police agency has been able to do—bring him down . . . and, an educated guess, get rid of him in the process."

"No further comment. I simply can't reveal any more.

However, I need any help I can get."

Summers looked at Chief. "Where does our Seminole friend fit in?"

"Chief is my cohort, a fellow soldier. He's donating his time to help."

"Uh-huh." Summers lapsed into silence, giving the appearance of deep thought. "I'll be upfront with you. One, I have to brief Richards about tonight and our conversation. I wouldn't be much of a cop if I kept it from him." He looked around. "Plus, the word will probably get to him before I do. Two, he's going to be madder than a junkie who paid top dollar for a bag of sugar that you're meddling again. Three, he's going to instruct me to keep a close eye on you and be ready to spring for an arrest the moment you step out of line. Four, you're going to see me around a lot until, sub-a, you bring down Blanc, or sub-b, Blanc eliminates you, sub-c, something of a higher priority comes along, or sub-d, Lt. Richards loses interest. Take your pick which will happen first."

"I'm betting it won't be sub-d."

"Most likely not."

"Fine. I can live with you in my hip pocket. However, while you're there, why don't you help us? I know you want Blanc, maybe as badly as I do. If we pool our resources, we'll get there faster."

"I . . ." Summers stopped and appeared to think some more. "Okay, I suppose I could drop a hint here and there."

"Such as?"

"I think I recognized one of the bodyguards. I've seen him or his mug shot before. I'm thinking he might have a record. If so, I'll sniff it out when I get to the station. If I were careless, you might learn his identity from me."

"Hmm, that could help." Josh considered it. "In fact that could help a lot. What say you, Chief?"

"Me?" Chief said. "I'm busy toying with the hundred thousand bucks you rejected for me. That's enough to keep me in beer the rest of my life. Darn careless of you, Josh. Are you that careless, Phil? If you are, you might just drop some information along the way."

All three laughed.

* * *

Josh and Chief drove toward Coral Lakes on I-95. Josh held it at a sedate seventy miles an hour, watching cars and trucks whiz by.

He glanced toward his passenger, whose eyes were closed. "What do you think of Blanc, Chief?"

His eyes opened, and he looked perplexed. "A strange one. I'm not quite sure what tonight was all about. Did he really think he could buy you?"

Josh slowed behind a white Toyota. The driver's head could barely be seen above the headrest. "Hard to say. Plus, that BS he put out about respect. I'm not sure we've faced anyone like him before, not even in our toughest ops."

Chief stayed quiet for a moment. "I didn't hear the part about respect. How did he handle that?"

"Basically, he said he read my file and had a great deal of respect for me. He claims to have flown with the Canadian air force in support of US Forces in Iraq." He shook his head. "What irritates me most is the ease with which people get access to our records. I guess there's no privacy in our 201 files anymore. This is the second time in a couple of weeks the personnel center has given them up. A classic example of who you know."

"Or who you pay," Chief said. "Doesn't make me feel too good either. Although I don't know why. There's nothing in there I'm ashamed of. In fact, I'm rather proud of my career."

"Yeah. But it feels creepy."

"Speaking of creepy," Chief said. "I have that prickly feeling on the nape of my neck. Are you watching your rearview mirror?"

"Yeah. There's something back there. They've been with us for a while. We might have picked up a tail. That set of headlights hasn't changed for the last few miles. Maybe our Mr. Blanc isn't as fair-minded as he made himself out to be."

"What are you going to do?"

"Let's find out if they're for real and not my natural paranoia."

"I'll trust your instincts. Wanna fight tonight?"

"Not really, but we'll see how they react."

At the next exit, Josh jumped off I-95 and headed west, watching his mirrors. The headlights stayed behind him. When he hit Military Trail, he turned north, and the follower turned with him.

"I'm convinced," Josh said. "Why don't we set a surprise for these guys?"

"I'm in," Chief said. "What do you have in mind?"

Josh thought a moment. "I don't want to get into a shootout with anyone. Too many innocent civilians around. Maybe we can use the police to do the job."

"Now you're thinking. How you going to pull it off?"

Josh activated his cell phone. "Call Phil Summers," he said into the voice recognition system.

Summers answered with, "Well, Josh, you know you're wrecking my reputation, don't you? I'm not up for any more beer tonight. You'll have to do better."

"Hello to you, too," Josh said, chuckling. "Strangely enough, I think I can do better. I can hand you a carload of Blanc's goons. Interested?"

"Maybe. What's up?"

Josh decelerated for a traffic light and watched the headlights do the same thing three cars behind. The lighting was not bright enough for him to identify the make, model, or color, and he couldn't see any silhouettes in the car. "When we left the Blue Line, we picked up a tail. They seem stuck on us. I'm thinking about stopping and letting them make their play. But, I'll need police backup fast or it could turn into a gunfight. I'd hate to have that happen. Some innocents could get hurt."

"How do you want to play it?"

Josh pulled forward when the light changed, sticking in the right lane. "We're heading north on Military Trail in Boca Raton. Suppose I turn west on Yamato Road and wheel into Coral Edge Park. If I remember right, it's only a few blocks down. Once we get there, I'll swing into the entrance and stop at the gate. The place will be shut down this late at night. If they follow us in, we'll front them and see what they want. Your job is make darn sure the police show up fast. We'll have them trapped between us. What do you think?"

"Sounds like you're banking on them being patient. Suppose they open fire as soon as you stop? Won't that mess up your night? Does Chief go along with this?"

Chief said, "I'm with Josh. We can always duck behind our car for protection."

Summers stayed quiet for a moment. "I hope the weapons you're carrying are legal. When the uniforms get there, they won't be inclined to sort out the good from the bad. They'll just grab everyone."

"I know, Phil," Josh said. "Been there, done that. I know the M.O."

"Okay. I'll get backup for you. Good luck."

"Don't be slow about it. We're only a few blocks south."

TWENTY-SEVEN

Josh disconnected. "Well, Chief, this could be fun. You ready to crack some heads? I'd love to get a couple of minutes with these guys before the police arrive."

Chief's grin was big. "Now you're talking."

Josh continued to travel at the speed limit, an act that made him stand out in traffic. It also convinced him he was right about the tail. Every other car passed him. The driver of the trailing vehicle was having a tough time keeping cars between them. Each time someone pulled into the space behind Josh, he quickly lost patience with Josh's speed, pulled out and passed, leaving the surveillant exposed. The situation allowed Josh to see two silhouettes in the front seat.

At Yamato Road, Josh turned and headed west. The second left took him into Coral Edge Park. He pulled to the gate, stopped, and killed the engine. Palm trees, growing in the swale, lined the entryway. A gentle breeze caused the fronds to sway, creating a rustling sound. Across the sidewalk, a well-manicured hedge rose to about six feet. From previous trips, Josh knew the vegetation grew wilder on the other side of the hedge.

He turned off the headlights, and he and Chief exited and moved to the front of the car, using it as a shield between them and what was to come.

"Jump through that hedge and be ready to circle behind

them," Josh said. "If the cops don't show, we might be able to catch them in a crossfire."

"Gotcha." Chief ducked out of sight.

The trailing car waited for traffic to pass, then followed Josh's path, stopping about twenty feet behind. Their headlights went off, and the front doors opened. Two men got out and knelt, partially hidden. "Hawkins, we need to talk to you."

The courtesy light bathed them. Pretty stupid, Josh thought. Must not be Blanc's top guns. He decided to see how much the guy wanted to talk and stayed quiet.

"Did you hear what I said?" the speaker said. "We need to talk to you." He didn't sound like the patient type. His voice was gruff, perhaps a bit of playacting in it.

"Sounds reasonable," Josh said. "Throw your weapons out, then walk over here with your hands on your heads. We're ready to exchange pleasantries. You can explain why you've been following us. Since you know who I am, it seems only fair that I know who you are. What's your name?"

"Are you nuts? You either toss your guns out and show yourself or we'll come after you."

Was there an edge of indecision in the voice? "Hmm, not interested. Looks like we have a Mexican standoff. We're not coming out, so it's up to you to make the first move. But, before you do, who're you working for?" *Wonder if Chief's in position yet.*

"Show yourself, and we'll explain all that."

Cars passed on Yamato Road, but none of them turned in. Between cars, the darkness intensified. Josh hoped he could keep the thugs engaged until the cops arrived—whenever that might be.

A gust of wind blew trash across the entryway, causing the palm fronds to create a bigger fuss. In the distance, a night bird sounded his call for a mate.

"Oh, yeah," Josh said, "I'm about to do that. Tell you what, you stay where you are, and we'll stay where we are. We can just keep at it until the sun comes up. Then I'll be able to see you and describe you to my psychotherapist. How does that sound?"

A shot answered his question.

"Take it easy," Josh said. "There's an over fifty-five neighborhood next door. Do you want a murder charge hanging over you? Besides, you'll have the police pulling in behind you if you wake those people up. They value their sleep. And they all have 911 on speed dial."

"Oh," the voice said, doubt showing. "Look, we need to wrap this up. Why are you being difficult?"

"Drop the guns and get your hands in the air."

Josh smiled. That was Chief's no-nonsense voice. It meant he had the drop on them. He rose from his secure position and hurried to the thugs' car. Pointing his pistol at the two, he said, "Isn't this nice? We can finally talk face-to-face. I'm Josh Hawkins. Who are you?"

The two hoodlums stood there, their guns down by their side. One of them said, "My name's Mike. Glad to see you decided to show your face. But, the joke's on you."

"Time for you to put down your guns."

Josh looked and was shocked to see the back door of the sedan open and a third nasty standing there, an automatic pistol in his hand. He waved it between Chief and Josh. From Josh's position, the barrel looked huge.

Damn, Josh thought. We've been had. Most basic rookie mistake. Don't commit your reserves until you're sure. "Well, Chief, we seem to have a bit of a pickle here. Five people, five guns, two versus three. What do you think?" Josh stepped to the side so the three of them were in a crooked line in front of him.

"Odds seem fair," Chief said, maneuvering in the opposite direction from Josh. "I think we have the upper hand."

"What the—"

"Don't get excited," Josh said. "Let's examine this like

gentlemen." He pretended to think. "Let's worst-case this situation. If all of us open fire, I figure at least four of us are going down. My friend and me, of course—three guns to two. But two of you will also most likely eat a bullet. The question I'd be considering if I were in your shoes is which two." He looked at the three, one by one.

"Chief, you take the guy on the left and the one in the middle. I'll concentrate on the right and the middle. That'll guarantee the two end positions are neutralized, and one of us will probably get the man in the middle, too. What do you think?"

"Sounds like a plan. I'm ready when you are."

"How about you guys?" Josh said. "Do you concur? I admit it's off the top of my head, but I didn't have time to come up with several options."

"You people are crazy," the thug on the right said. "Do you think we're going to stand here and let you gun us down?"

"Of course not," Josh said. "That wouldn't be fair. Everyone deserves an equal opportunity in a shootout. However, I don't see any other way out of this. You want us, and we have to defend ourselves. Do you have a different option?"

The leader looked at his cohorts. "Are you hearing what I hear? I wonder if the boss knows these guys are beyond help. He said scare'm off. This goes way beyond that."

Josh interrupted. "Would any of you like to change positions? As I pointed out, the center position has the best chance of surviving. If you want to shift, do it now. Then I'll count to three, and we'll start blasting away. Seems like the American way to end this. Is that okay with you, Chief?"

"I'm waiting for three. You count, I shoot."

"No, no," the thug said. "I can't believe how stupid this is. I'm not going to stand here and play *high noon* with you. All I'm supposed to do is scare you off. Nobody is paying me to die." Even in the darkness, his words showed what his face probably portrayed—fear and indecision. "Let us out of here, and we'll leave you alone."

"You mean nobody gets hurt?" Josh said. "That seems rather anticlimactic. I mean, you came charging in here like a herd of rhinos on uppers, making demands you can't back up. I feel cheated."

"We're out of here." He lowered his weapon and spoke to his friends. "Get in the car. I want to get away from these crazies."

"I think not," Josh said. "Take a gander behind you."

Two police cars pulled into the park entryway. They screeched to a halt and the officers jumped out, guns drawn. "Drop'm, all of you. Then face down on the pavement."

* * *

The following morning, as Summers predicted, the moment he set foot in the police station, he was summoned to Lt. Richards' office.

Richards set his coffee cup down and motioned Summers to a straight-backed chair. "I understand you had a busy night. Want to tell me about it?"

Summers chuckled. "Boss, no one can say you're not on the clock twenty-four-seven. It's only seven in the morning, and I haven't had my coffee yet. Too early to learn you've been spying on me."

"Didn't. But it's a small station and rumors fly fast. This one flew onto my desk in an anonymous note before I got here at six-thirty. You know, that hour when smart detectives who hope for promotion someday are at work. If I were you, I'd wonder if someone out there wants your job more than you do."

"If so, they probably haven't figured out I work for such a suspicious L T. If you'd given me a chance to draw a cup of coffee first, I'd have been in here to tell you about a strange evening. Do you mind?" He pointed at Richards' coffee pot.

"It was a late night."

Richards smiled. "Help yourself. I brewed it to your specs this morning. I expected you to come in whining."

After pouring a cup and topping up Richards' mug, Summers pulled the chair close to the desk and sat. "I'll pretend you don't already know everything worthwhile and start at the beginning."

Richards nodded.

Summers told about the call from Josh and his surprise when he arrived to find that Josh was meeting with Henri Blanc. "I couldn't hear their conversation, but it was obvious they didn't reach any kind of agreement. Blanc looked disappointed when he left. I don't know exactly why they met, only what Josh told me, but, as you know, I respect him and think he's a straight shooter."

"Yeah, sure," Richards said. "Why the hell didn't you put the collar on Blanc while you had the chance? You were in a bar full of cops, his bodyguards were gone, and Blanc was unprotected. What were you thinking?"

"Oh, unlawful arrest crossed my mind. Then, a picture of me in front of a judicial hearing having my badge taken away. Headlines in the newspaper about Phil Summers being a rogue cop, and a civil suit stripping me of everything I own. Probably jail time. And—"

"All right, all right. Enough. I get the point. So, what happened after the three of you came back together. And who is the big Indian?"

"Guy called Chief. He and Hawkins go way back." Summers continued his story, leaving out nothing pertinent. After telling Richards he thought he recognized one of the bodyguards and intended to check the databases on him, he sat back in his chair and sipped his coffee.

"That's it?"

"That's all there is, boss. What do you want me to do next?"

"Aren't you forgetting about having the Boca police

dispatched to Coral Edge Park where they arrested three men on gun charges?"

"Oh, yes. That was a minor part of the night. Josh thought he was being followed, so I gave him an assist."

Richards leaned forward, resting his forearms on his desk. "Sometimes I wonder who runs this shop. Sure isn't me." He paused and took a deep breath. "I know we have no paper on Blanc, but he's too big to ignore. This might be a golden opportunity for us. I want you to check out the bodyguard. Dig up everything you can on him. Then I want you stuck to Hawkins' backside. He's not to take a breath that you don't count. I don't think he's Sherlock Holmes like you do, but he might get lucky and cause Blanc to do something we can nail him for. Hell, Blanc might even put Hawkins in the hospital and get him out of my hair. If so, I want you there witnessing it. Understand?"

"What about my other cases?"

"I'll reassign them. Your one concentration until I tell you different is Josh Hawkins and Henri Blanc. If you can break both, so much the better."

Summers stood, smiling. "Good coffee. I'll wash out the cup when I finish."

"Get out of here and act like an up-and-coming detective. I want Blanc. If you deliver Hawkins at the same time, I'll be even happier."

As Summers walked out of the office, he couldn't help but grin. Richards had reacted exactly as he predicted. He sipped his coffee. It was excellent. Richards said he'd brewed it to Summers' specs. That caused a frown to hover as he wondered who had worked whom.

TWENTY-EIGHT

By the time Summers finished his conversation with Richards, Josh and Chief had completed their morning runs—five miles at a steady pace—and were sitting down to a late breakfast at the Dixie Grill. They had decided the previous night there was no point in hiding their partnership since Blanc knew about it. If Blanc came after them again, there was safety in numbers. It worked once, it would work again—Josh hoped.

Chief ordered a large meal times three while Josh picked a normal amount. The waitress didn't blink at Chief's order. Josh marveled at her self-control.

After the food arrived, they both dug in, the morning exercise having whetted their appetites. Josh swallowed and said, "It's an education watching you eat. Does Sandra feed you this much?"

"Yeah, and her sausage gravy is better—more sausage." He returned his attention to his plate.

They ate in silence, except for the clinking of silverware on china.

Josh's phone rang. He checked the caller ID, then looked at Chief. "Summers." Into the cell, he said, "Hey, Phil. What's up?"

"I met with my boss this morning, and things went pretty much as I predicted. I'm your shadow for the foreseeable future, my only assignment. I can tell you because he doesn't care if you know. Keep the pressure on, he said. Consider yourself pressured."

"Yeah, I'm all tensed up." Josh chuckled. "Chief and I are having breakfast now. Why don't you join us?"

"Can't. I have paperwork to wrap up so I can pass off my other cases. Also, I want to go through the books and see if I can locate the bodyguard. I'm convinced I crossed paths with him before."

Josh hesitated. "Don't get yourself in trouble."

"Not a chance. I look out for number one first. The lieut wants the same guy you're after and instructed me to do whatever is necessary—as long as it's legal. That's what I'll do. Oh, he also wants *you*, so don't screw up, or I'll be earning a promotion by dragging your butt in. You know Richards would recommend me."

"As if you could take me in," Josh said. "Call if you get anything on the bodyguard. Chief and I need that peephole into Mr. B's empire."

"You're on. Talk to you later."

Josh clicked off and placed the phone on the table.

"Anything good?" Chief asked.

"We'll be seeing a lot of him. For now though, he's trying to ID the bodyguard."

"Hmm." Chief took a bite of biscuit and gravy, then said, "If we locate him, he'll tell us where to find Blanc."

"That's what I'm hoping."

"He will. I know lots of bones to break."

Josh's phone rang its special ring, producing a smile. Jaden.

"Hello, Sunshine," Josh said. "Anything happening?"

"I'm on my way to the courtroom. The Rodriguez jury is coming in."

"Gut feeling?"

"No clue. No doubt in my mind about his guilt, but it's not up to me. What's done is done. I either convinced them or I didn't. I'll call you after the verdict announcement. Will you be home tonight?"

"I don't know. If possible, I'll get there. But this project is heating up, and I have to follow the temperature changes."

"I understand. Sometimes, I wish I didn't, but I do. Talk to you later."

Josh punched the off button, recognizing the irritation in Jaden's voice. He hoped the evening would be quiet. If the verdict came in against her, he needed to be there to console her. He knew she'd be upset. She invested her emotions in each of her cases, but even more so in this one. She blamed herself for not convicting him the first time he was in court. Josh's support would be appreciated—and expected—if only to hold her and let her vent. Of course, if the jury put Rodriguez away, it would be celebration time, and he wanted to be part of that.

"Anything new?" Chief said.

"Jury's coming in. Jaden will know soon."

"Better keep your mind on Blanc. He's the target. Rodriguez can wait."

"Yeah," Josh said and returned to his breakfast.

* * *

While riding the elevator to the eighth floor, Jaden could feel her heart beating, causing her to wonder if the other passengers could hear it and see her tension. Mentally, she admonished herself for allowing the case to get to her. She needed to be more like her co-counsel, Wilbur. He kept telling her they couldn't change the world, only affect it a small bit—or not. Try the case and move on. Close the old door and open a new one. But she wasn't like him, not on this case. She had talked with Sophia Rodriguez, had listened to the tales of a battered wife. And it was Jaden who had explained to Sophia why her wife-beater of a husband had been found not guilty of abuse. Now, Sophia lay in a grave, a direct result of his first acquittal. Jaden had respected her and now owed her, yet there was a distinct possibility she had failed again.

She pushed into the courtroom, walked to the front, and sat at the prosecution table. Taking a deep breath, she took out her files and spread the folders in front of her. To disguise her nervousness, she pretended to study them.

Samantha Kennedy, Rodriguez's attorney, entered and walked to Jaden's table. Jaden stood, not wanting to be seated in the subservient position. "Hello, Samantha. We'll soon know."

"No matter how this comes out," Samantha said, "it's been interesting sharing this trial with you. Although my client is innocent, I appreciate how hard you worked to convict him. I look forward to seeing you across the room again." She reached out to shake.

Jaden stared at the hand, then reluctantly shook it. In a soft voice she said, "You're good, Samantha. If I ever need a defense counsel who'll stop at nothing, I'll be on the phone to you. But you're wrong on one point. Rodriguez is guilty of murder, just as he was guilty of spousal abuse in the previous trial. Your witnesses perjured themselves. However, unlike you, I'll honor the jury's decision and close my file. I'm sure if you lose, you'll be drafting appeal papers."

Samantha's mouth opened, then closed. She walked away.

Jaden returned to her seat and looked at the files again, wondering for the thousandth time if she'd missed something. Perhaps there was an overlooked point, one tidbit that might have changed everything. Behind her, she heard the shuffle of feet and the low murmurs of the spectators as they took seats.

"All rise," said the bailiff.

The judge entered and took his position. He addressed the bailiff. "Bring the jury in."

"Yes, your honor."

A moment later, the panel filed in and filled the box.

Judge Germain addressed them. "Have you reached a decision?"

The foreman stood. "Yes, your honor."

"Bailiff?"

The bailiff walked to the box and accepted a folded paper from the foreman, then handed it to the judge. Judge Germain unfolded it and read, showing no emotion. He returned it to the bailiff who passed it to the foreman.

"What is your verdict?" the judge said.

"We find the defendant, Santiago Rodriguez, not guilty."

"Is your finding unanimous? Bailiff, poll the jury, please."

He asked each juror if he or she agreed with what the foreman had announced. In each case, the answer was affirmative.

The judge pursed his lips as he looked from one juror to another. "Thank you for your service. I know this has been a difficult time for you, and I appreciate your doing your civic duty. Our system of justice depends on citizens like you who are willing to give their time to make it work. Take pride in what you have done. You are dismissed."

As the jury filed out, he turned his attention to the defense table. "Mr. Rodriguez, you have been found not guilty by a panel of your peers. You are released from the jurisdiction of this court. I hope I never see you here again." He rapped with his gavel. "Court is dismissed." He stood, then exited through a back door.

Jaden dropped back into her chair, deflating like a spent balloon, feeling like a failure. Taking several deep breaths, she fought to keep her expression impassive as she packed her files. She looked up, sensing a presence nearing her. Rodriguez.

"Be seeing you around, counselor," he said, smiling. "Who knows? Maybe you can trump up another charge to get a third shot at me. But it won't work any better than it did the first two times. I got too many friends." He walked away, chuckling.

A chill rippled along Jaden's spine.

* * *

Jaden survived the rest of the day on remote control, studying her next case, reading without absorbing details. She continued, knowing she would have to start at the beginning again, but realizing if she stopped, Rodriguez would consume her. That couldn't be allowed. She'd spent too many hours with him already. He could not become an obsession. There was room for only one man in her life—Josh.

At five o'clock, Jaden put *homework* in her briefcase and headed for the exit. She cleared the entrance and stopped, breathing in the heat and humidity of South Florida. After being in air conditioning all day, it felt good, even though she knew the feeling would be temporary. Before she reached her car, she'd be looking forward to cold air blowing over her.

"Have a nice evening if you can, counselor. You don't have much to celebrate, do you?"

She turned to see Rodriguez leaning against the wall. He locked eyes with her, grinned, pushed off, and started toward the sidewalk. After a few steps, he stopped and turned back. "See you around."

Jaden stared, confused, not knowing whether to be scared or contemptuous of him. Goose bumps laced her arms.

TWENTY-NINE

Two days later, Henri Blanc sat in a recliner, a book open on his lap, but making no attempt to read. Instead, he was deep in thought. He had been in that position for thirty minutes.

Collette, his wife, walked over and rested her hand on his shoulder. "*Mon cher*, what is bothering you? You seem so far away."

Blanc grinned and pulled her into his lap. "Never far from you, *ma chère*. I have a heavy decision to make, perhaps the biggest of our lives. There are many details to consider."

"Would it help to talk about it? You said *our* lives, so I assume it affects me, too."

"Yes, everything I do concerns both of us. I know I should confide in you more often. It's not an easy thing for me to do sometimes."

"We've been married for thirty-five years. Don't you think I feel pain when you hurt? I may smile, but inside, my aches are as intense as yours."

Blanc kissed her on the cheek. "What would you say if I told you I'm weighing retirement—returning to Canada and never visiting the USA again?"

She hugged him. "I would say it'd be nice to spend more time with the children and our grandchildren. I would say I'll go with you wherever you choose. But then I'd say you need to tell me why. I've known you long enough to know you wouldn't do something like that without a strong reason. Share with me."

Blanc didn't respond for a moment, then he sighed. "As you know, I've done some terrible things in my life. Sometimes to protect myself, sometimes because people proved themselves untrustworthy, and sometimes to further our business interests. I'm not proud of them, but, at the time, it was crucial to our survival."

He paused, formulating his next thoughts. "The people I disposed of were no loss to society. Only their mothers could love them. Not one life was lessened because they no longer walk the streets. But now, things are spiraling out of my control. A few days ago, I met a man who does contribute to society—a person I would be proud to call a friend."

"He must be quite a man," Collette said, squirming in his lap. "Do I hear a but coming?"

"Yes, I'll explain later. More about this man first. Perhaps for the first time in my life, I have met a truly honest person."

"Impossible. You say all men have an Achilles' heel, every man has his price, every person has a crack in his veneer."

"True, and I believed it. I now realize I might be wrong. I sat across from him and stared into his eyes, the entryway to the soul. What I saw was someone who will not be bought."

"Is he a threat to us?"

"*Pour sûr*, the first part of my dilemma. He is sworn to destroy me. He works for people in Washington who want me out of business, and they're not choosy about how it happens." He paused. "I have studied his background. He is an incredible man. I am overmatched."

"Surely not. You have Gustave and Marcel. They would never let him harm you."

"And that leads to the second half of my dilemma. In the past, I have kept tight reins on the organization. Nothing would be done in my name which I did not command.

Yesterday, I discovered one of the underlings took action without my knowledge. And that action reflects poorly on me. I'm very disturbed."

"I understand. Is it so bad we need to retire?" Collette said, kissing him on the cheek. "You've spent years developing this business."

"It's complicated. The action was against the man I met. We drank together under a flag of truce. He lived up to his end and made no move against me, although he had the upper hand and plenty of backup. Without my knowledge, someone dispatched three men to scare him off. They followed him from our meeting. There is no way he can think I didn't plan it. Which, my love, impacts my credibility. Once the word spreads that I went back on my word, no matter how much I defend myself, others will begin to question me. My so-called empire is built on my name and fear, more my name than fear. If I lose my credibility, those below me will lose the fear. When that happens, I'll become the target of every wannabe in the country."

Collette pushed herself up and looked into his face. "I love the idea of retirement, but I don't want to live with a beaten man the rest of my life. Especially, when he's not defeated. You're as strong today as you've ever been. Gustave, Marcel, and I stand with you. You've stood up to attempted coups before. You can do it again."

"Perhaps. But what about the man I told you about? This will add to his incentive to kill me."

"Same answer. Gustave and Marcel. They'll stand between you and him. I'm sure they are loyal, and no one is so good he can get past them."

"I'd like to think that, but I'd be fooling myself—and that could prove fatal. They are good friends, willing to give their lives to protect me. With this man, I fear they would do just that. He would cut through them like an épée through Brie. I would be sending them to their deaths. I don't want their deaths on my conscience."

"That cannot be. You make him sound like a superman."

"Superman?" Blanc thought for a moment. "Perhaps he is. I've studied his military records. He survived in situations where normal people would have failed—and died."

The room went quiet as Blanc retreated into himself, and Collette appeared to be equally deep in thought. After a few minutes of silence, she said, "It appears there are only two options. The first is to run, to retire, and leave the country, never to return. The second is to befriend this man, to find a way to make him an ally, rather than an enemy."

Blanc examined her words. "In your voice, the first option sounds cowardly. I will attempt the second. He met with me once. Maybe he will do it again, and I can explain. However, my expectations say there is little chance it will happen. Running may well be the solution we must choose. But again, I fear this man would follow me through the gates of hell to carry out his mission. He has that kind of perseverance."

"Call him. If necessary, tell him we will abandon our business interests, leave the USA, and never return. Perhaps his blood lust will be satisfied."

Blanc sighed. "I'll try it. At least in years to come, I can tell myself I did my best."

* * *

Josh lay on the couch, his mind drifting. Chief was in the bedroom, stretched out across the bed, his snores proof of his sleep. Josh hoped Summers would call soon with information on Blanc's bodyguard. Without it, he was pretty much stymied. He wondered if he should have followed Blanc from the Blue Line and tried to get a handle on where he stayed while in South Florida. No, that would not have fit his code. The meeting was under a white flag and no advantage should have been gained—no matter what Blanc had done.

He considered Blanc, the overall impression he'd made. He was not the man Josh expected. He didn't deny his activities or attempt to excuse them. Josh wondered if he was married. Did he have children? He said he was in the first Gulf War—a pilot in the Royal Canadian Air Force. Had he flown any of the air cover Josh had heard stories about? According to the old vets he served with, those jets screaming in over their shoulders were the most beautiful sounds and visions in the war zone. Under different circumstances, Josh thought he could enjoy a social evening with Blanc. Or, if he had a wife, the four of them having dinner. Jaden would like him—trust him.

Yet, it could never happen. The man who appeared so earnest had violated their flag of truce and sent his henchmen after him. Josh had to ignore the good vibrations he'd gotten about Blanc. He had to remain the target, a duplicitous target who could lie with an honest face. Josh had to keep his concentration on center mass.

The phone rang. He checked the caller ID and saw it was a blocked number, a favorite telemarketer's trick. Then he remembered the call he received from Blanc was also blocked. Could it be him again?

The phone rang a third time. *May as well find out who's there.* "Hello."

"Mr. Hawkins?"

"Yes. Who's calling?"

"This is Henri Blanc. Can we meet again?"

"Why?"

"That's the subject of the meeting. I need to explain a few things. Do you have time for me? I'd prefer we do it soon."

Josh hesitated, his mind swirling. What was happening here? They had met. They agreed to stay enemies. Blanc had stamped that agreement by sending thugs after him. That phase was over. "Mr. Blanc, I really don't see any reason to sit down with you a second time. I thought we pretty much established our positions. Not to mention you proved I cannot trust you."

Blanc was silent for a moment. "I agree things did not go as they should. But it was not what you think. It's important to both of us you know the truth."

"Excuse me, but this is nuts. We're sworn enemies. You turned your goons loose to kill me before I take you out. That was the outcome of our first meeting. Wait a minute. I smell a rat. You're trying to draw me into the open where I'll be an easy target, aren't you?"

"I assure you, Mr. Hawkins, your opinion is not true. The confrontation you incurred was not of my making. I'd like to explain what happened, and how the situation is different now."

Doubt surfaced in Josh's mind. Blanc sounded sincere. But why, what could another meeting accomplish? No, it had to be a trick, an opportunity for Blanc or one of his people to gather intelligence—or, perhaps, finish the game. "No, Mr. Blanc. I think not. From here on in, if I see you, I'll try to take you out. I expect you to do the same."

"I was afraid that would be your position, and I am sorry to hear it. *Au revoir*, Mr. Hawkins. I'm sure you'll be a worthy adversary. I'll be sorry to see you die."

Josh hit the off button. Had he missed an opportunity? Could Blanc have been on the level? No. It didn't make sense. The three thugs who cornered him in Coral Edge Park were real, carrying real guns. The door had slammed shut.

* * *

Blanc placed the phone on the table, his face long, sadness permeating his soul.

Collette said, "I gather he wouldn't meet with you."

"No. He didn't trust my words. In his world, the attempt on his life after the first meeting proved my lack of integrity. He says we must fight."

"Have you considered picking him up and forcing him to listen?"

Blanc thought about what she'd said. "Not impossible, my love. I'll give it some thought, then run it past Gustave and Marcel. No matter what, we must formulate a plan to thwart Mr. Hawkins. Once we neutralize him, I'll announce my retirement. If all goes well, we should be home in Canada within thirty days, ready to enjoy the rest of our lives."

THIRTY

Jaden slowed as she approached the front doors of her office complex. The people behind flooded around her, each apparently anxious to head for home. So was Jaden, but she grimaced, thinking of what might be waiting on the other side—Rodriguez. Several times since the trial, he had greeted her with a smile at the beginning and the end of the workday. His comments of "Good Morning, Ms. Archer," "Have a nice day, Ms. Archer," "Enjoy your evening, Ms. Archer," or whatever other neutral expression he used were not something she could report to the police. What would she tell them, "He smiles and wishes me well?" They'd laugh her out of the building.

She could tell Josh, perhaps *should* tell Josh, but she feared his reaction. He was a direct person, no nuances. To him, the shortest solution would be the straight-line between him and Rodriguez. And that would prove unhealthy for Rodriguez. Ultimately, it could produce criminal charges against Josh, and Jaden could not allow that.

No, she'd smile and take it. When and if he did something illegal, she'd bring in the police. She took a deep breath and pushed through the door, her eyes scanning left and right.

"Have a nice evening, Ms. Archer," she heard from in front of her. Concentrating on that space, she spotted

Rodriguez through the other employees leaving the building. He leaned against the railing in the middle of the steps. When she locked eyes with him, he saluted, pushed off, and walked down and onto the sidewalk. He turned left and continued, in no hurry, without looking back.

Jaden realized she had stopped and blocked the stairs. A shudder passed through her, but she pushed it away and forced her steps. Walking to her car, she couldn't help checking over her shoulder. He didn't follow her. He never did. Why was he harassing her in this manner? It didn't make any sense.

Crawling into her car, she yearned for someone to talk to. Not for the first time in her life, she wished for a sister. So many times she'd heard other women speak about how close they were to a sister, and how they shared their deepest secrets. Several said they spoke with them almost daily, using them as sounding boards, or burning off frustration, or celebrating the good in their lives.

In Jaden's world, though, it hadn't happened. One brother, five years younger. They had never been close, respectful of one another, but not bonded. Her mother, apparently noticing the distance between brother and sister, had often remarked she wished she had had more children, another son and another daughter.

Her mother. Too bad she wasn't still alive. She had cheered for Jaden during the good times and propped her up during the bad. She would understand Jaden's confusion about what to do about Rodriguez and whether she should trust Josh. It seemed her mother was blessed with common sense far beyond the norm and an innate ability to come up with the right words. Jaden hoped that if she and Josh had children, she would find she'd inherited those traits from her mother. "Mom, I'd sure love to ask your advice," she whispered.

Then the answer hit Jaden. She knew exactly how her mother would react. She'd say, "If you love Josh enough to marry him and bear his children, you'd better love him enough to trust him. Talk to Josh."

Smiling, Jaden relaxed. That's what she needed to do, what she should have done before. But, Josh was so wrapped up in his current case she wasn't sure when she'd see him again. However, when she did . . .

* * *

Josh stared at his cell phone. What was the point in having the darn thing if it never rang when he wanted? Three days had passed with no word from Summers. Josh could contact him, but figured there was no point. He'd call when he had something to report.

But, if he didn't come up with information on the bodyguard, Josh would go after Felipe Estrada, the name Tony Carrillo had revealed. Carrillo passed his collections upward to Estrada, but swore he didn't know anyone else in the system. Also, he said he didn't know how to contact him. His last phone call had answered as a disconnected number. While waiting for Summers to come through, Josh could practice his computer skills by trying to find Estrada. Everyone left a trail in cyberspace.

He walked into his home office and moved the mouse, waking the CPU. Then he logged on, smiling as he input his password. He knew it was weak, but it felt good to type *JadenArcher*. She should be on the way home about now. Perhaps he could afford to take the night off and spend it with her. No, until the Blanc case was resolved, he needed to stay away from her. He had little doubt Blanc's people were watching him, and he didn't want to lead them to Jaden. As long as he stayed away, she would be safer.

Josh opened a search engine and entered *Felipe Estrada*. He flinched when he saw the results—approximately sixteen million, five-hundred thousand hits. He added South Florida to the search and reduced it to about seven-hundred-seventy-four thousand, a number he still found impossible to comprehend. He opened a Word document and headed it Felipe Estrada along with the number of responses. Under that, he wrote *Felipe Estrada, South Florida* with its number. If necessary, he'd work his way through every city and town until he found the right one. Of course, the question was how would he know when he hit the right Felipe Estrada.

He leaned back and stared at the screen. Maybe it would be quicker to visit the Trungs and hope a new collector had stopped by. However, if that were true, Ms. Trung would have called him. *I sure wish Summers would call.*

As if in answer to his thoughts, his phone rang. Staring at the caller ID, he smiled. Perhaps he did have an angel on his shoulder. Summers was on the line.

"Hey, Phil. I was thinking about you."

"Sure, and you have some choice ocean-front property about twenty miles west of you. You'll cut me in at bottom dollar, right?"

"C'mon, Phil. You know I'd never scam you."

"Uh-huh. Not as long as I stay ten yards in front of you, you won't. And rest assured, I'm there. But enough of your moneymaking schemes. I have info on the bodyguard. You'd be surprised how tough it is to find someone simply from a picture in your head. Now I feel sorry for the victims we bring in and pop in front of a computer with thousands of mug shots."

"So, give."

"The name is Pablo Figueroa. I was in on his arrest three years ago on assault and resisting a police officer. He was involved in a brawl with two other guys. He broke the arms of both of them. It took four cops to subdue him. Strange part was when it went to court, he only received probation for resisting arrest. The assault charges were suspiciously reversed—the two men decided they had attacked him. I remember wondering at the time how he, the victim, had no marks on him while his attackers looked like they'd been run through an old-fashioned meat grinder. Anyway, I have an address on him. Don't know if it's good now, but it was then."

"Thanks. Did you check it out?"

"No. I figured we'd get together and formulate a plan."

"A plan? Me? Don't you listen to your lieutenant? He says I never know what I'm doing."

Phil laughed. "That's why it's my idea to come up with a plan. You'd screw it up if I left you alone. What say I hit your house in an hour or so? It'll be after five somewhere, and I'll be off-duty. We can split a beer while we think things over."

"A clear winner. I'll be here. But it'll have to be a three-way split. Chief's with me."

"Even better."

* * *

Josh turned to his computer and renewed his search for Felipe Estrada. He thought for a moment about how to narrow the search, then typed in *Felipe Estrada, Broward County Florida*. That produced over 65,000 hits, helping very little. He sat back, realizing he needed more hard info on Estrada before he could track him. The Internet was good, but the old adage, garbage in, garbage out—GIGO—still applied.

Nothing to do but wait for Summers. Josh hoped Chief would be back before then. He'd gone for a walk about thirty minutes before. Hard to say how far or how fast he'd return. Chief was accustomed to being on his own in the Everglades. A neighborhood, such as Josh's, was a novelty for him. Josh hoped he didn't get lost.

He walked into the kitchen, thinking he'd get a soda out of the fridge. Maybe make a sandwich. He hadn't eaten since breakfast, and hunger gnawed at him. As he reached into the refrigerator, a shadow—or something—flitted across the corner of his eye. He looked up, but saw only the glass patio doors. Frowning, he walked over and looked out. Nothing.

Well, if you called an overactive imagination nothing, it fit. Probably just a bird flying by. As he moved back to the fridge, he heard a noise from the front of the house. Chief had returned.

Grabbing two sodas, he walked into the living room, figuring Chief would be thirsty after his walk. The person standing there was almost as big as Chief, but it wasn't him—and the pistol he held was not Chief's type of weapon.

"Good afternoon, Mr. Hawkins. Hope you don't mind that I let myself in. You really should lock your door. Never know when a burglar might be in the area."

Josh heard his patio door slide open and footsteps in the kitchen.

"Baptiste, search the house. Mr. Hawkins is with me," the uninvited guest said without taking his eyes off Josh. "As I was saying, Mr. Hawkins, you really should learn to lock your doors—windows, too."

"Okay, you're in," Josh said. "What do you want?" His mind raced. The man looked familiar. He'd seen him before. Where? The sound of bar noise filled his memory. Blanc. Henri Blanc's bodyguard. He must be Pablo Figueroa. Now that he had a name, he felt better—and worse. Figueroa's visit could not be good. Once again, Blanc had grabbed the upper hand.

"Want? Not much. The first thing is that you contact your partner and have him come over here. Mr. Blanc wants to see both of you. He says you turned down his offer of a meeting. That was unacceptable. When he wants something, he gets it. Baptiste and I will escort you."

"Good," Josh said. "I changed my mind. I'd like to see him, too. But we'll have to go alone. I have no partner. He went home."

Pablo chuckled. "You are too obvious. Mr. Blanc predicted you'd say something like that. He told me to remind you he saw him—along with another man. However, he discovered the third person is a local cop and no threat to him. Have a seat. We'll wait until you decide to cooperate. I should tell you, though, Mr. Blanc told me to keep you alive. He did not say *healthy* and alive."

Baptiste came into the living room—the second bodyguard. "House is clear. No one here. But there is evidence of another man staying in the guest bedroom."

"Too bad. Now we'll have to *encourage* Mr. Hawkins to do as I asked and bring his partner in." He stepped to Josh and backhanded him across the face.

Josh reeled backward, stumbled, and would have fallen except the wall caught him. He shook his head and rubbed his jaw.

"I can do that all day," Figueroa said, pulling on a leather glove. "However, I'd prefer not to. Take out your phone and call your partner."

Josh wiped at the corner of his mouth, his hand coming away red. "You wouldn't want to get blood on that nice glove."

The front door opened. "What th—"

"Ah, the missing partner," Figueroa said, spinning toward the opening, his gun at the ready. "Do come in, sir. We've been waiting for you. Now, the party can begin."

Chief stood there, the doorknob in his hand. "Who the hell are you?"

"Either come in, or I'll ask Baptiste to blow your friend's head off."

Baptiste grunted as he trained his weapon on Josh.

Chief stepped into the room.

"Close the door."

Chief complied. "You didn't answer my question. Who the hell are you?"

THIRTY-ONE

"Chief, let me introduce our guests," Josh said, pushing off the wall. "The heavy-handed one is Pablo Figueroa, senior bodyguard to Henri Blanc. His friend is Baptiste. You might remember them from the Blue Line. They've come to issue us a personal invitation to meet with their boss. He thinks I was hasty when I turned him down."

Chief shrugged. "Makes sense. I'm ready if you are."

"Just a moment, gentlemen," Figueroa said. "I realize you've met some of the street-gnomes who pay tribute to Mr. Blanc. Don't make the mistake of thinking we're as careless or stupid as they are. Baptiste, remove whatever weapons they're carrying."

"That's not necessary," Josh said. "I'll—"

"Oh, I'm sure you would. Either Baptiste does it his way, or we proceed to a strip search. Which is your preference?"

Josh grinned. "I'll lean and spread. Baptiste, don't miss my ankle gun and the knife on the other leg."

"Me, too," Chief said. "But don't jump to conclusions when you don't find anything. I'm not carrying." He took a position beside Josh, who leaned against the wall, his legs spread in the body search position.

Baptiste performed a pat down with the expertise of a twenty-year detective, removing Josh's gun and knife and tossing them onto the couch. He found nothing on Chief.

When he finished, he stepped back. "Okay, they're clean."

Figueroa picked up Josh's knife and examined it. "Nice piece. Where'd you get it?"

"I designed it. Not another one like it."

"If you don't make it back here, think I'll stop by and pick it up. Do you mind?"

Josh shook his head. "If I don't make it back, it won't really matter, will it? You'll be welcome to the knife. Of course, you probably should know it's registered with the police."

Figueroa laughed. "Good point. Baptiste, get them ready to travel." He turned to Josh. "You do know you'll have to be incapacitated and blindfolded for the trip. Any problem with that?"

"Your politeness is killing me," Josh said. "Let's get on with it."

"Excellent attitude," Figueroa said. "Cross your arms over your chest and reach for your backbone."

"Huh? Say that again."

"Straight jacket style. Baptist will use plastic ties to simulate a straight jacket. Understand?"

"Interesting," Josh said, smiling at Chief. "We'll have to remember this technique. Don't think I've ever seen it before."

"Just do it, please," Figueroa said. "We need to be moving along."

When Josh and Chief complied, Baptiste secured each man's hands and immobilized their arms by pulling ties from wrist to wrist around their backs. Each man could walk, but was effectively neutralized from taking any action with his hands. Baptiste then slipped behind them and put a blindfold over their heads, leaving their eyes uncovered.

Figueroa checked the ties. "Good job. I think they'll agree you developed a technique superior to handcuffing."

"My congratulations," Josh said. "Your name will go down in history."

"Okay, that's enough," Figueroa said. "Let's get on with it. Walk straight to my Escalade and get in the back. Baptiste and I will be behind you, so don't get fancy. And don't drag it out. I'm not interested in your neighbors watching through their windows and calling the cops."

"Got it," Josh said. "Then what?"

"Baptiste will seatbelt you in and lower your blindfolds. After that, we'll be off to meet with Mr. Blanc. From that point forward, he'll make the decisions. Baptiste and I will be with you to do whatever he says. The good news is not all the people who meet with him die. Some are smart enough to agree with him, and I bring them home. Others . . . Well, you probably know."

"Yeah, yeah, I get the picture," Josh said.

Chief grunted.

* * *

Time and distance are difficult to judge when a blindfold covers your eyes. It seemed to Josh they'd been on the move at least a half hour, but it could have been only ten minutes or so. Likewise with how far they'd traveled. It could be one mile or ten miles. He knew they made lots of turns—right, left, left, right. Centrifugal force told him that as he swayed from side to side, the seatbelt holding him upright. After ten turns, he quit counting since there was no way he could translate the turns into where they had been or were going.

Josh sensed Chief sitting beside him, but made no effort to communicate. What was the point? Nothing to say. Chief was as much a pro as he and would be looking for any opportunity to escape their kidnappers.

After that indeterminate amount of time and the unknown distance, they drifted to a stop. The crunching of the tires led Josh to believe it was a gravel parking lot.

"We're here," a voice said, sounding like Figueroa, which was logical since he appeared to be the leader. "Sit tight. We'll come around and help you out."

"Take your time," Josh said. "I'm in no hurry."

Someone chuckled. Probably Baptiste.

Josh's door opened, then the door on the other side.

Figueroa said, "Just follow my lead, and I'll get you out of there. Chief, you do the same. Baptiste is on your side." He unbuckled Josh's seatbelt.

"If you're paid extra for courtesy, I'll be sure and let Blanc know you earned a bonus," Josh said, forcing a chuckle. "Never been kidnapped by such nice people before." He felt a hand on his elbow, turning him.

"Enjoy yourself while you can. I'm sure Mr. Blanc has plans for you."

With Figueroa's help, he made it out of the Escalade without falling. A hand in the middle of his back steered him as he walked forward. A door opened, and he stepped from gravel onto a solid floor, then kept moving for several more seconds. Another door opened, and they passed through.

"Mr. Hawkins, I'm going to seat you now, but don't lean back. It's a stool. When you're down, I'll take off your blindfold. Same for your friend."

Josh let himself be settled onto a hard surface, then felt a hand on his brow as light flooded in. He squinted and shook his head. Whether it helped clear his vision, he didn't know, but it felt the natural thing to do. He would have rubbed his eyes except his hands were still secured in their wrap around position.

"Relax," Figueroa said. "I'll let Mr. Blanc know you're available to speak with him. Baptiste, keep a close eye on them. They're tricky." He left.

Josh gazed around the area. They were in a small room. Chief, like him, was perched on a three-legged stool with a small seat. Also, the stool was short, no more than two-feet tall. He supposed it was to discourage him from launching himself at his guards.

The sparsely furnished room held a scarred, wooden

desk with chair, a couple of straight-backed chairs, and the two stools. The walls were bare, nothing to identify where they were. It could be a backroom any place in South Florida.

"So, Baptiste, do you know why we're here?" Josh asked.

"Keep your mouths shut," Baptiste said. "You'll find out soon enough."

"Your wish is my command," Josh said.

Baptiste frowned.

The door opened, and Josh turned to see who entered.

Figueroa came in, checked the bonds on Josh's and Chief's wrists, then turned back to the doorway. "It's clear, Mr. Blanc."

Henri Blanc entered, walked around the desk, and sat. "It's good to see you again, Mr. Hawkins. I'm glad you decided to visit and brought your friend along. I gather that you two share everything, so this will save your having to brief him later."

"Later? I like the sound of that. But visit? Somehow, I think you received an inadequate briefing. Being cuffed, blindfolded, and driven here by your goons doesn't fit my definition of a visit."

"Come now, Mr. Hawkins. Let's not be melodramatic. I'm certain they treated you with the utmost respect."

"Okay, you score on that point. Your people were courteous. However, my hands are going numb. How about getting these ties off?"

Blanc waved at Figueroa. "Cut them loose, but keep a close eye on them. Stand directly behind where they can't see you."

Figueroa followed through, and Josh spent a moment rubbing his wrists. "Much better. Now we can move on. Your goon says you want to talk to us. What's on your mind?"

"I wish you wouldn't call them goons. Actually, they are nice people—and loyal to me." He smiled. "To answer your question, it's simply to talk. As I said on the phone, I need to explain a few things, then tell you of my plans. Perhaps the knowledge will encourage you to abandon the chase."

Josh considered Blanc's comment, wondering what it meant. *Abandon the chase? Not likely.* "As I replied when we spoke, the time for talking passed. The moment you violated our truce with your three punks, it was over. By the way, how are they doing? Did they have your *insurance?* It's time for action now." He scanned the room. "Although, given the circumstances, I wouldn't mind a long chat."

Blanc chuckled. "You are an interesting man, Mr. Hawkins—an assassin with a sense of humor."

Josh looked over his shoulder toward where he thought Figueroa stood, but couldn't see him. "It would seem, Mr. Blanc, that Chief and I are at your disposal. So, if you want to have a conversation, I want to participate."

"Good. First, the three people who followed you after our first meeting. I had nothing to do with it. An overzealous underling *thought* he was doing what I wanted. He has learned the error of his decision."

"Oh? Last I heard your hirelings were out on bail, free to resume their attack on me."

"Wrong. Your information is not current. They are back in jail, their bail revoked. And to put to bed another potential thought of yours, their *insurance policy* has been rescinded. They'll be represented by a public defender."

"Interesting," Josh said. "You're telling me you took revenge on them. What about the guy who sent them out?"

Blanc rubbed his chin. "Even in surroundings like this, there are some questions best not answered. But I can assure you he'll never do it again."

Josh glanced at Chief and shrugged. "Mr. Blanc, you're a fascinating man and have a fantastic way with words. Did you have us dragged in here just to spin that tale? You know I can have it checked in thirty seconds or less."

"When you do, if you do, you'll find I told the truth. However, that's not all. Over this past week, my wife and I had several conversations about the future." Blanc hesitated and raised an eyebrow. "I see from the expression on your face that hearing I have a wife is a surprise. Well, get ready for more. I not only have a wife, whom I love dearly, but I have two children and three grandchildren. The wife is with me, and the others live in Canada. They are legal—not even a traffic ticket. Furthermore, they have no idea how their father and grandfather got his riches. They are a major reason I have never violated the law in Canada and never will. I don't want my family embarrassed."

"Mighty noble of you," Chief said.

Blanc turned toward Chief. "Oh, you can speak. You had me wondering." He smiled.

"I don't waste words on people I don't like. I much prefer to interact with them in my own way."

Blanc nodded. "Understood." He turned his attention to Josh. "It appears you're a well-matched pair. Something I don't understand, though. How did someone with your integrity become a hired assassin? The same for your friend. I haven't read his file, but, if he's with you, I assume he's the same kind of person. How can you be so desperate you'd track down and kill a man who means you no harm, who is a devoted husband, father, and grandfather? I don't understand."

Looking at the ceiling, Josh digested what Blanc said. They were good questions. Had he become nothing more than a hired killer? He didn't see it that way, but he could understand Blanc's point of view. "Mr. Blanc, isn't there a Bible passage that says something like, *Judge not, that ye be not judged?* I suggest you heed its message. You are in no position to judge anyone. Even if I believe your fairytale about the night we met, your so-called insurance business has caused the death of several people, not to mention losses to many innocent people. You might call me an assassin, but I think of it as doing a service for my country. You and others like you need to disappear."

Blanc pursed his lips as if in thought, then nodded. "One of those times when we must agree to disagree. Back to why you're here. My wife and I spent hours discussing the future. We're in total agreement that we do not wish to spend it ducking people like you. Oh, yes. I'm quite sure that if you fail, Newsome will trot out someone else to hunt me down. People like him have endless resources. And he has bottomless pockets—the US Treasury. How much is he paying you?"

"Can't see how that's any of your business," Josh said. "Continue with your story."

"My wife and I decided I'm retiring. Within the next few days, I'll be gone from the US, never to return. Even now, she is in our temporary home, packing. I'll be finished with the business and, I hope, you'll be finished with me. Would it satisfy you to know you were successful in ending the career of Henri Blanc?"

Josh was at a loss for words. He'd expected threats, perhaps a beating, and even death, but not Blanc's retirement. What was he pulling? It had to be a trick. But why? He had the upper hand. In fact, he had total control. Josh and Chief were helpless with Figueroa and Baptiste at their backs. All it would take was a nod from Blanc. He searched for the gimmick. What was Blanc's trick?

"I see by your look of confusion that you don't get it." Blanc scratched his cheek. "Am I right?"

Josh sighed. "Yeah. I don't get it. What are you up to? Where's the twist in your story? I've always heard if it sounds too good to be true, it isn't."

"Yes, I have heard the same thing—many times—and the adage carries the truth more often than not. However, I assure you there is no twist. I'm getting out. That's it. Breaking all ties with the insurance business. From now on, I will spend my time making my wife and the rest of my family happy. I've ignored them for too many years."

"Sounds nice—like mom and apple pie. Who's taking

over your business? I might want to buy stock."

"Sorry, Mr. Hawkins. You know I won't tell you that, even if I could. I'm sure Newsome and his bloodhounds will discover it—after I'm home in Canada, lounging with my feet up, I hope. Who knows, you might get a new assignment."

"I'm glad to hear you speak of my future. Does that mean you're releasing Chief and me? If that's your plan, can we speed it up a bit? I didn't have lunch."

"Perhaps. That remains to be seen. Will you give up the chase? Will you go to Newsome and tell him you won't hunt me any longer? Same for your friend. If you're willing to make that commitment, I can probably turn you loose. Otherwise . . ." He shrugged.

"Interesting," Josh said. "Of course, before I can answer, I need to consult with my partner and then with the task force."

"With Chief, yes. With Newsome, no." He rose. "I'll give you ten minutes. Figueroa and Baptiste will stay with you."

"I prefer privacy."

"I'm sure you do, but you're my guests. It would be rude to leave you unattended." Blanc came around the desk and left the room.

THIRTY-TWO

When the door closed behind Blanc, Josh spoke to Chief, "What do you think? Is he on the level? Want to trust him?"

Chief looked at Josh, then turned on his stool and stared at Figueroa. "Me? I'd rather talk about these two. I say we can take them. I say their squinty eyes come from lying on the beach, and their muscles come from a gym. We faced a lot tougher in jungles and deserts around the world."

Josh turned in time to see Figueroa flinch—not much, but he flinched. "Yeah, probably. What about their guns?"

Chief stroked his chin. "I figure Blanc told them to take it easy on us, don't hurt us unless he gives a specific order. That's why we've had such good treatment. If we move on them, they'll hesitate. And you know what they say. *He who hesitates is lost.*"

Josh continued watching Figueroa, then cut his eyes at Baptiste, who wore a quizzical look. Ignoring the guards, he concentrated his words on Chief. "This reminds me of when we were trapped in the mountains of Colombia. Remember that? Blood thirsty bandits all around us. I thought for sure we'd bought the farm that day. But, you know what? I learned to trust your judgment. You said hit'm in the middle, and I followed your lead. An hour later, twelve bandits were down, and you and I were rendezvousing with our chopper. If you say we can do it, I'm with you all the way."

"That's crap," Figueroa shouted. "If you move, I'll put a bullet in you."

"I figure you might be half-right," Chief said. "One of us might catch a bullet, but that won't stop the other. You know, the funny part about the episode Josh and I were in." Chief shook his head. "When we inventoried our ammo 'board that chopper, we realized we hadn't fired many rounds. That left us to guesstimate they mostly shot one another. Crazy what happens under the stress of battle."

Josh looked at Baptiste. "You ever been in a shoot-out with this guy across from you? He nodded toward Figueroa. "Can he control that thing when he starts squeezing the trigger?" He shifted his gaze to Figueroa. "How about you? Can you trust Baptiste to shoot the right people?"

Figueroa and Baptiste glanced at each other, doubt reflecting in their eyes.

The door burst open, causing the four heads to swivel.

Phil Summers stood in the doorway with Blanc in front of him, the barrel of his police-issued Glock pressed against Blanc's right ear. "You boys need to put those guns down. Either that or my finger might twitch and cut a new channel through your boss's head."

"Do as he says," Blanc said. "I've come too far to have it end this way."

Figueroa and Baptiste stared, then lowered their pistols.

"All the way down," Summers said. "Drop them."

"For God's sake, do what he says. This guy's a policeman. He has nothing on us. My lawyers will have us walking free in a few hours."

Figueroa and Baptiste looked at one another as Josh and Chief leaped to their sides, disarming them.

"Took you long enough," Josh said. "What'd you do, low-crawl here?"

"I thought I'd give you time to get yourself out of the mess. When I saw you were helpless, I figured a rescue was in order."

"Is that right? What you don't know is Chief and I were about to make our play before your grand entry. You messed everything up."

"Oh, sure. What do you want me to do with these three? I'm guessing you're not willing to swear out kidnapping charges."

Josh stared at Blanc. "Earlier, you spun an interesting story. You tried to convince me you're retiring, leaving the country to never return. Is that true?"

"Yes. As I told you, my wife and I are going home to spend what's left of our lives with our children and grandkids. We'll be gone in a few days, leaving no trail behind. It'll be like we were never here."

"Not true. There are widows and fatherless children who will remember. In addition, you questioned why I'd hire on to anyone as an assassin. Remember that?"

"Yes. I've seen your file. It still doesn't compute for me."

"Maybe you didn't read in enough detail. You missed the part where I love my country so much I'd do almost anything to protect it. Including squashing vermin like you."

"Hey, you guys," Summers said. "Can we wrap up this love fest and make some decisions. My finger on this trigger is sweating. It could slip. What do you want me to do? I have no paper on Blanc. I can drag in his cohorts on weapons charges, or I can take in all three for kidnapping. But the latter means you have to come in and fill out the paperwork to press charges. Also, folks will be curious as to why you were grabbed, especially the lieut. Might mean you have to tell stories that probably shouldn't be told."

"Yeah, I'm considering that. Give me a couple of minutes to consult with my protégé. Chief, let's step outside."

* * *

A couple of minutes later, Josh and Chief returned to the room. "Okay, Phil. We have a plan. Maybe not the best one, but it's all ours." He looked at Figueroa and Baptiste. "You two have a choice. You either find a new line of work, or you're going to end up in jail, or dead, or worse. You're lucky this time. Your ex-boss and I will be moving out soon, leaving you to sort out your futures—that is, if Detective Summers decides to turn you loose. What say, Phil?"

"I might take them downtown and run them through a few warrants, just for practice. Maybe they have a parking ticket or some such."

"Your choice. Thanks for showing up. You saved Chief and me from skinning our knuckles on these guys' hard heads. Mr. Blanc, we have a rendezvous to make. We'll take your car. I'm sure you didn't walk here."

* * *

Josh pulled into a parking space in front of the police station. Isaac Newsome was on the sidewalk, pacing back and forth. Josh shifted into Park, put the windows down, then got out. "I'll only be a minute, Chief," he said into the backseat.

Chief sat beside Blanc, whose wrists were laced together with plastic ties. "We'll be fine. My guess is our friend isn't in any hurry."

Newsome headed toward Josh, but Josh cut him off. "We need to talk a moment," Josh said. "Then I have a present for you."

"This had better be good. I was in a meeting. Your message said if I dropped everything and rushed out front, you'd make me a national hero. So what gives?"

"Patience, my friend, patience. Walk with me." Josh moved down the sidewalk.

Newsome caught up with him.

Josh filled Newsome in on his and Chief's kidnapping and the story Blanc told him, emphasizing the part about *leaving the US forever.* He left out the part about Phil Summers rescuing him and Chief, not wanting to drag Phil's participation into the spotlight.

When he finished the story, they were two blocks from the police station. He doubled back, and they walked in silence for a few minutes.

Newsome said, "I almost hate to ask. Did you take care of Blanc?"

"In a way, yes. Let's go back to the car. That's where your surprise is."

"Explain," Newsome said. "I'm not into playing games."

"Funny. You expected me to dance to your tune. However, this is not a game. Just pick up the pace, and it'll be over soon."

Upon arrival at the car, Josh opened the back door. "Isaac Newsome, meet Henri Blanc. Henri Blanc, this is Isaac Newsome. I know each of you is fully aware of the other, but I'm guessing you never met face to face before." He turned back to Newsome. "He's all yours. This is as far as I take it."

Josh stepped back and stared at Newsome. "Mr. Blanc asked how I'd come to be a hired assassin." He returned his attention to Blanc. "The answer is I haven't. I'll do what's necessary to keep my country safe, but not to protect an inept justice system." He faced Newsome. "While you have him, I suggest you find out who his mole is. Perhaps, the two of you can work out a trade."

"You can't—"

"Oh, yes I can, Mr. Newsome. I'm a civilian. Remember? I don't work for you or any part of the government. Your tasking to me was to take Blanc out of the game. There he sits, totally in your control without the ACLU or any other bleeding hearts looking over your shoulder. I delivered. Now it's up to you. Let me know how it comes out."

He spoke to Chief who still sat in the car. "Let's go, Chief. We can get a cab to my place. Then you can head for home. I think we've done as much as we can."

THIRTY-THREE

Josh and Jaden shared a quiet evening at home. At dinner, he told her his current assignment was finished. When she questioned what it was, he ducked. "Sorry, still can't tell you. Too many secrecy agreements."

She laughed. "The day you share with me is the day I'll wonder if someone took over the body and soul of the man I adore."

In return, she caught him up on the cases on her docket. Nothing glamorous. The most serious was a hit-and-run against a bicycle. A young woman clipped the bicyclist and kept going. One pedestrian wrote down her license number while another took a picture of the car. Open and shut case. The defense council was begging for a plea deal. Jaden was being difficult, but admitted she'd probably give in. The woman seemed contrite and was footing the biker's medical bills.

Jaden frowned. "I feel like I'm being punished for losing the Rodriguez case. John says it's my imagination, but—"

"John?"

"My boss, John Fellows. Remember? You met him at the cocktail party a couple of months ago."

"Yes. A short, rotund fellow named Fellows. How'd I forget that?"

"Never mind your sarcasm. It's only that I . . . I feel like

I'm doing penance. My cases are so insignificant. Yet, I don't know how I could have done any better than I did."

Josh led her to the sofa. "Speaking of Rodriguez. Any word on his recent activities?"

"If you mean illegal, no. Nothing has come through the office." She took a deep breath and appeared to think. "Okay, here goes nothing. Please don't comment until I'm finished. Rodriguez is doing something strange. I see him twice a day. When I show up at the office, he's there to wish me a good morning. And at the end of the day, he's outside waiting for me. He says something like, 'Have a nice evening' or 'Hope your day was nice.' It's innocent, but it's spooky. I can't call it stalking because he walks away as soon as he greets me. He makes no attempt to intimidate. He doesn't even try to talk to me. A greeting and he's gone. I don't know what to do about it."

Josh frowned. He had Rodriguez on his radar as his next project, and this upped the ante. Rodriguez had to disappear. However, as asked, he said nothing.

Jaden continued, "I'm not saying this for you to do anything. I don't want you near him. What he's doing is harmless, showing off. If he does anything threatening, I'll turn it over to the police. I only need to share." She sighed. "Talking about it takes the edge off. I feel better. That's what families do."

Josh smiled, liking how she said families. "So, you're saying I should let the woman I love be harassed and do nothing about it?"

"That's exactly what I'm saying. Besides, it's not harassment. It's more, uh, more . . . Oh, hell. All you have to do is promise me. I want to be able to share without expecting you to go ballistic. Do I have your word you'll stay away from him?"

"No. You tell me this man is hounding you, then ask me to sit on my hands. I can't do that. You know I'm not built that way."

"If you love me, you'll do what I ask. I can't have you roughing up every man who looks crosswise at me. It's inevitable in my job. If I win, the perp is going to hate me. If I lose, he'll want to gloat. That's all Rodriguez is doing—rubbing my face in his victory. Promise you won't touch him."

Josh said nothing, thoughts ripping through his head at sonic speeds. He'd promised himself Rodriguez would pay. However, Jaden was his life mate and he didn't want to lie to her. Then he rationalized, she said I should stay away from him. I can do that, if . . . He stayed quiet, deep in thought for another moment. "If that's what you really want, you have my word. I will not go near him."

"I hope you're not lying to me. If I find out you hurt him, I'll never trust you again. Now, let's clean up the kitchen and get ready for bed. I want proof that you're all here for me tonight."

* * *

The next morning, Josh kissed Jaden out the front door, then returned to the kitchen and poured a third cup of coffee. Settling at the table, he took out his cell phone and punched in Chief's number.

When Chief answered, he said, "Hey, sorry to bother you again so soon, but I need another favor."

"Nice to talk to you, too," Chief said. "And how was your evening. Mine was wonderful, like every night with Sandra."

Josh chuckled. "Sorry. Heavy thoughts this morning make me forget my manners. Glad y'all keep renewing your wedding vows. With Jaden, everything is wonderful. But then, things are always wonderful with her."

"You are such a romantic. The difference this time is you have someone to be romantic with. What's on your mind?"

"Remember I told you about this guy Rodriguez that

Jaden prosecuted—the one who killed his wife and got away with it?"

"Yeah. What happened? Did he strike again?"

"Not exactly. But he's harassing Jaden." Josh filled him in on Rodriguez's actions and Jaden's fear of him. "She made me promise to not go near him. But she didn't say a friend of mine couldn't treat him to a personality-expanding-experience. I think he and Miss Allie would make a fine pair. What do you think?"

Chief didn't hesitate. "You and Jaden need to go away this weekend. I'll come in Thursday afternoon, and you can point out this Rodriguez to me—from afar, of course. When you get home on Sunday evening, you will no longer have a Rodriguez problem. How's that sound?"

"Spoken like a true friend. Give Sandra my best."

* * *

At Josh's urging, Jaden arranged for a three-day weekend. Friday morning, they headed for Sarasota. Without telling her either their destination or the reason for it, Josh bought tickets to the Ringling International Arts Festival. They had missed the first two days, but there were enough activities on Saturday and Sunday to keep them occupied and entertained. It would especially direct Jaden's mind away from Rodriguez, which was Josh's primary goal—that and to share time with the woman he loved.

The weekend was everything that Josh wished it to be.

THIRTY-FOUR

During the next month, Josh returned to the routine investigations he ran for Irving and Irwin, the law firm from which he drew a retainer. He uncovered a phony *cripple* who was defrauding the insurance company, found an heir to a will, and tracked a disappeared wife and mother to her new boyfriend and living arrangements in Bermuda. His good luck seemed to have no end, and Robert Irving was gracious in his praise, promising a bonus when the cases were paid.

He dropped by Mo's and returned the GPSs, explaining they were unused. Mo wanted to know the details of the case, but Josh told him he couldn't talk about it. That, of course, earned Josh several good-natured insults from Mo and a demand for at least a six-pack of Killian's.

At the end of the first week of that month, Jaden gave him a suspicious look. "I haven't seen Rodriguez this week. The last time he greeted me was the Thursday before we went to Sarasota. Is there a specific reason for that?"

Josh tried to look puzzled. "I haven't been near him, if that's what you're asking. Maybe the heat got to him. Awful hot standing in front of your office all day. The sun can be brutal."

"Are you sure you didn't do something to him? Remember, you promised not to bother him."

Josh shook his head. "Aw, my doubting woman. I

251

promised I wouldn't go near him, and I assure you I haven't. If you hadn't made me promise, I admit I might have broken his face with a two-by-four. But, a promise is a promise— especially to the woman I love."

Jaden stared a moment longer, then leaned over and kissed him. "I'll accept what you say. Don't make me regret it."

On Friday morning of the fourth week, Josh sat in Jaden's kitchen, enjoying a third cup of coffee. She had left for work ten minutes prior, leaving him to sort out his day. He had nothing firm on the schedule. Even Irving and Irwin seemed to be in a lull. His cell phone rang.

The caller ID showed a familiar number. Josh looked at it, couldn't place it, then shrugged. "Hello."

"Mr. Hawkins, this is Isaac Newsome. We have unfinished business. Meet me in the conference room this morning."

"Conference room? There are lots of those in South Florida."

"I think you know which one. Where we've met before. I'm assembling the team. The conversation needs a secure setting. Be here at ten."

Josh drove to police headquarters, was met at the front desk, and escorted to the conference room. When he opened the door, four heads turned toward him. He frowned. Someone was missing.

"Come in, Mr. Hawkins," Newsome said from his position at the head of the table. "We have much to discuss."

"Does that mean *the check's in the mail?*"

Newsome chuckled. "Not exactly." He tapped a piece of paper lying in front of him. "It's on the agenda though."

Josh looked around the room. "I suppose we can't begin until Roz gets here. Do you have any coffee?"

"I'll have some brought in." Newsome hesitated. "Roz won't be here."

"Oh? Why not?"

"It's on the agenda." He kept his head down when he said it. "We can begin as soon as you take a seat."

Josh frowned, but pulled out a chair and sat. "Ready when you are."

"First, I have briefed the team and those upstairs about your resolution of the case. Some were happier than others. You didn't do anything to enhance your reputation, but you didn't hurt it too badly either."

"Gee, I'm thrilled," Josh said. "Guess that means I won't get recruited again. Breaks my heart."

"Don't count on it. Now, let's discuss payment for your services." Newsome looked at his three operatives—Randolph, Kelly, and Sutherland.

All but Sutherland kept their heads down. He glared at Josh, a lack of respect glowing in his eyes.

"Since you didn't carry out your assignment," Newsome continued, "I have chosen to change the terms of our agreement. I'll be transferring one-hundred-thousand to your bank account. You can split it up among those who helped you however you see fit."

Josh chuckled. "Wish I were surprised, but I'm accustomed to bureaucrats like you. I expected you to double back on me. What do you mean, I didn't *carry out my assignment?* Last I remember, I opened the back door of a car and handed Blanc over to you. Did he get away? If so, it wasn't on my watch."

"No. On the contrary, we had some interesting conversations. Lest you forget, your task was to kill Mr. Blanc and dispose of his body so it could never be found."

"Hmm," Josh said. "Not exactly the way I remember it."

"Then your memory is faulty." Newsome's voice carried a *don't contradict me* quality.

Josh reached into his shirt pocket and brought out a small recorder. "There's an old adage that goes something like, those who don't learn from history are doomed to repeat it. Perhaps, we should visit a piece of history. Maybe we'll all learn something." He punched the play button and leaned back in his chair.

Newsome, Kelly, Randolph, and Sutherland hunched forward.

Newsome's voice came from the recorder. "*Another point for you. Okay, no more games. I'll go a half-mill—five hundred thousand—if you produce absolute proof Blanc is out of the game.*"

Josh's voice said, "*Tax-free and no IRS snooping?*"

"*I can slide it under the table, if that's what you mean, but tax-free if it's found? I'm sure you're aware no one controls the IRS—not even the President.*"

There was a sound of shoes clicking along a sidewalk. Then Josh said, "*I don't like it. You hand me a half-mill, then the IRS swoops in and takes it back. While they're crowing about their coup, they put me in jail on a trumped-up tax charge. You get Blanc, and I get time with nasty people who'll let me know exactly what they think of me. Sounds like a win-win for the government and a lose-lose for Josh Hawkins.*"

"*That's the best I can do. We're at the take-it-or-leave-it stage. I'm trying to meet you more than halfway, but if it's not to be, it's not to be. I'll find another operative. You're my first choice, but not my only choice. Make up your mind.*"

"*The half-mill plus a written explanation from the Attorney General.*"

A pause, then Newsome's voice. "*That might be possible— or not. But what is possible is a written explanation signed off by me. You'll have my words to help if IRS targets you.*"

Josh clicked off the recorder. "Your exact words were *if you produce absolute proof Blanc is out of the game.* Don't know how much more absolute it can be than putting him in your hands. After all, you're the one with all the clout in D.C. You have many ways to bury him and many agencies to do it. In my simple mind, I delivered. Now it's your turn."

The room grew tense as Newsome stared at Josh. "How dare you record me."

The three members of the task force stared at Newsome,

smiles ticking at the corners of their mouths—even Sutherland's.

"Yeah, I remember," Josh said. "You were the only one allowed to have a recording device. However, you weren't as thorough as I was. I might respect you, Mr. Newsome, but that doesn't mean I trust you."

"I think he's got you, Mr. Newsome," Sutherland said. "I'm sure Ms. Morgan would love to hear that tape. You remember her, don't you, sir—Director of the FBI? You spoke to her about me."

"Shut up, you twerp," Newsome said. He spun on Josh. "You win. Two-hundred-fifty thou. Not a dime more, and you'll get a 1099 on it. Make sure you save at least half for the IRS."

"I can live with that," Josh said. "But I still want a letter from you, explaining that I was on a secret mission for the government. Might not save me any money, but it'll look good framed in my office."

Newsome took a deep breath. "And in return, I get the recording?"

"Oh, I can give you this one, if you like." He slid the device toward Newsome. "However, you should be aware I transferred it to my hard drive and a couple of thumb drives and . . . You know, I can't remember how many copies I made."

Newsome's face flushed red, and his fists clenched. He took a deep breath and let it out slowly. As his complexion returned to normal, he shook his head. "Remember when I said I was beginning to like you? Scratch that. You're not a nice person—competent, but not nice. You'll get your letter."

Sutherland said, "Mr. Hawkins, if you please. I badly misjudged you. I figured you were just another of his groupies. I apologize for my words and actions."

Josh looked at Sutherland. "You just grew a few inches. Remember the old adage of *Don't judge a book by its cover?* Well, don't judge anyone by your preconceptions. Keep thinking independently, and you might qualify to be a G-man." He returned his attention to Newsome. "No problem on the money. It's worth it to see you lose your composure. Mr. Cool, you ain't today. So, what about Roz. Where is she?"

Newsome took a deep breath and looked around the room. Then he tapped the paper in front of him. "Need to stick to the agenda."

"Oh, what's next? More government bureaucratizing to obfuscate facts?"

"You're so eloquent, Mr. Hawkins. Let's lose the humor. If you remember our first meeting, you asked what I ultimately hoped to accomplish since any vacuum at the top would simply be filled by the next leader."

"Yes. And you said there would be a bloodletting among those vying for power. That would, in turn, supply the authorities with the leads they needed to break up the whole mess. Is my summary correct?"

"Close enough. I was right. The revolution has begun. Blanc had two lieutenants to whom he handed off the reins of power when he left the country. This morning—"

"Whoa. What do you mean, he left the country?" Josh realized his voice contained a hint of incredulousness, but a comment like that was one of the last he expected.

"Yes, Mr. Hawkins. We struck a deal. In consultation with his wife, he gave us certain information we wanted, and we escorted him to the border. He assured us he won't be back—plus we took certain precautions to ensure he keeps his word. Does that surprise you?"

Josh tapped his fingers on the table, then smiled. "Mr. Newsome, everything you say or do surprises me. Sometimes I wonder what country I'm living in. Seems like something important got lost between the Founding Fathers and today."

"Perhaps," Newsome said, a touch of sadness in his voice, "but there are those times when expediency is more important than the *letter of the law*. It was my call, and I decided this was one of those times. May I continue with my report—following the agenda?"

"Please. I'll try not to interrupt again."

"Good. Our principal's lieutenants were Gustave Archambeau and Marcel Latourette, two French-Canadians like him. They'd been with him for years. It took some doing, but his wife convinced him to give them up. As I said, he handed off his empire to them. Latourette washed ashore this morning. It looks like he took a bullet in the face from close range. His fingerprints identified him. There have been several other bodies discovered in alleys and alongside less used roads—dead. Also, one chopped up in a suitcase beside I-95. The police are in active pursuit and will be making arrests soon. I believe this empire, as it existed, is fragmented, finished. We'll be better prepared when the next one comes along."

"So, it's happening as you expected. Congratulations. I admit I doubted your rosy beliefs. Guess that proves the difference between you high-level executives and us ground pounders."

"Thank you. I suppose that's the closest thing to a compliment I'll ever get out of you. One more thing, and I'll never bother you again—well, not unless we need your specific skills."

Newsome stopped, and Josh heard a deep intake of breath as a look of sadness took over. "He also gave us the mole."

"Oh," Josh said. "Who was it? Couldn't be Sutherland. He's here today."

"No." Newsome spoke directly toward Sutherland. "His major shortcoming—that I know of—is being a spoiled brat." He turned back to Josh. "Our traitor was Rosalyn Waters. We confronted her, and she collapsed. Her brother is a junkie. He's tried to kick it on several occasions, but failed each time. Latourette approached her and threatened to cut off her brother's supply if she didn't cooperate. She said she's seen him in withdrawal before and couldn't stand to have him go through it again. She gave in and fed Latourette info from inside the task force. A black eye on our operation, but a human one. It reminds me that none of us is perfect. I accept full responsibility. When we outed her, she appeared relieved, broke down, and sobbed, saying she was glad it was over. I almost felt sympathy for her."

"What will happen to her?"

Newsome looked over Josh's head. "She's fortunate. We can't allow any of this to go public. Instead of jail time, she'll be drummed out of the service, her reputation in tatters. Anyone who checks will get a summary that says *released for the good of the service*. That language will follow her for the rest of her life."

Josh grimaced. "Kinda like a General Discharge from the military. I'm sorry to hear that. She must have gone through hell. She struck me as a dedicated DEA agent."

"Yes, she was. A real loss to the government. Sad isn't it how the smog of evil envelops the innocent?"

THE END

RANDY RAWLS BIOGRAPHY

Randy Rawls is a retired U.S. Army officer where he served in an intelligence and security capacity. Following retirement, he continued serving in the Department of Defense.

He recently completed a term as Chapter President of the Florida Chapter of Mystery Writers of America, an organization he has supported through voluntary positions since joining in 1999. He was the Chairman/Co-Chairman of SleuthFest for five years, during which time SleuthFest was a resounding success each year. SleuthFest is one of the premier mystery writers' conferences in the country.

He has twelve published books in three series and one historical plus several short stories in various anthologies.

Randy writes because he enjoys it and smiles, because life is fun.